The Whistleblower

Samuel Wachira

Published by

Longhorn Publishers (K) Ltd,
Funzi Road, Industrial Area,
P.O. Box 18033 – 00500,
Nairobi, Kenya.

Longhorn Publishers (U) Ltd,
Kanjokya Street,
Plot 74, Kamwokya,
P.O. Box 24745,
Kampala, Uganda.

Longhorn Publishers (T) Ltd,
New Bagamoyo / Garden Road,
Mikocheni B, Plot No. MKC/MCB/81,
P.O. Box 1237,
Dar es Salaam, Tanzania.

Longhorn Publishers (R) Ltd,
166 KG 13 off KG 11 Avenue
P.O. Box 5910
Kigali, Rwanda

First published 2016
Reprinted 2016

ISBN 978 9966 31 240 2

Printed by Printing Services Ltd.,
Factory Street off Commercial Street,
Industrial Area, P.O. Box 32197-00600, Nairobi, Kenya.

Dedication

To Sr. Pasca, for her unwavering support and ceaseless encouragement.

Chapter 1

Call me Sherriff, for that is what everyone calls me. In the beginning, I hated the name for it was coined as a form of mockery, but as time passed, the name stuck and I came to accept it. Indeed I even started feeling proud of it.

Once I used to adore Sundays but now I loathe them for they remind me of my beloved Sarah. I always called her Sarah although she always insisted that I address her by her cultural name. I remained adamant and this only changed when she gave birth to our first-born son and I substituted Sarah with the fond name Mummy, which she very much appreciated and indeed she in turn always called me Daddy.

In normal circumstances, I always spent my weekends in my rural home and Sarah would always insist that we go to church as a family. We would sit next to one another and receive the Holy Communion together. I had never given religion a deep thought but Sarah waved the magic card that converted me first during our courtship and later in marriage life. It was my love for her, buoyed by her relentless pleas that dragged me back to the sheepfold of the Lord, until I finally found myself becoming an active and devoted Christian.

Now, here I sat on the sofa, a cigarette hanging on my lips and bored to the bones, without even a minimal intention to attend mass. My bloodshot eyes shifted to the wall and with a lost look, I started viewing the pictures that hung there, an exercise that only aided the pangs of solitude and redoubled their stings. These photos marked the most cherished moments of my life: the day of my passing-out parade, our wedding day, the first birthday of my first-born son and so on. Before disaster struck, I would always look at the photos for they gave me an injection of new hope but on this fateful day, looking at them left a hollow void in my stomach.

I looked at the hopeful faces of my late family and my heart snapped, making me bury my mournful face in my palms. I could hardly believe that after having worked so hard to build a stable future for them, all that remained were precious memories. My eyes moved on to the last plaque that I had made for Sarah on our first wedding anniversary. It was a romantic poem, the fruit of a genial mind and which I had felt could best express my love for her. *When life will age and time will faden, thou'll need a soul transplant and I'll donate mine.* This writing always made me feel proud of myself but this morning, it made me feel like a solitary soul abandoned in the middle of a deep forest. I moved my eyes to the next writing. This one was a batik, which Sarah had bought in one of our religious pilgrimages. *'Come to me all you who labour and I will give you rest.'*

'These words pierced my heart the way a pin would pierce a ball of wool. Perhaps this is what I needed most now so as to give my battered spirit a facelift, I thought. Perhaps I needed to go to church, kneel on the pews and pour my heart out to the Lord. Yet, however much I tried, I realised that I had neither the energy nor the will to drag my broken heart to church for mending.

I would have done with the company of a close friend just to slay the loneliness, if not to seek for a word of advice. However, all had gone with the funeral of one of my close friends whose killing was as mysterious as it was bizarre. A crime-bursting guru, Bob Smart was arguably the best police officer and the most brilliant detective we had in the force. He was a man who believed in fighting crime with fervour and who was infallible when it came to investigating crimes. That was until unknown assailants sprayed his car with bullets, killing him instantly, an episode that left everyone wondering whether this was a case of assassination or robbery.

I would never have chosen to become a policeman but fate and desperation drove me into it. Like everyone else, I went to school hoping that one day I would land myself a plum job. I dreamt of becoming a lawyer, or an engineer, or an accountant, something that could give me a higher standing on the societal ladder. Although I was not very poor in school, I failed to clinch a berth in the university for my marks fell short by two points. When I realised that the dream of having a degree was sheer wishful thinking, I shifted my attention to the less lucrative careers like teaching or clerical jobs. I wrote one application letter after another but all I received in return were regrets and desperation. No one had told me that the deadly bug of corruption had bitten almost everyone in Ndiambo-land and that you needed to have a godfather somewhere or to grease someone's palms before you got a slot in any college. When I failed to clinch a berth in any of the colleges, I decided to try my luck in the police force.

The first hurdle involved a gruelling eight-kilometre race that was followed by a physical scrutiny and finally a session of answering idiotic questions, which any primary school leaver could have answered. When the recruitment exercise was over, I was among the lucky few. One month later, I was at the National Police College as a recruit.

The six-month training elapsed without a fuss and the day of my passing out came. Owing to my discipline and devotion to duty, I left the college with a shining curriculum vitae and it came as no surprise when I was assigned to the traffic department.

Ever since my school days, I had always been a fan of justice and a firm believer in seeking the common good. When I became a policeman, I thought that my principal duty was to enforce the rule of law but alas, I soon discovered that I had dived headfirst into a sea of evil. I needed only a few months as a policeman for the bare truth to dawn on me: the police force was just a hub of thieves in uniform; a bunch of crooks who shamelessly abetted crime while filling their pockets with bribes. I soon found myself hating my job and if I had an alternative, I would have opted out. I hated doing what was being done but the reality on the ground and shortage of artillery drove me into it. I did it because it was the fashion of the day and everyone was doing it anyway. From the most junior officer to the highest-ranking commander who sat at the headquarters, receiving a bribe was the hit-song of the moment. When I heard how the irredeemably corrupt top brass was pocketing hundreds of thousands, I justified receiving a fifty-shilling note from a wayward *matatu* driver for to me, it seemed a drop in the sea. I continued living in self-denial, although my conscience kept reminding me that what was being done was wrong.

While we were filling our pockets, road accidents were the order of the day and the roads had been turned to something akin to the Cambodian killing fields. Every weekend, the roads were filled with caravans of cars as people went to bury their loved ones, victims of grisly road accidents. Whenever I saw these caravans, my heart always got pricked and I wished I never took bribes. Many a time I would drop into a moment of reflection over what was happening and

I would feel ashamed of myself and like the biblical Cain, I would hear God's words: 'Where is your brother, Abel?' Looking at the state of things, I knew that our answer would be: 'I am not my brother's keeper'.

Money was collected from the roads and when evening came, it was spread on a table and everybody got his share. A fraction of this money would be sent to the top cadre as tax. All the same, as they say, every cloud has a silver lining. I willingly took my share because it boosted my earnings and helped me give a hand to my parents in educating my younger siblings.

Little did I know that the acid test would come knocking one year into the job.

It was on the eve of Christmas and I was busy manning a roadblock. This was the time when the roads turned into a beehive of activity as people travelled home to join their kith and kin for Christmas festivities. To us the men in blue, it was the time to make hay while the sun shone. We all called it the season of ripe berries, for this was when business boomed and money flowed in, making our pockets burst at the seams. Thus, when the station commander sent a message that I was urgently required at the station, I felt like a lion that had been pulled away from its prey. Little did I know that what awaited me was something that would change my life forever.

I only needed to look at the face of my boss to know that a bombshell was just about to explode. When I walked into his office, he pointed at the telephone receiver that lay on the table without uttering a word. I picked the receiver with shaky hands and listened to the voice at the other end.

When I heard the unmistakable voice of my mother, I immediately sensed that something bad was afoot.

"Hello mother," I said hoarsely, struggling to catch my breath.

When she heard my voice, she immediately burst in tears and I had to wait for what seemed like ages before she regained her composure. Finally, she managed to speak but only in monosyllables.

"My son… your father… I am at the mortuary…"

I swallowed dry air and before the message could sink, another voice came on the line. It was my uncle, Gichero.

"My son, you have to come home immediately. Your father has been killed in an accident," he said without beating about the bush.

I stiffened into a statue and I could barely feel the hand of my boss as he seized the handset from my weak grip. My eyesight became blurred and I felt like I needed air. Slowly, I sank into a nearby chair and passed out.

The funeral mass was filled to capacity and all my father's friends were there to give him a worthy send-off. As the first-born son, I saw the whole burden of taking care of the family being shoved squarely onto my back. My father was, by the time of his death, working in the city and like everyone else, he was rushing home to spend Christmas and New Year festivities with his family when the accident occurred. When I got the whole story of what exactly had transpired, I found myself hating my friends, my job and myself. According to the survivors, the minibus in which my dad was travelling was carrying double the number of passengers it was supposed to, and the half-drunk driver was cruising at a daredevil speed when the front wheel burst, sending the minibus rolling down a cliff. Half of the commuters lost their lives while most of the survivors were left maimed for life.

When the ritual of viewing of the body came, I looked

at my dead father's face and read all my guilt scribbled on it. I saw myself pocketing a bribe to let an overloaded matatu pass through I saw myself standing next to the table of death waiting to receive my share of the bribes collected and felt ashamed. When I thought of what my colleagues and I were doing, I could barely hold myself to look at him.

It was as if I had killed him myself.

As my family wailed in grief, my eyes wandered to my colleagues who had come to mourn with me. What I saw in their eyes shredded my heart into ribbons. In them, I saw a bunch of butchers. Men and women who heartlessly opened the gates that led to the gallows, a band of guilty monsters who sold innocent souls for a price as low as fifty shillings. When I thought of the number of roadblocks that the killer mini-bus had sneaked through, I hated my profession and myself. After long moments of soul-searching and deep reflection, I finally saw the light. Receiving a bribe was akin to signing the death warrants of innocent passengers, meaning that we cops were indeed killers. To me, our blue uniform was no longer blue, it was red: smeared with the blood of innocent people who had spilt their blood in the road carnage that had become a common occurrence on our roads. I looked at my grief-stricken mother and silently wondered how many women had been rendered widows just because of our greed for blood money. How many families had lost their breadwinners and how many children had been orphaned by our greed? Well, they normally say that it is only after one has experienced the sting of death that he or she knows what truly death is. After losing my father, I experienced the implications of pocketing a bribe.

As I watched my father's body being lowered into the grave, I decided to bury my passion for bloodied money with it. I vowed that I would rather die a pauper than pocket a bribe.

If you want to know who the devil is, just convert from your wayward ways and he will come to you firing from all cylinders. My new vow immediately landed me into troubled waters and earned me a host of enemies. When my colleagues who had been my comrades-in-arms in the get-rich-quick scheme noticed that I had converted, they started looking at me with eyes of suspicion. They immediately isolated me making me feel like an outcast, but I stood to my ground. It was not long before they got tired of looking over their shoulders whenever I was around.

That is when I earned myself the nickname Sherriff. As days passed, my friends who were now unable to put up with me, grew even more wary of the enemy from within. I was now living like a lone buffalo and whenever I passed, whispers of my comrades followed me. The loathesome eyes that I saw around me were enough to tell me that I was surrounded by foes. To them, I was an ungrateful person who had bitten the fingers that fed him, a man who had committed the sin of hubris. They saw me as a dangerous person; someone hell-bent on blocking the taps of the water of life. Yet others viewed me as a fool; someone who had received the key to the gate of quick riches on a silver platter and had thrown it inside a pit-latrine instead.

The acolytes of corruption must have sent a word to their high priests warning them that there was a cat amongst the pigeons, a kind of an angel who had descended from heaven with the sole mission of slaying the sacred goose that produced the golden eggs. Hence, when I received a letter informing me that I had been moved to the Directorate of Criminal Investigation, I knew what had hit me.

The gods of corruption had cracked the whip. Although I knew I was being punished, I received the letter with a mixture of relief and doubts. True, by moving out of the traffic department, I had bid farewell to the horrific career of helping butcher innocent people but on the other hand, it meant that I would come face to face with hardened criminals bearing sophisticated weapons. When the day of moving out came, my friends looked at me without hiding their smiles of sarcasm. It was as if they were saying, "He wants to fight the devil. Well, let him meet him in the real battlefield now!"

I knew that tribulations had begun and although I had lost the battle, I vowed to soldier on hoping that one day I would win the war.

I had successfully spearheaded an investigation into a bank robbery when I received an unexpected call from a senior police officer. The robbery had been pulled by a couple of robbers who were working in cahoots with some bank employees. It was a superb job, the kind that you can willingly entrench in the annals of investigative history and when I wound it up, I was left basking in glory. No one thought I could work it out so fast but when I finally uncovered all the culprits, both friends and foes viewed me with admiration.

The telephone call was from Muli, a provincial police boss whom I had not met since I left college. Back then, he was in charge of the college and one of my greatest admirers. He always gave me the impression of a man of sound morals and I willingly reciprocated the esteem he held me in. Although he never told me, I knew that he was the man who had manipulated the levers to make sure that I was posted to the traffic department when I left college. Thus, when he called to inform me that I had been moved to the anti-fraud department, I knew this was more of a favour than a promotion; a gift from an old friend.

I viewed my promotion as sheer luck because working in the anti-fraud department meant an increase in my pay, better working conditions and above all an open chance to pursue my career as a professional detective. To crown it all, my new posting meant that more often than not, my finger would seldom be around the trigger and this sounded like music to my ears.

When I bade farewell to my colleagues and moved out of the 'ghettos,' as we called the police quarters, I could hardly resist a smile. When I watched their envious faces, I remembered the sarcasm that had followed me when I left the traffic department and murmured to myself, "Well, its pay-back time." I was now leaving the awesome police quarters and moving into a comfortable two-bedroomed house. Although I was still struggling with the burden of educating my younger siblings, I managed to secure a loan and buy myself a decent second-hand car. One month into my new job, I won myself a one-year scholarship for an in-service course abroad. I studied banking security and when I returned to the country, I was attached to the central bank. This kind of course could only be accessed by the lucky few who had a big uncle somewhere up the ranks or those who could manage to part with a hefty bribe. So when I received the news, I mused that maybe lady luck had finally decided to get married and she had chosen me for a groom. However, I would occasionally have moments of reflection over my achievements and thank God that I had maintained my vow to be bribe-free. In a way, I thought God was rewarding me for reaching greater heights without coughing up any bribe. My life was now flowing sweet and I reckoned that I had already hit the roof of success. Little did I know that the icing on the cake - my better half - was just around the corner.

It was just after Christmas and I decided return to the city so that I could beat the New Year rush. I had just passed Matata town when I came across a lone lady waiting for transport to the city. Although I had vowed never to go picking up strangers, I decided to turn into a Good Samaritan at least this once.

It was only after she had entered the car that I realised that I had indeed picked a real queen. She was chocolate-brown with a bewitching smile and a pair of seductive eyes. Her jet-black hair was beautifully done and she had the right height and a figure that could make any model burn with envy. We started chatting and I learnt that her name was Sarah and she was a student in a teacher training college somewhere in the Northern Province. She was travelling to her aunt's place in the city so that she could catch a bus to college some days later. I told her my name but I avoided telling her what I did for a living. I would have willingly told her but I wasn't sure whether she too formed part of the club that had the police phobia disease so I thought it wise not to risk. If I told her what I did, I reckoned, this could end up upsetting my apple-cart midstream and spoiling the party.

I dropped her at her aunt's place in Sunset Estate and when I asked her for her phone number, she declined weakly but after my relentless pleas, she finally caved in and gave me her number.

This meeting sparked off a close friendship which grew roots until it matured to a full-blown relationship. It was not long before we both realised that we were made for one another and we started laying the ground for a life together. I would regularly travel to the north to see her and she in turn would come to my place and spend a couple of days whenever she was going for her vacations. When she asked me what I did for a living, I told her that I worked in a bank but I did not tell her that I was a police officer. When the day of her graduation came, I went to grace the occasion and this gave me a chance to meet my future in-laws for the first time. When the ceremony was over and her parents had gone away, I took her for supper in a posh hotel and officially proposed marriage to her. It was then that I decided to own up and tell her the truth about my profession. When I told her that I worked for the Directorate of Criminal Investigation and explained why I had been reluctant to tell her the truth, she looked at me fondly and said, "You don't look like a policeman. You are too soft and tender to harm a fly."

I joined her in laughter, with a feeling of relief. I hadn't thought that she would take it with such serenity.

"The first thing I want you to teach me after we get married is how to fire a gun," she went on, this time seeking for my hand.

"Why on earth should you want to use a gun," I asked with feigned curiosity.

She smiled at me charmingly then said, "It has never been my dream to use a gun but you can bet I will use it on the first woman I catch messing around with you."

I bent over and kissed her while our laughter went on.

"That makes us a pair because I will do the same thing if I catch another man smiling at you," I said.

Our wedding was fabulous and I had never felt this happy in my life. One year later, we were blessed with a first-born son who was later followed by another boy. We then joined hands and secured a loan, which we used to buy a five-acre piece of land near Northwest town and on which we built a permanent house. Life flowed smoothly and we looked forward to the joyful tidings ahead. Whenever I looked at my life and my achievements, I could hardly resist a smile of pride. A beautiful and devoted woman for a wife, a cute family, a wonderful career; everything a man would dream of. This made me feel like I was sitting on the seventh cloud. That was until doom and gloom descended on my dreams shattering whatever I had constructed and leaving it lying in debris.

Everyone knew that it would be a hotly contested election but nobody expected that this cut-throat race would lead to an Armageddon of such a magnitude. During the campaign period, the politicians went around trading hate speeches, firing inflammatory projectiles and inciting tribes against other tribes, but no one could imagine that they were preparing the ground for the seeds of genocide and ethnic cleansing that would follow later. During the day, they drummed up support for their candidature but when nightfall came, they sounded the war drums and planted the demonic seeds of violence.

This exchange of ethnic innuendoes and generosity in vitriol between the warring sides was supposed to be a kind wake-up call, something that would have elicited for a quick intervention from the authorities, yet no one moved a finger. By the time voting day came, the seeds of genocide had already sprouted and the air in all the corners of Ndiambo-land was polarised with ethnic hatred. The political climate was fully charged, yet no prophet foresaw the looming disaster that lay ahead.

The bungled election was the trigger that helped to ignite the already charged environment to an explosion.

As a man who had never taken interest in politics and the

razzmatazz that comes along with elections, I did not go to vote and I preferred to stick in the city doing my job but like everyone else, my ears and eyes were glued to the local media as we waited for the results. Patiently, the country waited but no results were forthcoming. Then all of a sudden, it was reported that the elections had been bungled in some areas while one side claimed that it had been rigged. Hell broke loose and by the time push came to shove, news started streaming in that spates of violence had erupted in various corners of the country. The air in the country suddenly turned tense and volatile and intense anxiety gripped the citizenry.

Real fear gripped me and I went into panic mode. I knew where my family was and with the memories of past cases of ethnic cleansing and inter-tribal clashes still in my mind, I knew that if there was an area that was an epicentre of ethnic suspicion and a real hot-bed of tribal animosity, then this was it. I had to act and act fast. I picked up my phone and called my wife instructing her to board the nearest vehicle and head for the city. I then called a close friend who was a native of the area and begged him to offer a safe haven to my family in case things spilled over to the worst.

By the time evening came, the media was awash with horrific images of rioters, looters and dead bodies. The whole country was now aflame with hatred and anger. Neighbour was turning against neighbour and opposing tribes were baying for each other's blood making it look like the apocalypse had finally come. What the people had taken to be normal electoral mudslinging and campaign vitriol had snowballed into an astronomical crisis and the whole country was now leaning on the brink of a precipice. While all this was going on, I could barely manage to remain seated and I kept pacing around the room like one infested with deadly ants, all the time praying. My fear had now reached a crescendo and I was losing control of my nerves. All I wanted was to see my family safe and sound.

Then came the telephone call that slashed my heart, leaving me gasping for life.

When the phone squealed, I immediately knew it was Sarah.

"Daddy! Please come and save us!" she wailed breathlessly. "The house is surrounded by militias!"

I swallowed dry air. I thought about my sons whose wails I could hear over the phone as they cried calling for Daddy.

"Sarah, please be calm," I pleaded. "Dress the boys in girls' clothes and prepare to get away. I have already talked to Mwalungu. He will come around and pick you then whisk you to somewhere safe until peace is restored." I had hoped that dressing the boys in girls' clothes would save them as the tribal militias were known to spare women and girls.

What I heard next was something that I would carry with me for the rest of my life like an indelible scar.

The loud bang told me that they had brought down the iron door and gained access to the house. I then heard the helpless screams of my wife and sons as they called out for me. I heard the voice of my wife as she offered them money to spare her and the two boys but her pleas fell on deaf ears.

There and then, my world ground to a halt and time ceased to move. I just stood there like a zombie, sporting the far away look of a desperate man who was caught between the devil and the deep blue sea. I was dazed to the bones and with nothing to do except to listen to the eerie cries emanating from my phone. I heard the last cries of my sons as the cruel hand of death snatched them away from me and listened to my wife's cries as they gang-raped her. One of them grabbed the phone that was still on and spoke rapidly in Swahili.

"We don't care whether you work for the Directorate of Criminal Investigation or the Federal Bureau of Investigation but we advise you to stay in your native province and never come back here!" he said arrogantly.
The last thing that I heard before passing out was the weak voice of my wife as she bade me farewell, telling me that she loved me.

I spent the first three months doing nothing except drinking, counting the spoils and thinking of how to reconstruct my tattered life. Both friends and kith and kin rallied around me in a bid to help me revive my withering life and wriggle out of the despair but their efforts came to naught. The loneliness, the pain and the emotional anguish tore me apart and I hit the bottle as if I was born for it, until a kind friend rang the alarm bell and warned me that I was headed to the ruins. For weeks, lunacy stared at me in the face and although I fought hard to reclaim my former state of mind, no exorcist could drive away the dickens that had invaded my life. The traumatic memories of my deceased family, the ugly scene of my razed home, the charred remains of what used to be the dream of my life, the new tag of a refugee: all these proved a burden too heavy to bear. Some of my friends organised that I go to the Coast and relax in a house of a friend but, even though my host was very helpful and did everything to lift up my fallen spirit, wading out of the sea of despair, proved to be a tall order. My host, noticing that I had yielded to despair changed tack and helped me enrol in a counselling centre where I undertook a psychological accompaniment course, which helped me a lot since it offered me a chance to embark on a mission of soul-searching. After deep reflection, I mustered courage and decided that my rebirth would have to be marked by a resignation from my police job. In a way, this was a kind of a personal revolt against a system that I felt had betrayed me. As one who had given a lot in terms of service to my country, I felt that I had received the raw end of the bargain and felt cheated. It was due to this that I felt that my resignation would be the first milestone in the journey towards rebuilding my wrecked life. I didn't know what I would do for a living; all I knew was that I wanted to be out of the police force.

Having made this decision, I found myself relaxing and gaining peace of mind.

I finished writing the resignation letter and went to the fridge to fetch another cold beer. I then switched on the television and sat down to enjoy my beer. I was not following the television keenly but the voice coming from it gave me company and added some spice to the deathly aura that held my house hostage. Then something appeared on the breaking news that made my heart race with fear. What I saw and heard made me wish I hadn't switched on the television.

The reporter, who was standing at the entrance of a hotel, said that a popular journalist had been found dead in his hotel room. When he mentioned the name of the slain journalist, the glass of beer fell from my trembling hand and crashed onto the floor.

Chapter 2

I had met Larry when we were in secondary school. He had struck me as a likeable boy who could fall into company with anyone. I was one class ahead of him hence I acted as his bodyguard against the bullies who were fond of harassing the newcomers. He was by nature a very lively boy and it was because of this that a close friendship sprouted between us until we became inseparable. He was a little bit of everything; a wag, a trickster, a joker, an interesting liar, an entertainer, just the kind of harmless boy anyone would love to have around. We all called him *simba,* owing to his idolatrous love for the local club, the Lions. Coming from the Ambuya tribe in a school dominated by the Kuyumba tribesmen made him an an easily notable favourite to all. When we completed school, he was among the lucky few who managed to clinch a slot in one of the colleges and there and then, our paths separated.

We never met again for years until we unexpectedly bumped into each other in the streets. He was surprised to see me in a policeman's uniform, for he knew since our school days that I hated policemen.

I learnt that Larry had studied journalism and that he was now a reporter with one of the popular media houses. When I remembered our high school days, I told him that he was tailor-cut for the job. One of his fortes was that with his rhetorical flair and a natural talent to entertain, he could hold a multitude spellbound for hours. He was a master of satire and when we were students in high school, he would keep us busy with his endless sweet stories while we lay on our beds at night.

We revived our old friendship since our paths frequently crisscrossed, especially when I was working in the crime department. When I was moved to the anti-fraud department, I smelt out a mega-pyramid scheme that aimed at robbing innocent citizens millions of their hard-earned cash. It was a case too hot to touch for it involved getting into a warpath with a couple of political sacred cows and stepping on some sensitive political toes. My boss congratulated me for a job well done but he regretted that the job was too dangerous to touch.

"I know how it feels to work for nothing Sheriff, but this is the far we can get," he told me. He was an experienced man and when he told me of the dangers of touching off a war against the high and mighty, I believed him.

"The big shots always have ways of getting around things and I would not be surprised if everything backfires and we find ourselves on the receiving end," he told me. "They know where to get the best lawyers; the kind that studies the law with a tooth comb in search of escape routes which they always end up finding. Consider that these lawyers wine and dine with the judges and you can figure out the rest for yourself."

I agreed to let things rest at that, although my conscience refused to see no evil and hear no evil. I still felt that there was a way of getting around things and after giving it a thought, I went back to my boss and told him there was another way of making sure that the scandal did not see the light of day. He listened to me and when I told him that we needn't take the centre stage, he gave me the green light to proceed.

That is when I leaked the secret information to Larry. He was salivating like a mad dog as I leaked the works to him and since I had already given him enough flesh, all he had to do was to stick it on the skeleton and present it to the citizenry. This is how he finally blew the whistle and uncovered one of the biggest and dirtiest pyramid schemes of the day. As expected, the revelations felled a couple of big names and provoked a series of high-level resignations. While heads were rolling, a hitherto unknown lowly reporter was propelled to the heaven of courageous heroes, transforming him into a national hero overnight. Due to this courageous act, Larry's fame shot to the limelight and he became a household name in the media circles and having turned into a media celebrity, he jumped ship from the local daily and joined an upcoming media house *Mambo-Leo* as a chief reporter.

But one truth had escaped the ears of the citizenry. They did not know I was the real hero and Larry had only stolen the show and ended up scooping the prize. This, however, did not worry me for I had obtained my objective albeit by proxy.

The uncovering of this scandal offered Larry the springboard on which to catapult himself to fame. He started writing a weekly article entitled 'The whistleblower' in which he stripped naked the day-to-day scandals in the government. He peeped and eavesdropped and encouraged the public to help him raise the alarm whenever they sniffed anything fishy. He became allergic to all form of corruption. He defended the common man and the downtrodden from the excesses of the ruling class. If you had something important to say but you thought that saying it would put your life in jeopardy, you called Larry and he helped you say it. If you smelt a scandal involving the high and mighty, you called Larry and he helped you uncover it. He enjoyed every moment of it and saw his work as a divine calling. To him, the pen and the microphone were the guns and swords to fight scandals and protect the populace.

Larry the journalist had finally turned into an activist. The poor loved him; the common man adored him while he became a darling to the lovers of social justice. On the other hand, the rich and the powerful abhorred him. To them, he was an eyesore, a constant thorn in their flesh. They nicknamed him the mad monkey with a loaded gun, and made it no secret that they would throw a party if he dropped dead. The article proved to be a success in keeping the authorities on their toes making him to extend the initiative to the airwaves where he ran another successful weekly talk-show which served the same purpose:exposing scandals. It is this weekly radio talk-show programme that finally gave him his popular pet name 'The Whistleblower'.

When the genocide was raging, Larry picked up his equipment and bravely headed to the hotspots. It was a dangerous initiative but he braved the guns and the machetes in the line of duty. He updated the people with all that was happening, giving the truth without holding anything back. Indeed, he ended up becoming the face of the genocide and this made him very famous. When normalcy returned to the country, he scooped the prize of bravery which was awarded by the national media fraternity.

Larry never made it secret that he owed his climb to the summit of success to me and this helped cement our friendship. When he found his better half and time came for him to walk down the aisle, he chose me and Sarah to act as the best couple. The last time I had met him was at the funeral of my family, then he had dashed back to the hotspots of the genocide to make sure that the people learnt the truth. After I returned from the Coast, I called him but like all my other friends, he had gone to attend Bob Smart's funeral. Thus, when the news came that he was the journalist who had been found dead in the hotel, I was so shocked. I forgot about my impending resignation, holstered my gun and left for the city centre.

* * *

The entrance to the Gossip Hotel was littered with police officers and teeming with the press when I reached there. Police officers who were also fighting hard to keep the press at bay beefed up security in the vicinity. A crowd was milling around making the job of the police a bit hectic. After digging my way through the milling crowd, I flashed my badge to the policeman manning the barricade and I was let through. Larry was arguably the best and most controversial journalist in the country, so the security at the scene of crime had to be watertight. I walked rapidly through the corridors until I reached the scene of crime, where I found the scene-of-crime team taking photographs and dusting for fingerprints. I watched the body of my friend in shock. It was now covered with a white sheet. I uncovered his body just to be sure that it was him. He was lying on his tummy, naked but with no visible injuries, although I could see some dried-up white foam around his mouth. I gazed around the neat room and my experience as a sleuth told me that there was no sign of a struggle and this to me looked strange.

"Seems like a professional job," replied the pathologist when I asked him what he thought of the case. "This is a typical case of drugging. There are no signs of a struggle but I can't tell you more until I have carried out a full autopsy."

I leaned down and observed his neck. I noticed that there was a strange line running around his neck; like somebody had tried to wring him. I did not comment, for I thought it wise to wait for the doctor's autopsy report.

After I had talked to some of my colleagues, I slowly started knitting the pieces together. From what I gathered, the police were making enquiries about a certain woman who had last been seen with Larry. I entered the bar where a man I easily recognised as the police commandant was grilling the workers. Most of them remained tight-lipped, but this did not worry me. I knew that with some extra coercion, one of them would buckle and offer some leads.

Come afternoon, the press went wild, leading to a stream of all kinds of news. The police finally gave their version: Larry had picked up a prostitute who had ended up drugging him. According to their hypothesis, the woman must have applied an overdose, leading to his demise. Investigations revealed that a briefcase that contained his laptop and digital camera were missing. His wallet and his phone were also missing. The police circulated the woman's descriptions to the media houses while at the same time chanting the usual police refrain of not leaving any stone unturned until they nailed this prostitute who had robbed the media fraternity of a rare gem. To the police, this could be summed up as a case of a robbery gone sour.

From the outset, I refused to believe this. The version looked foolproof yet at the back of my mind there was a lingering feeling that something precious was missing. I decided to visit his wife and see whether I could pick up some valuable clues. Larry would have been a Casanova but we all knew that he loved his wife and confided in her always. If there was something fishy behind his sad demise, then she had to have a clue, so I thought.

She was too grief-stricken to give me full attention but she was still able to answer my questions. I started by asking her whether Larry had received any death threats but she answered in the negative. I asked her if she knew if Larry had an enemy and she shook her head.

I exhausted my questions without getting anything valuable, yet the signal behind my mind refused to go off.

"I know Larry used to work a lot at home," I said. "Could you allow me to look at his study room?"

Again she shook her head. "I guess you have come too late," she said amidst her sobs. "The police came an hour ago and requested the same thing. They carried away his computer and files saying they needed to look at them."

I immediately smelt a rat.

This could only mean one thing: if the police were not convinced that this was a mere robbery gone sour, then they must have fed a half-baked story to the press just to cool the public tempers and this could only mean that there was something sinister behind this affair. That was when I decided to place a call to the editor- in-chief of *Mambo-leo*.

The editor formed part of my very limited group of peers. He was a pleasant and easy man to get along with whom I met regularly due to my close relationship with Larry and like all the others, I also addressed him as Editor. Although he was the boss, he and Larry were more than comrades-in-arm, they were soul mates and the cordial relationship that existed between them was something that would have elicited jealousy even from the trinity. I always considered his idea to start another media house as both novel and brainy and I always teased him that his media house was the best idea after bottled beer. When I reached his office, he was still yet to pull himself out of the grief.

"This is the worst thing that has ever hit me," he said as he pulled a chair for me.

I was careful not to share with him my suspicions, so I started by asking him if he knew whether Larry had been working on a case. He brooded for a moment, pulled a face and said, "This I can't tell but yesterday he called me sounding like someone who had hit a jack-pot. He was in an upbeat mood and I could guess that he had stumbled onto something interesting. 'Boss', he told me, 'Cross your fingers and pray to all your saints. I have stumbled into something precious. If it works, our sales will shoot above skies.' I asked him what he meant by this. "You know how Whistleblower is…he can even crack jokes in hell." Then he told me, "If this is not the key to paradise, then I am the president of the world."
I didn't take him seriously so I decided to wait till morning. Unfortunately, from the look of things, I won't be getting any key to heaven after the loss of one of my best reporters and friend."

He pulled his handkerchief and wiped his tears. I could see that he was trying hard to fight back the tears.

"Can I have a look at his office? Perhaps I could get a clue."

He cut me short by shaking his head emphatically. "There is nothing for you Sherriff. That was the first place the police raided immediately his body was found. They carried away his computer, flash disks, files, everything they could lay their hand on."

I raised my eyebrows and faced him with eyes of suspicion.

"What reason did they give to warrant this kind of act?"

He threw his hands in the air as a sign of desperation. "Well, the police are the police. All they needed to tell me was that they were not treating this case lightly and that they could not write off the possibility of an assassination. They claimed they were hunting for all the clues and that made me soften my stand."

The red light grew even redder.

So the police were giving a fake version just to lower the tension among the populace!

All the doubts now vanished from my troubled mind. I now knew for sure that Larry had been assassinated.

"Editor," I told him without mincing my words. "Right now I have no evidence in my hands but I can assure you that our friend has been assassinated. I can't bet my life on it but it seems clear, like a neon sign in a dark street."

He gazed at me with round eyes full of disbelief but I was unfazed.

"We shall leave it to the police for the time being but I want you to burn the midnight oil until you discover what case Larry was working on because there must be something."

He picked up his pen and started toying around with it. I could see that he was fighting hard to avoid my searching eyes. Finally, he managed to look up towards me. "Sherriff, I don't know whether to buy your idea or call it a bluff but rest assured that should I stumble onto something valuable, I will let you have it," he said hoarsely.

My next stop was with the police pathologist. He was a middle-aged officer who dealt with all cases involving homicide. We knew each other since the days I worked in the crime department but that did not mean that he had my full trust.

"Well, the chemical used is chloroform, the usual drug that prostitutes use to drug their clients," he told me after I told him what I wanted. "You can get it from any pharmacy although both of us know that this is illegal."

"But in most cases the victims just pass out for a while then regain their consciousness," I said, cutting him short.

He made a face, smacked his lips then said, "Sherriff,

remember we are talking about a lethal substance that is being administered by someone with no medical know-how. True, it need not be fatal but an overdose can lead to death and this I think was the case with this particular victim."

I didn't buy his theory but I made it look like I was fully contented with his half-baked explanation. I bade him farewell and I headed back to my flat.

As I sat on the sofa emptying a bottle of cold beer, something kept ringing at the back of my head like a persistent alarm bell; something that kept reminding me that I owed Larry something after many years of brotherly friendship. I fought hard to shake off the assassination idea but it kept on forcing itself back into my mind. I remembered his humorous and easygoing way of savouring life. Just like in the good old days, he was never short of jokes and never ceased to tease me because of my profession. While I referred to him as a mad monkey with a loaded gun, he in turn referred to us the police as thugs in uniform.

"The police are magic workers when it comes to manufacturing evidence," he would say. "They can even find a crime in a saint! They apprehend a teetotaler today and tomorrow he is in the dock facing charges of being drunk, disorderly and behaving in a manner likely to cause a breach of peace!" At times, when he joined me with some of my friends for a drinking spree, he would entertain us with the usual police drama that he was never tired of repeating.

As I thought about all these memories, I stared at the resignation letter that I had written in the morning and which was still lying on my table and I found myself landing on the horns of dilemma.

Should I go ahead and hand it over?

This turned out to be a maze that I found difficult to

untangle. I toyed with the idea of shelving it until I got to the bottom of the case but I shied away from the idea. I was no stranger to homicide cases and I knew that some of them took years to unravel. I was still haggling with the idea of postponing my resignation when my cell phone squealed, a squeal that left me completely rattled.

I picked up my cell phone and I stared at the unknown number. I was tempted to ignore it but when I remembered the events that had rocked my day, I decided to hear who it was.

"Yes," I answered to the growling voice of the caller.

"I presume I am talking to Sherriff," a voice I had never heard before growled.

I could not recognise the voice but the fact that he addressed me by my nickname told me that he knew me.

"Yes, it's me. Who are you?" I asked in an anxious voice.

The caller drew in a deep breath then said, "I am the police general and I want to talk to you. It's urgent."

Without knowing why, I felt electric shocks slashing all over my stomach. By now, the news of Larry's killing had sunk among the citizenry and wagging tongues were almost provoking a tempest. The swirling of hearsay in the air had started provoking ripples in the populace and rumours, both weird and imagined, were already doing the rounds. Although the police commandant had already briefed the press promising not to leave any stone unturned, this did not whittle down the rumour mill and the speculations that came along with it. Thus, when the caller said he was the police general, I guessed what the intended topic of discussion was.

"Are you still there, Sherriff?" he insisted.

"Yes, I am. Where can we meet?"

I noticed with shame that there was a strange stammer

in my voice and I sounded like a scared man.

In the brief silence that followed, I could hear his heavy breathing over the line, like that of a man under hysteria. He came in again.

"I am waiting for you in my residence. I am sending a driver to pick you up. He should be with you in half an hour."

Before I could say anything, I heard a click on the phone that told me that he had cut the connection and this could only mean one thing: this was not a request, it was an order.

As I placed my phone on the table, I started feeling unsure of the new set-up. Why the principal of the police service was insisting for a nocturnal meeting started giving me ideas. This call could only mean one thing: Larry's murder was giving the authorities cold feet but why he insisted on talking to me left me baffled. True, many people knew that Larry and I were inseparable friends but the general's entrance into the scene made me feel unsure of myself. Well, I finally decided to go and hear what he wanted. I half-heartedly picked up the resignation letter and shelved it, then holstered my gun and sat on the sofa to wait.

* * *

The moment I stepped into the lavishly-furnished and kingly mansion, I knew I was standing in front of a very big man. The general had a gait and a demeanour that left no doubt that he was the country's top officer. Tall and massively built with shifty eyes and a hard face, he had a gait that could have forced any potential criminal to chicken out at the eleventh hour. I had seen his face in the newspapers and in the TV screens a number of times but it had never crossed my mind that one day I would find myself facing him amidst a tension that I could almost touch with my hand. In spite of the small successes in my life, I always counted myself as a member of the hoi polloi, someone who had no business rubbing shoulders with members of the upper crust of the society. The moment I set my eyes on him, I detected that whatever reason had made him summon me was giving him sleepless nights. He was holding a glass of liquor in his unsteady hand and he kept pacing around the spacious room the way a lawyer paces while arguing his case in front of an attentive jury.

It was the first time that I was stepping on the holy grounds of the exclusive and posh King's Park Estate, where the noble and the members of the high caste of the society lived. Poking my nose here meant that I had a chance to breathe the fresh air that was reserved for the top echelons of the society and this I didn't mind. The heavily guarded gates, the kingly palaces and the wall fences drove back my mind to my life as a constable, when three families shared the same house divided only by curtains. Well, I wasn't here to ask him why he was living like a king while junior officers who did the donkey work lived like paupers. I was here to know what he wanted. Nevertheless, I made sure I hid all the telltale signs that would have made him see that I felt uncomfortable in this royal ambience.

He fetched another glass and poured some liquor into it and then handed it over to me saying, "I guess we just have to drink without any toasting. After what has happened, I guess we have no reason to toast."

I accepted the drink and joined him. It was Scotch whisky and well blended. The entire house lay in deep silence and this made me wonder if he lived alone. Except the two guards at the gate, I hadn't caught sight of any other soul in this hallowed place.

I noticed that he was moody, so I kept my peace. He kept

brooding for long intervals, staring fixedly like someone in a trance. There was no doubt that whatever lay in his heart was weighing heavily on him.

After a lengthy and tense silence, he caressed his clean-shaven chin, then turned to me.

"I called you because I want you do to me a favour," he started, keeping his voice as low as he could, maybe to hide the tremor that accompanied it.

A favour?

I couldn't follow him but I decided to wait until he finished.

"I know it is hard for you to understand but first I will fill you into the set-up. Yesterday, my wife left for shopping accompanied by my chauffeur. Normally, she likes to stay out so I was not worried even when the clock struck 21;00 hours without any sight of her. However, when the hour hand crawled to midnight, I started getting jittery, so I called her, but her phone was off. I started making marathon calls to our friends, but none of them had seen her. I spent a difficult night hoping that when morning came she would arrive but when I went to take my breakfast and didn't find her at the table, I started getting jittery. I now knew that something had happened to her and I decided to inform the relevant authorities and order for a manhunt. However, before I could do that, I received a call from them."

"Who?" I asked impatiently.

He drew in another heavy breath, sipped his drink and set it on the table. He then licked his rubbery lips and said, "The kidnappers."

I felt a lurch in my bowels but before I could not say anything, he went on.

"They told me that they were holding my wife and they

asked me to deliver five million shillings in cash if I wanted to see her again. After the usual stuff of not trying to contact the law, they gave me an ultimatum of twelve hours to gather the money. They called me again at mid-day and told me that they would instruct me on where the money should be delivered."

I looked at him searchingly without hiding the feeling that what he had told me had left me both dazed and speechless.

I, like everyone else, knew of the spate of kidnappings that were rocking the city, but the news that the wife of the police general had fallen victim would surely make banner headlines. Kidnapping and asking for ransom was turning out to be the crime of the moment. Many children of the moneyed had been kidnapped and their parents had parted with heavy ransoms, figures which only helped to motivate the kidnapping rings even more. I was still at pain to understand why he had summoned me, until I remembered a landmark episode during my stint in the crime department.

On that occasion, I had commanded an operation to rescue a victim in one of the most chilling kidnap episodes I have ever been involved in. A daring gang had kidnapped the son of a prominent politician and had gone ahead to demand a hefty ransom. The father had informed the agents of law and using technology, we had traced the calls of the gang to a house in one of the city estates. The commando-style rescue operation that left four of the kidnappers dead had been successful, for it had been organised to the tiniest detail but it required iron nerves and was highly risky. I knew how tricky it was to crack such a calibre of crime. Dealing with a kidnapper falls in the same line as dealing with a lunatic serial killer. In most cases, kidnappers have nothing to lose, making them some sort of terrorists. At times, paying the ransom helped nothing and in many cases, the victims got knocked off even after the ransom had been paid.

"What are you planning to do, Sir," I asked for the sake of it.

He rubbed together his giant palms then placed them on his head in a gesture of resignation.

"If I make one false move, these lunatics may end up killing my wife," he said sullenly.

I said nothing. With my experience in the world of fighting crime, I knew that negotiating with kidnappers was tricky as it was difficult especially if the victim happened to be the wife of a police general, but what he said next made me raise my eyebrows without wanting to.

"I will follow their instructions and pay up. I can't sacrifice my wife for five million."

I could hardly believe my ears. I was aware that it was a tough dilemma but on the other hand, I knew that paying ransom was what was maintaining these rings in business. When people paid, they played right into the hands of the kidnappers, making it hard for the law enforcers to eradicate these gangs. To curb them, and to deny them air, the authorities always advised the public not to pay the ransom. Now that the police general was playing ball with them, I knew things were really bad.

I hadn't yet understood why he had summoned me. In the beginning, I thought he wanted me to command an operation to free his wife but now that he had said that he was ready to part with the money, I found myself foxed.

"Have you talked to anyone?" I asked plainly.

He shook his head without saying anything. "I will not be doing that. If I squeal these lunatics may end up harming my wife. Above all, this affair may get to the public domain and this is something I wouldn't want to happen. Public opinion is dangerous to toy around with especially if you occupy an office like mine, hence my decision is to pay the money silently then everything will go on without a fuss."

I decided I had enough of this boring wait. I had to know why he had called me.

"What do you want me to do?" I asked unceremoniously.

He dropped into another moment of boring silence; a silence that seemed to last for ages and that left me anxious to the bones and stretched my patience to near breaking point. He then slowly lifted up his head and fixed his scared gaze on my face.

"I called you because I want you to help deliver the ransom," he said in a low voice that denoted a lot of inner pain.

The whisky went the wrong way and I found myself coughing persistently. I composed myself, then faced him with eyes of disapproval.

I was now a scared man and I had every reason to be. While I was organising the rescue operation of the kidnapping case I had solved before, I had a chance to read enough about cases involving kidnappers, so I was aware of all the risks involved. Messing around with ransom money was akin to walking into a cave full of vipers blindfolded. Many a time, the victim got knocked off and the person who delivered the ransom money got knocked off too.

"This is not an order, Sherriff, it is just a request," he said in a beseeching voice. "I will pay you handsomely if you accept this job. I know you won't understand but all I want is to have my wife back."

A strong feeling of solidarity with him gripped me as

I gazed at his mournful face. He reminded me of my own desperation when my wife and children were crying for me to save them. I felt my heart soften.

"The money is already here with me," he continued, "I will pay you one hundred thousand to deliver the ransom then to fetch my wife from a place that they will indicate."

In spite of my soft heart, I was still not sure whether I wanted to dip my oars into this one. At the back of my head, a siren kept warning me that this affair could end up backfiring and if it did, the person who would pay the price was me. All the same, his look of desperation kept dragging me to his side.

"How sure are you that they will release her after the ransom is paid?" I asked without looking at him. I hated asking him this but I thought it wise to let him know the gravity of the situation and the risks involved.

"They gave me their word!" he retorted, almost in a shout. "They promised me that they would send her back to me so long as I did not attempt to pull a fast one. I promised I would not try any trick and I intend to keep my word."

I decided to change the topic, just to help him relax. "Sir, do you think the chauffeur is part of the gang?"

He rapidly turned his head like an aroused viper and stared at me inquisitively. There was a strange hardness in his eyes, which left me perplexed.

"Jackson has served me diligently as a chauffeur for ages. I don't fancy him doing this."

"But have you heard from him?" I insisted.

"No, I have not," he said, this time avoiding my eyes. I was now very sure that if the chauffeur was not part of the scheme, then he was dead. You don't just kidnap the wife of a police general unless someone gives you a hand; someone who knows how the inside works. I abandoned this kind of thoughts for it was like placing the donkey in front of the cart. Right now the most important thing was to save the kidnapped woman.

"Sir, I think if we organise ourselves we can beat them. We can…"

"No!" he shouted, almost bringing down the roof of the house. He then thrust his fleshy finger towards me and hissed, "Sherriff, I don't want any heroism in this affair. Don't you see that if we try anything these bastards may end up harming my wife?"

I decided to leave it at that. Well, it was his money. If he lost it, that was no pain in my neck. In a way I understood him although I did not wholesomely excuse his fears. I finally accepted to help him deliver the ransom after deep thinking. However, I made it clear that I was not ready to receive any unofficial pay.

"Good," he said with a note of gratitude. "They promised to call any time from now. Once they call I will have a car waiting for you."

"Will I go alone?"

"Yes. They insisted that whoever delivers the money must be alone and I don't want to risk."

I felt a cold chill run up my spine. Initially, I had thought that he would come with me but now that he had told me that I would go it alone, I felt unsure of myself and I almost chickened out at the eleventh hour.

He offered me another drink but I flatly declined. The whisky was beginning to get the better of me and I thought it would be better to stop. If I had to face this one, I thought, I had to have a sober head on my shoulders.

He left me in the living room and disappeared to another room. After about two minutes, he came back carrying a shiny briefcase and placed it on the floor. I did not need to be told that this was the ransom money. I viewed the briefcase with a little bit of remorse since I knew there was a big chance that he could end up losing both the money and his wife, although I did not tell him this. Well, I had tried to help him but he had closed his ears to counsel.

I watched him as he walked towards the telephone and lifted up the handset and talked to someone. After a minute, a girl appeared.

"Yes Sir?" she said in a musical voice.

I could not help noticing her striking beauty. She was around twenty-five with a figure worthy wasting your time staring at. She moved in an elastic way, something that told me that she must have been a dancer at one stage of her life. Although she was perfectly dressed, I immediately guessed she was the housekeeper. The only thing that spoiled her dark looks were the dark smudges under her eyes, which told me that she must have had some long sessions of weeping.

"Jackline, this is detective Sherriff. He looks very tired and I guess he will need a shower and a good rest. Take him to the visitors' room," ordered the general.

She did not say anything. She just motioned me to follow her then walked out.

The clock struck 23:00 hours and a sharp rap came at my door. I hurriedly rose from the bed and opened the door.

The long wait was starting to weigh on me and without knowing it, I had found myself dozing. Had the knock not come, I could have drifted into slumberland.

I opened the door and found the general standing outside, still dressed in his suit.

"They have contacted me," he said breathlessly. "The money is to be delivered within one hour from now then they will tell us where to find her so get ready."

I gulped down some dry air and caressed my face. I still wasn't sure whether I wanted to take the risk but I was aware it was too late to turn back. I went back into the room and picked my up jacket. While I was harnessing my gun, a scared voice brought me to a stop.

"Sherriff?"

I turned my head like a lion that had been disturbed at feeding time. He was still there watching me, his face still submerged in fear and worry.

"Yes, Sir."

"I don't want you to try any senseless bravado," he said in a voice that sounded threatening. "If they kill my wife you will have her in your conscience for the rest of your life."

We stared at each other like two boxers sizing up each other before a fight. It was as if he had read my thoughts.

I had been turning my brain over and over thinking of how I could pull a fast one on the kidnappers. The only thing that worried me was the amount of money at stake. Like a trained officer, I knew the higher the ransom, the higher the risk that the victim could die and this made me rule out any possibility of bravado. I hadn't lost hope but his words made me whittle down my ambitions of carrying out a rescue.

I left King's Park and headed to Forest Road. When the gang said that the money had to be delivered somewhere near Forest Road, I knew that we were not dealing with babies in the world of crime. Owing to my long stint in the crime department, I knew all the hotspots in the city like the back of my hand and I knew that by choosing a less inhabited area, which was flanked by a forest, the kidnappers were not taking chances.

There was less traffic since it was at night and so I could drive moderately fast. According to the general, they had spelt their terms very well: the money was to be placed inside a public toilet and that is what showed that they had brains.

It was not difficult to pick out the toilet. When the flashlights of my car picked it out, I drew in a sharp breath and touched my gun. I parked my car at the verge and leaving the engine running, I clutched the briefcase and walked towards the toilet. There was no soul in sight and a deadly silence hung in the air, broken only by the undeterred crickets that continued to fill the night with their rhythmic noise. As I walked towards the door of the loo, I dipped my hand inside my coat and felt for my gun while at the same time surveying the hideous vicinity. I could see no one but I knew that somewhere, a couple of eyes were lurking in the dark watching me. The toilet had no door so I just walked in. Typical of all public toilets, it was littered with human dung all around and a strong stench engulfed the entire space. I moved my flashlight around and selected a dung-free space where I slowly placed the briefcase. Covering my mouth with one of my hands, I carefully walked out and headed back to my car.

I closed my car door, shifted the gear and drove away as the kidnappers had ordered. Nevertheless, one of my eyes did not leave the side mirror for I wanted to be sure that no one had followed me. I hadn't driven for more than three hundred metres when I heard the faint noise of what sounded like the cracking sound of a motorcycle engine. I immediately looked at the side mirror. That is when I caught sight of the tail light of a motorcycle as it branched into the main road and sped in the opposite direction. It was dark and so I couldn't catch the sight of the rider but I knew that he was the man who had been assigned to grab the ransom. There was nothing we could do now. All that was left was to cross our fingers and wait for them hoping that they would honour their part of the bargain.

* * *

The long wait was beginning to break me down and my head now felt heavy like a stone while my eyes grew red with sleep. Such a tedious and nerve-wrecking wait was something I abhorred. At a certain moment I excused myself and walked to the garden outside for a smoke. I left the general sipping his whisky while at the same time pacing around the hall like one who had black ants in his pants. I had a nagging feeling that all was not well, but I would have hated to pour paraffin on a blazing fire. I would have wanted to tell him that he had seen the last of her but I decided to wait. The clock on the mantlepiece struck midnight. That was when the long wait was interrupted.

I was busy walking around the well-trimmed lawn, smoking a cigarette while I racked my brains when a whistle came. I looked behind my shoulders and caught sight of the general standing at the doorstep. That told me that something new had cropped up. I crossed my fingers and hoped for the best while at the same time bracing myself for the worst.

"Did they bring her over the phone?" I asked as I picked up my jacket from the sofa.

"No," he replied in a flat apprehensive voice. I looked at his face and what I saw told me all was not fine. He now looked older than his age and I could see there was not a single spirit in his facial expression.

I made a last-ditch effort to make him accept that we call for reinforcement but he insisted that he wanted this episode hidden from the public ear and eye.

I let it rest at that.

I took the car and drove towards the city centre. Apart from the twilights and nocturnals, the city was deserted and this facilitated speeding. I branched to Freedom Highway and then towards Ocean Road. I was beginning to curse and to respect this gang at the same time. They were fond of choosing the most bizarre places; where they knew that it was easy to cover their trails. I passed the airport and headed towards Santos River, still maintaining an average speed. I hadn't driven more than ten minutes before I caught sight of a cluster of half-finished storey buildings.

I gave them full marks.

By choosing a building site where they knew there would be a number of idlers walking to and fro, the kidnappers showed that they were experts in the art of camouflage. I branched off into a dusty road, at the same time counting the houses. Some of the houses were half finished while others were just at the foundation level. When I counted the seventh house, I slowed down and started looking for a place to park.

I opened the car door and lit the grassy path with my powerful flashlight. Though I felt no fear, I had made sure I brought my gun with me. I walked through the opening that looked like a door and found myself in a large hall littered with sand, concrete and pieces of half-cut wood lying all over. I found my way to the second floor climbing through a half-finished stairway. The second floor was a step ahead in construction, for it had rooms with doors and the walls had already been smeared with cement. I opened the first three doors but I found nothing.

Suddenly, I felt afraid. I stopped for a moment and listened, just to be sure that I was the only soul in here. The house now felt like a haunted hall with a deadly silence that sent chills roaming all over my body. I slowly pulled out my gun and pulled back the safety catch.

I fixed my flashlight on the fourth door with my gun

held at the ready. I wasn't taking chances so I used my foot to push the door open.

I found myself in an empty room. My heart was thudding. I swung my flashlight around and the light picked out a wooden door at the right side of the room. I slowly moved towards the door then used the tip of my shoe to push it open.

It did not move an inch.

I leaned on it, placing the whole of my weight and using my shoulder, I attempted to push.

The door moved but something told me that there must be some weight interfering with it. Finally, I pocketed my gun, mustered all my strength and pushed the door open.

I entered into the room that had nothing to show for furniture. There was a mat on the rough floor and it seemed as if the room had hosted a group of people. The plastic papers that greeted my eyes told me that whoever had been living here had been surviving on junk food. I moved my flashlight around but I saw no one. Then I fixed the light behind the door and I grimaced.

Her body was hanging behind the door with her hands tied behind her back. She looked beautiful even in her death but the mottled colour of her face made me almost vomit. There was a trickle of blood running from her mouth down to her chin. I looked at her half-naked torso and the marks I saw told me she must have been tortured before her death. I moved the light from her and surveyed the room again. That is when I caught sight of an empty briefcase lying in the farthest corner of the room. I moved nearby and surveyed it. I did not need to touch it to know that this was the briefcase in which I had carried the ransom money, although I did not need to open it to know that it was empty.

I sighed deeply and pulled out my handkerchief to mop my wet face. As a professional, I knew that the rest was best left to the scenes of crime team. All the same, I had to call the general. I didn't know how to select my words but I knew I had to break the news to him in one way or the other.

"Sorry Sir, but I have bad news for you," I said mournfully without mincing words.

I heard him gasp and I could tell from his fast breathing that he was fearing for the worst.

"They have not killed my wife Sherriff, have they?"

I was afraid to tell him but then I had to.

"Unfortunately they have killed her, Sir,"

"What followed was a long silence during which I could hear his heavy breathing over the line.

"What should I do, Sir?" I asked, just to break the silence.

After another brief moment of silence he said, "Just go home Sherriff and leave the rest to me. Once again, thank you for your help."

This left me dazed to the core.

The wife of the country's top police officer is hanging from a hook, dead and the bereaved husband is not even talking about calling the police!

"Sir, don't you think we should send for the law?" I insisted.

He paused for brief moment, drew in a deep sigh and said, "You have done your part, Sherriff. Just go home and leave the rest to me."

The click on my phone told me that the line had gone dead.

I dropped my phone in my pocket and cursed the royalty and their fear of publicity. I half-heartedly walked down the stairs and headed to my car.

Chapter 3

The traumatic events of the previous day had rocked me hard but I still managed to pull myself up and push on with life. The first thing I did after waking up was to rush for a newspaper. The screaming headlines spoke of nothing other than the killing of the general's wife. This I expected considering that she belonged to royalty but what surprised me was the way the story read. The story, which dominated the front pages of the local media and which according to me helped to dilute and overshadow the death of an iconic scribe like Larry, was completely altered to the point that it sounded new to me. According to the police, the victim had been kidnapped and a ten million ransom demand had been made. The general, unwilling to bow to the demands of the kidnappers, was busy mounting a rescue operation when the kidnappers killed her then melted away. Her body was later found in an abandoned warehouse somewhere on the outskirts of the city. According to the report, the police were hunting for the chauffeur who was the last person to be seen with the victim and who was yet to resurface after the ordeal. When I read this, I immediately raised my eyebrows. Why the police had falsified the facts, altering the entire flow of events, left me baffled. I remembered that the general had insisted that he didn't want this case to become a public case. Maybe that is why the events had been altered, I reasoned. All in all, there was a lingering feeling at the back of my mind that there was something fishy.

Below the story, there was a short column where the

general was advising the public never to collaborate with kidnappers so that they help the police block the windpipe of these gangs. Although I was the man who had risked his neck, it was the general who emerged from this affair as a hero. He was canonised for his coherence and was heaped with praises as a man who was not ready to negotiate with evil, a selfless and principled man who was ready to sacrifice even his treasured self in the name of upholding the law!

Astonished and baffled, I almost spat on the floor in disgust!

I read the story again, then my eyes settled on the photo of the presumed villain in the piece - the chauffeur whose description the police had circulated to the media houses. There was a public appeal for anyone who sighted him to report to the nearest police station.

But why the change of story?

This still left me baffled and however much I tried to understand the awkward position of the general, something still told me that there was more than met the eye in the whole story.

I shook my head and turned to the next page.

Larry's death had been given a full page. When I read the story and viewed the pictures, my soul was slashed into ribbons and I felt that I had to do everything until the killers were brought to book. I had a feeling that the law was dragging its feet over the matter and this is what pushed me to make the hard decision: before handing over my resignation letter, I would make sure I solved this case.

That evening I felt obliged to visit the general and convey my message of condolence. After all, he had put his trust in me by assigning me the mission to save his wife and so I thought it would be a polite gesture to just pass by his home and give him a shoulder to lean on. I would have wanted to ask him why he had fed lies to the press but I decided that this would have been a question too severe to pose to a mourning person, so I discarded the idea. Above all, I knew what his answer would be so I decided to let the matter rest at that. In a way my hands were tied. Certainly, if I went ahead and let the cat out of the bag, I would have ended up contradicting him and that would be juice to the press. Well, it was his wife and his money and if he thought it wise to put a stone over the case in the name of saving his public image, so be it. However, the fact that he had shown his trust in me made me feel indebted to him, so I took my car and drove to his home.

The parking space was littered with top-of-the-range cars and the faces I saw inside the living room made me feel like a goose amongst hens. Looking at them was like reading the list of who is who in the top echelons of the society. There was a collection of members of parliament, cabinet ministers, senior civil servants, political bigwigs and prominent businessmen, all who had come to offer the general a shoulder to lean on. But there was one odd thing that struck me and left me wondering: there seemed to be more of merrymaking than mourning. Everyone was chatting animatedly and there was not a single tear on their faces. Beer and wine flowed freely and the aroma of roast meat engulfed the entire house. Waiters had been hired to serve the guests and soft music gave company to the mourners. Well, considering that this was the first time that I was mixing with the cream of the society, I fancied that maybe this was their style of mourning. I felt lonely and this made me yearn for a cigarette. I sat down and I was served with a plate of food and a bottle of beer. As I chewed the juicy meat and washed it down with the cold beer, I threw my eyes hither and thither searching for the general.

He was seated on the high table surrounded by a group of prominent men. They were laughing heartily while they relished the roast meat. Although I felt uneasy, I gathered my courage and walked over to this table of the high and mighty. I gave the general my handshake of condolence but the odd stare he gave me did not escape my notice. He looked at me – like someone who had gatecrashed into the party – with repellent eyes and a hard unwelcoming face. I interpreted this to mean that I had interrupted a group of people to whose class I did not belong, so I immediately backed away and went back to my meal. I hurriedly finished what was on my plate for I wanted to get out of the uncomfortable ambience. Although everyone was smoking freely inside the living room, I reckoned it would not be polite to copy them. I walked out into the compound. I sought refuge under a well-trimmed bougainvillea shrub and lit my stick.

The night air was cool and soothing and while I smoked and listened to the music, I thought about what had happened in the past two days.

"Would you do with some company?" a voice said behind me.

I turned around and I found myself facing the girl I had met the night before. She almost startled me for I was not expecting that someone would be interested in me. I had not talked to her since the day she had shown me to my room. On that night, she looked very appealing but now, with a dull face and mourning eyes, she looked less appealing.

"I wouldn't mind," I said politely.

She offered me her feeble hand and I gave it a tender squeeze. To me, she appeared as the only person that was mourning.

The music in the living grew louder and I saw her bite her lips. Without being told, I knew that the whole scenario irritated her. While she sat in silence, I noticed that she would occasionally wince in suppressed anger and I could see from her facial expressions that she was fighting hard not to show it.

"Seems more of a wedding than a funeral," she said indignantly.

"What do you mean by this," I queried curiously.

She ignored my question. After a while of silence, she came in again. "Now that she is dead, I hope they will find the peace they have always yearned for."

The way she talked surprised me. She was talking in soliloquy; as if she was alone and the note of disgust in her voice was obvious.

Although I could still not follow her, the carnival mood that I was witnessing told me that there was more into this affair than it seemed to me. I remembered the night when the commissioner called me to deliver the ransom. He looked so worried, so shaken. But when I went to greet him this evening, what I saw in his face was a complete contradiction of the man I had met the night before. He looked jovial although he tried hard not to show it but when I looked into his eyes, they gave me the impression of a very relaxed man and this I found to be odd.

"You seem to be the only one who is mourning here," I said as a matter of concern.

"Yes. After all, I am the only one who has lost a friend. To them, it's a case of good riddance; a heavy load off their back," she answered.

A very strange answer, I thought. Although I had not gone there with the intention of snooping around, I decided to dig deeper, if only to pass time.

"Sorry, what do you mean by this?"

She paused to dry her tears, then said, "Today is the last day for me to work here. With Tracy gone, I guess I better un pitch my tents and seek for greener pastures."

I noticed that she kept looking furtively behind her shoulders while she talked. It was as if she was worried that what she was saying may be blown into some undesirable ears.

"I am happy for what you did for Tracy. Frankly speaking, I guess only you and I hoped that she should come out of this ordeal alive. Unfortunately, the gods of evil have won."

I was now sure that I was on to something.

"Have you read the newspapers?" I asked cunningly.

Again she chewed her lips in suppressed anger.

"Yes, I have and I had been expecting that the story would read that way."

"You mean there is more than meets the eye in this case?" I asked, putting my hand on her shoulder.

Again, she looked behind her shoulders then told me in a whisper. "They say walls have eyes and bushes have ears. If you don't mind, I can give you a date then I can tell you something that may interest you."

I was perplexed but I made sure I hid this from her. I too had been having jitters over this bizarre set-up, although I hadn't given it much thought.

"Do you believe the chauffeur is behind it?" I asked.

She looked at me and grinned. "You cops are all the same. You never see a question that you cannot ask. Well, I will yield to that one but it's the last." Again she looked behind her shoulders. "I know appearances can lie but knowing the closeness that existed between Tracy and Jackson, I don't believe a hoot that the latter is the mastermind of this heinous crime."

“Then where is he?” I insisted.

Again she grinned, this time sarcastically. “That is the mystery that the police must unravel.”

I did not press her anymore. I decided it would be better to wait for the date.

* * *

Die-hard fans surrounded the giant screen. Some yelled, some shouted while others quarrelled and this I understood. The big match between Arsenal and Chelsea was a dish too sweet to miss. Unlike the other matches, this particular match had a unique flavour for it was a do-or-die affair. It was the last appointment of the premier league and only a single point separated the two archrivals, meaning that whoever won this mouth-watering derby would automatically run away with the coveted silverware.

The two teams made their entrance into the pitch and the yells and shouts increased, but this did little to fire my interest. I kept looking at my watch while at the same time cursing. Luckily, the cold beer and the soothing music helped lift up my patience.

While I waited for her, my mind drifted back to the events of the night before.

I had gotten bored with the unfamiliar environment and was contemplating sneaking away. I hurriedly swallowed my beer and was just about to raise myself from the chair when someone tapped my shoulder.

I turned my head and I found myself facing one of the waiters.

“Your name is Sherriff?” he whispered.

I nodded in affirmation.

“Somebody wants to see you,” he went on. Before I could ask who it was, he gestured with his finger, “Come.

Follow me."

I rose up and followed his broad back as he meandered through the guests, finally stopping in front of a door. He opened the door then gestured to me that I could enter.

Like a hypnotised person, I obeyed.

The general was sitting behind a desk in what looked like a small office. There was a half-filled bottle of liquor and an empty glass on top of the desk.

His eyes were bloodshot and he looked as if he would have needed some extra hours of rest. Nevertheless, he gazed at me benevolently and even managed a weak smile.

"You can sit down," he said with a husky voice.

I sat down and placed my hands on my laps. Since I had already conveyed my message of condolence to him, I didn't know what to tell him. A quick glance at him convinced me that it would be better if he did the talking and I did the listening.

He filled the glass with liquor, took a long swig then placed the half-filled glass on the table.

"I have been nursing a strong desire to meet you and thank you but time has been scarce," he said lowly. I could see that he was forcing himself to speak.

"I know what you have read in the newspapers has left you baffled but I know you will understand," he went on. It was interesting how he was anticipating all the questions that were disturbing my mind.

"If you were in my shoes you would have done the same. If I weren't the police general, I would not have altered the facts but negative publicity is known to have killed many careers."

He caressed his clean-shaven jaw then looked at me like a trapped mouse begging for mercy.

"Mourning my wife is almost breaking me down. Imagine how the situation would be if I also had to deal with the disquiet that would have been provoked if the truth had come out."

I said nothing for I had nothing ready. Of course I had guessed why the course of events had been altered but I did not tell him this. However, there was one thing I would have wanted to ask him: whether he would have liked the events leading to his wife's death to be investigated. Before I could ask him this, he opened a drawer and drew out a bulky envelope. He drew in a deep sigh then stared at me imploringly.

"This is to pay for your troubles," he said, handing the envelope to me.

I was caught flat-footed. The night before, I had told him that I was not ready to receive any back-door pay and I could not understand why he was giving me the money. Nevertheless, although I would have wanted to decline, I found myself half-heartedly accepting the envelope.

His mournful face and beseeching eyes had disarmed me.

I had walked out of his office and headed home. I was both ashamed and angry with myself for having betrayed my principles but I had to accept that he had caught me unawares.

I stopped thinking of the general and shifted my eyes to the giant screen. They were still running the 'commercials' but I knew that soon the match would begin.

Then she appeared.

She was dressed in a deep-blue hipster, a matching jacket and a dark-red blouse. She looked a bit more jovial than the last time I had seen and that made her look like a woman whom any man would waste his time feasting eyes on.

"I wish we hadn't made our date on a day like this," she said while I pulled a chair back for her. I could see that she was a bit agitated and even though she gave me her soft hand, she had her eyes stuck to the screen

"I am a die-hard fan of Chelsea but I have a strange jinx, which I have never broken. Every time I watch an important match involving Chelsea they always end up losing but if I fail to watch, they win," she said as she placed her handbag on the table.

I laughed and then I asked her what she would want to take.

As we waited for the barman to deliver the order, we got into a casual talk although I could hardly wait for the time to talk real business. I realised that she was by nature a very talkative person and now that she was talking in her normal voice, it felt nice to listen to her. Now that she had shaken off the mourning dust, she talked freely and could even afford to crack a joke.

The waiter delivered the cold malt and I helped pour the drink into her glass.

We lifted up our glasses and she proposed the toast.

"To our victory," she said with a chuckle.

She took a long sip from her glass, then gave me another warm smile saying, "I know you are dying to fire questions but first you must promise that you will let me talk first then we leave the questions for the end."

I willingly obliged to her request although I knew it would be hard to stick to this vow.

"I met Tracy some years ago in college where we were fashion design students and we instantly became inseparable friends. We both loved fun, although I was later to learn that she had an insatiable hunger for big money. She was the one who introduced me to the lucrative trade of the day. We would prey on rich gentlemen who needed the much-desired youthful warmth of beautiful girls but who also had deep pockets and wads of big cash to dish."

She sipped her drink, cast a quick glance at the giant screen then went on.

"The public calls us gold diggers, although I think it's out of jealousy. Many women would want to be in our place for I believe no woman hates money and comfort while many men would want to have us but they carry the curse of having shallow pockets. To the self- proclaimed gatekeepers of morals, we are prostitutes but to me it's nothing more than taking one's opportunity and drawing all the profit out of it while warm blood is still flowing in your veins. Call it making hay while the sun shines."

Shouts of *oohs and aahs* filled the air and we both simultaneously shifted our eyes to the giant screen. The shouts of despair were coming from the Gunners side, for their team had just lost a clear chance to net their first goal while the Blues applauded for the close escape.

"Phew! That was a close shave," she said, scratching her head. She then took up her story again.

"Sweet life flowed like an eternal stream that never dries up and the fun that came along made us feel like queens. Although we were still college students, we were living in a good apartment in the most exclusive city suburb, which only a very rich woman can afford. We had a car and the net wage of each one was almost touching the six-figure level. The other students envied our flashy clothes and our carefree lifestyle. Things were now dandy and we were both looking forward to happy times ahead. The icing on the cake came when Tracy met the general."

She took a long gulp from her glass, smacked her mouth then went on.

"I don't know how she came to fall into the arms of the general, though I guess that the aroma of big money was too much to resist. The night she hooked him, she burst into our apartment in an upbeat mood, like one who had landed in the seventh heaven. She told me that she had not only found the key to paradise, but also its security. Though I didn't understand what she meant, it took me only one week to feel the true weight of these words. The general handed us sweet life and luxury on a silver plate. We were treated like royal poodles with a mountain of money to spend as we wished and a chauffeur and a bodyguard to accompany us for shopping in a sleek car and this to me is the kind of chance that falls in your path once in a generation. From the outset, I was a bit sceptical about the match since he was double her age but the hefty pay package, his extraordinary largesse, holiday trips abroad and exorbitant shopping finally won me over. When they started living like husband and wife, Tracy invited me to be her house help. The request was mouth-watering for it meant that I would now have a secured six digit payslip, a dear friend next to me, less work to do and freedom of fun-seeking thus I found myself falling for it."

Shouts of "Goal! Goal!" filled the air and a part of the crowd waving red shirts went into a frenzy.
Arsenal had drawn first blood.

"I told you!" she shouted while at the same time banging the table with rage. "Every time I watch these matches, we always end up losing!"

"Don't you let it bite you! He laughs loudest who laughs last so pull yourself together for all is not lost," I said in sympathy. She mopped her wet face with a handkerchief then continued with her tale.

"The general had lost his first wife with whom he had sired four children, all grown-up and independent. They hated Tracy at first sight and they made it clear with their body language that she was *persona-non-grata* in the family. Little did they know that they would soon reckon with her charms and supernatural feminine prowess. Tracy had a natural talent and she could draw any man to herself like a ringed bull. It was not long before she put her charms into play, stamping her authority in the home and making her presence felt. The 'big mama' act was an instant success and it was not long before the general called his children together and read them the riot act. He told them to shape up or ship off, threatening to crack the whip ruthlessly if they did not accept his new wife. To show them that he meant his words, he installed Tracy as the bona fide manager of the vast family business empire. Dejected, hopeless and unwilling to swallow the bitter pill, the children stormed out of the house and left the two love birds alone never to return again."

I poured her another drink and she took a couple of sips then went on with her story.

"Old habits die hard, thus goes an old adage. As I had told you earlier, Tracy loved big money and luxury but she also loved fun. She wanted to eat her cake and also keep it and this is why she started cheating on him. Unlike in the years before when she used to dig for moneyed middle-aged men for cash, now she dated young men in their mid-twenties for love and warmth. With cash, a free hand and lots of time, it was not hard for her to hook the money hungry toy-boys. She was a sly schemer and shrewd in her activities so this small secret was only known to me. I guess because of this, problems started brewing between her and her husband. Slowly, the love started to erode; the warmth of the bedroom began to fade and finally, the gulf between them widened till it became irreparable. Indeed, by the time their love touched rock bottom, they had become estranged and had ceased to share the same bedroom. While she was running after young men, her husband in turn became mysterious and sought refuge in his office and in golf clubs in the company of his prominent buddies. To Tracy, this was godsend, for it meant free space for her Casanova escapades. This was until she met and fell in love with a prominent youthful DJ who worked in one of the city-clubs."

She paused, shifted her eyes to the screen and sighed deeply when she looked at the time.

"This DJ was handsome, he had a talent in handling women and above all he was free and bubbling with the sap of youthfulness; the kind of man whom any sex-hungry and spoilt-rich woman would willingly snatch without a second thought. In the beginning, it looked like just normal truancy of a woman in search of warmth and love but as time passed, it progressed into a serious affair. It was at this point that Tracy began to lay a fertile ground to sow the seeds of divorce. The love between the two lovebirds grew roots and blossomed, hence it was not long before she finally confronted her husband requesting for a formal divorce. The latter remained adamant and went ahead to threaten her with dire consequences if she ever made her request again. Since Tracy knew that he was a man who wielded the big stick, she cowed in a tactful retreat and decided to bid for her time. Then something happened two weeks ago that changed the tune of the music."

The tale was turning juicy and I was now alert, like an aroused viper. Even the beer I had taken lost its inebriating power and I opened my ears the way an insect spreads out its feelers.

"On this fateful day, her husband came home so dead drunk that he could hardly find his way to his bedroom unaided. He accidently dumped his briefcase on a sofa in the living room, then staggered to the bedroom. Since their quarrels began, he never left his bedroom keys to anyone, not even to me. I had to go and help him open the door when he had found the key for he couldn't manage by himself."

The two teams made their entry into the pitch for the second part of the match and the crowds clapped to rally them on.

"When Tracy saw the briefcase, she grabbed it and took it with her to her bedroom. She remained locked up in her room for about an hour and when she walked out, she was wearing a gleaming face, like one who had struck gold. Looking at her strange aura, she reminded me of the Tracy of the good old times. She was holding a brown envelope in one hand, which she showed to me saying: "I have finally laid my hand on the key to paradise baby."

"I drew close and my eyes looked at the envelope. There was nothing on it except the writing 'TOP SECRET' written in bold letters. She placed the briefcase on the table, opened it and replaced the envelope. She then closed the briefcase and hurled it on the sofa, then turned to me and smiled widely saying, "All I need now is to find a good journalist and you and I will fly to paradise where we shall live like angels." She then hurriedly dressed up, walked out, drove out and remained out for the better part of the night.

"One day later, she gate-crushed into her husband's bedroom in the morning and what followed was what I would describe as the 'morning of raw nerves'. Their heated argument sent cold chills down my spine. At one point I even thought of asking for outside help. Although I was now used to their bitter exchange of words and endless morning showdowns, none of them would have outmatched this one and if I could, I would have awarded it the gold medal. It was so heated that I feared he may lose his mind and be compelled to shoot her. I tiptoed to the door and since it was half open, I had a chance to get a blow-to-blow account of the whole verbal inferno.

"You either give me a legal divorce or the contents of that envelope will land into the wrong hands!" Tracy kept shouting at the same time pointing at him threateningly. These words led to an unexpected turn of events. Her husband – who seldom ceded any ground – coiled and even toned down his language. He discarded his baritone voice and started begging her not to act foolish, warning her that she was toying around with a very dangerous thing, but Tracy would hear none of it. Before walking out of the bedroom, she gave him a two-week ultimatum within which he was supposed to have filed for divorce. Unfortunately, the two weeks did not elapse before she met her end."

My heart was now racing with excitement and I could hardly hold my patience. I had a million-dollar question that I was dying to ask and I wished she put a full stop to her story so that I could put it across. But what she told me only helped to increase the beating of my heart.

"Now we come to the kidnap episode. I had told you that Tracy had been having an illicit affair with a popular DJ. Only three people were privy to this affair; Tracy, I and Jackson, the chauffeur. Tracy would go to town ostensibly for shopping and the two would meet in a secret love nest and they would have a good time while Jackson would go to a bar and wait for her call. Tracy paid Jack extra money to tighten his lips. Now, this is where the numbers don't add up. Tracy is kidnaped and twelve hours later she is found dead. The next day, the charred remains of her lover – the DJ – are found in the burnt shell of his car while Jackson the chauffeur who happens to be her closest confidant has disappeared into thin air. Glue these pieces together and you will see why I suspect foul play in the whole set-up."

"I don't follow," I hissed impatiently. "You want to tell me that the DJ too is dead?"

She gave me a strange look, like I had made a sacrilegious remark then said, "Are you the only stranger in Jerusalem? Today in the morning there was a major demonstration of music lovers who had flooded the streets demanding action for the murder of a popular DJ. Didn't you hear about it?"

I would have wanted to tell her that I had enough troubles of my own that I had ended up disconnecting myself from current affairs but I decided to save that for another time so I flatly told her that I had heard nothing."

She looked furtively behind her back and her eyes had that fearful sparkle that told me that what she wanted to tell me was meant for my ears only.

"What I will tell you is what the newspapers have written. The charred remains of the DJ were pulled out from the burnt-out shell. The police are saying that his death can be attributed to a love triangle gone sour." She leant closer to me and whispered, "No one has glued together the link between the two killings. No one knows that the slain DJ was having an affair with the general's dead wife. If someone comes to find out the truth and then shouts about it, then be sure that hell will break loose and there is going to be a lot of disquiet in the media. Do you now see why I was telling you that there is a lot that meets the eye in these mysterious events?"

My whole body was now trembling with suppressed curiosity, for I was now sure that I was on to something interesting.

"For how long have Tracy and the DJ been in this game?" I asked. I had already broken my vow of silence once hence I saw no use in sticking to it.

She tapped her forehead as she dug into her memory. "Six months to be exact. I remember this because they met one day after my birthday. On this day Tracy walked in with the air of a princess and told me that she had finally met her prince charming with whom she intended to spend the rest of her life. She went ahead to tell me that all she needed was to legally divorce his husband, rake off a good chunk of his fortune and the two would fly away to glory-land rolling in dough."

"Are you sure the general did not know about this affair?"

She shook her head emphatically.

"It was impossible for him to know unless Jackson told him and this I find improbable."

"Then how do you link the two episodes together if no one knew of this affair?"

She ignored my question then after looking furtively behind her back, she leaned forward and whispered, "Strictly between you and me, this is the way I can figure it out. The general, unwilling to bow to her blackmail must have decided that the best solution was to silence her. This can only mean that he is the one who engineered the kidnap."

I was not listening to her for my sleuth mind was already at work. As a trained cop, I knew that you don't just blackmail a general of the police unless you are holding a very strong weapon and that to me spoke volumes.

You are joking around with a very dangerous thing.

These words sounded like a bombshell to me.

All I need is to find a journalist and then we fly to paradise and live like angels.

I remembered that Larry had been found dead twelve hours before I found the general's wife.

Was Larry the journalist that Tracy was talking about?

I put myself in Tracy's shoes. You are the wife of a prominent man and you have some sensitive information. You would want this information to get to the public domain and the only person who can work in aid of this is a competent journalist. Now, if you lived in Ndiambo-land and you are looking for a fearless journalist, who would you go for if not the Whistleblower?

Slowly a hunch started to form in my mind and I vowed not to go to bed until I gave it an acid test.

Chelsea scored the equaliser and the 'blue sea' went into a devilish delirium. Jackline almost knocked me over as she hugged me and planted kisses all over me. The match was now in the homestretch and that meant that whoever scored a goal would automatically run away with the coveted prize. The atmosphere was now fully charged and both sides were tense like a tight rope. I was dying to ask her whether the journalist whom Tracy wanted to contact could have been Larry but the emotions of the dying minutes of the game had stolen both her heart and her attention. We could barely hear one another however loud I attempted to speak. I decided to give her time until she got over the emotions of the game. To kill time, I rose up and walked to the loo.

Hardly had I finished unzipping my trouser when shouts of goal came thundering shaking the club to its foundation. When I finished urinating and walked out of the loo, I was greeted by shouts of 'Arsenal! Arsenal!'

This conveyed the message that Arsenal had scored a last-minute goal, sealing both the game and the championship. I fought my way through the mad crowd who were now pouring beer on one another in celebration until I reached our table.

She was resting her head on the table like one in mourning, with her hands spread in front of her head. I resisted a chuckle for I thought she was mourning the historic loss of the team of her heart. I called out her name and when I got no answer, I caressed the top of her head in a gesture of solidarity.

Still she didn't move.

I shook her shoulder and when she didn't react, I flinched. I slowly lifted up her head and what I saw sent my heart sinking to my bowels.

Her face was resting on a pool of blood, which filled her eyes and her mouth. I looked at the side of her head and when my eyes caught sight of the gunshot, I quickly felt for her neck hoping that there was still a chance to save her. That is when I realised with a sinking feeling that she was dead.

I woke up half-heartedly, hoisted my tired body from the bed and lazily walked to the kitchen to make myself a cup of tea. I would have willingly done with some extra hours of sleep but the call-in duties made me discard the idea.

The night prior, I had hardly slept a wink and only in the wee hours did I manage to doze off. What had happened to Jackline had left me shocked and rattled to the bones.

I had first called the police before I tried looking around, hoping to catch the killer. The melee of celebrating fans worked as a wave against me, so I could not pick up anything of value. No one had seen anything, no one had heard anything. Whoever the hit-man was, he must have been a very lucky opportunist for he had struck in the right moment; when all the attention of the people was focused on the giant screen. The fact that no one heard the shot told me that the killer had used a silenced gun and that was enough to convince me that I was dealing with a trained professional.

The police had arrived faster than I had expected and I was surprised to notice that the man in the lead was the commandant. This I found to be odd though I could not tell why. This man seemed to hover around like a hawk and was always at the right place at the right moment! I remembered that when I arrived at the Gossip Club the morning Larry was found dead, he was the man directing the operations. When I found Tracy's body and I called the general, the commandant was the man who took over. Whenever I called the headquarters asking for any developments on Larry's case, I was always referred to the commandant! And now Jackline is cleared from the way and he is still at the centre of the scene! I took this as a clue and stored it in the archives of my mind for as my instructor used to say, never ignore a pattern when investigating a crime.

I hurriedly swallowed my breakfast and then I went to the shopping centre to buy myself the daily paper. Unlike other days when I would hang around joking with my friend Kabs, whom I fondly referred to as Ma-plan, today I was in a big hurry. I bought the day's newspaper and asked him if he had the leftovers of the newspapers of the last three days and he gave them to me.

I went through the newspaper with a hair comb looking for the story of Jackline's assassination but I found none.

My mind now went alert.

Considering that Jackline had been working for the general as a maid for years, I found it strange that her murder did not receive any media coverage. Come to think of it! The general's wife is kidnapped and assassinated. Twelve hours later, her maid and best friend is felled by a gunman's bullet while she was talking to me.

And the newspapers do not find this as newsworthy! Surely, there was more than it seemed in this case, I murmured to myself.

I picked up a past newspaper and started looking for a story on a dead DJ.

It was hidden somewhere in the middle pages, between two columns. The DJ, according to the story, had been kidnapped and his charred remains were found some hours later in a burnt shell. Very little was said about him except that he was a talented crowd puller. From the story, I picked up the facts that he was a Congolese national and a prominent DJ in one of the city's most frequented discotheques. No witnesses had recorded a statement but the police were treating it as a case of a love triangle gone sour. The DJ's remains, according to the report, had already been interred. Above the story was a picture of a placard-waving mob, all demanding to be told who had snatched away the life of their music icon. Some of the demonstrators carried twigs while others carried musical instruments. There was a giant banner 'DJ Cool Lives', towering above the mob.

I started thinking about the whole set-up, putting into consideration all the clues, hints and hunches, yet one question kept disturbing me, like a nagging thorn held in a vein.

Was Larry the journalist whom Tracy had contacted and what could have been the big story?

The more I thought about this question, the more I became convinced that the answer to this question is what held the key to the mystery. It was a pity that Jackline had been assassinated before she could answer this question and now that she was gone, I had to seek the answer elsewhere.

I shifted gears and trained my focus on Tracy. Discretion told me that you don't box the police general into a corner unless you are holding a very lethal weapon. This left me wondering what weapon Tracy was holding to warrant sending the general on his knees. If Jackline was to be believed, Tracy had stumbled onto a 'Top Secret' envelope. There was no doubt that she wouldn't have used the contents as the threatening weapon unless the content was something filthy that implicated the general.

But what was it?

Unfortunately, even on this, I found myself hitting the dead end for the only person who could answer this was either Tracy or the general himself.

The former was already in boot hill while making this question to the latter was strictly for the gods.

"Now all I need to do is to look for a good journalist."

These words still resonated in my mind and there was something in them that told me that they had something to do with Larry's death.

After studying my notes carefully, I concluded that if I hoped to crack this case, I had to dig up something about two prime characters in this act: the prostitute who was last seen with Larry and Jackson the chauffeur.

I zeroed in on these two and decided that this is where I would begin.

I went and took a shower, then made sure that I dressed in a very natty way. I knew the first impression is always very important so I made sure that I camouflaged myself very well with my mode of dress. A grey suit, a white shirt with a matching red and shiny-black shoes to complete the act looked like cool touches. I went to the table and picked up the newspaper cuttings I had made and stuffed them inside my satchel. I then picked up my gun and my car keys and walked out.

Chapter 4

It was not difficult to trace the chauffeur's home. All I needed was to study the newspaper reports carefully for me to know where to find it.

While I sent my car through the sparse traffic of Dinka Road, I found myself losing some of my motivation for I didn't know the kind of reception that was in store for me. Nevertheless, buoyed by the old adage 'if you don't seek, you don't find,' I pressed on the gas pedal and placed all my hopes on lady luck.

I arrived at the countryside just before midday and finding the home was not a Herculean task. When I reached the dusty shopping centre, I stopped my car and sought directions from an idling young man who was seated next to the road gnawing at a sugar cane. He willingly gave me the directions and after thanking him, I entered into my car and drove on.

I found myself stopping in front an iron gate painted black and after cutting down the engine, I walked to the blind gate and looked for a bell.

There was none.

I tried to push the gate but I realised that it was locked from the inside.

"Another cul-de-sac," I murmured to myself.

There was only one thing to do now; go back to my car and attempt hooting.

I went back to my car and hooted, first gently then when no one answered, I hooted like a lunatic pushing the whole weight of my hand on the horn.

Half a minute passed and was just about to repeat the hooting when the smaller part of the gate opened and a young man stepped out. He first eyed me meanly before walking towards me. Perhaps my demeanor convinced him that I could not hurt a fly.

"Can I help you?" he said without offering me his hand.

He was dressed in a dusty overall and the leaves sticking out from his hair told me that he must be the *shamba* boy.

Without introducing myself, I explained to him that I wanted to talk to the wife of the owner of the homestead. He eyed me suspiciously then probed me keenly from head to toe, brooded for a while then said, "Mama is in school but lunchbreak is a couple of minutes away. She never stops anywhere so you can come in and wait for her.

When I saw him swing the gate open, I thanked the gods of luck for I was expecting to have the doors slammed in my face. Although I knew I was far from hitting dry land, I thanked the heavens for at least I had covered the first milestone.

I was entering my car when my eyes wandered to the main road and my eyes caught sight of something strange.

A plain white Nissan saloon car passed by driving at a very low speed and I got the sensation that the two occupants in the car were looking towards my direction. I remembered that when I had stopped to refuel at Dinka Town, I had seen a white Nissan saloon with two beefy figures inside. I had not given it a thought but just when I was branching off the Dinka Fly-over I saw the same car some hundred metres behind me. When I stopped my car to ask for directions, the same car had driven by. Now I was seeing it for the fourth time and without consulting an oracle, I knew I was not alone. Somebody was trailing me.

I parked my car in front of the red-tiled farmhouse and stepped out. The lawn was neat and the Kay-apple hedge well-trimmed. The well-tendered flower beds in front of the house betrayed the hand of a professional gardener. I looked at the house and whispered in awe when I remembered the police ghettos. A simple chauffeur could not afford this kind of luxury, unless he had an extra hand that helped him to pluck the fruits of success or he had a tall uncle somewhere in the ranks. Well, they say that a rat that lives inside the palace of the king is not similar to a countryside rat, for while a countryside rat is used to living on grains, the palace rat lives on cheese and bacon. Being a chauffeur to the police general meant that even though he was a junior cop, he was bound to be strategically positioned in the gravy-train. However, looking at the house, it did not look like it housed a kidnapper on the run.

The young man led me inside and I found myself in a clean living room whose floor was covered with a blue carpet. There were two sofa sets covered with red linen, a huge study table and a couple of shiny mahogany lounge chairs. I sank my frame into one of the sofas and started admiring the framed pictures that hang on the cream-painted wall.

Three photos caught my attention.

The first photo was that of a young policeman in a neat police uniform, which told me that this photo was taken on the day of the passing-out parade. The second photo had the same man but this time he was in the company of a beautiful maiden dressed in a bridal gown. The last picture had the couple with two toddlers and a birthday cake.

Although the photo that had appeared in the papers looked old, the features had not changed much. The young man in the photos I was looking at had kind eyes and a fleshy face and looking at his calm posture, he could not pass for a kidnapper.

I was still admiring the rest of the pictures when the front door opened and a woman in her mid-thirties walked in. She was dressed in a pink-flowered dress and she carried a handbag that was hanging from one of her shoulders. Although years had passed, I could tell that she was the woman in the second picture wearing bridal robes.

She looked at me with inquisitive eyes then managed a weak, forced smile. I stood up and offered my hand without introducing myself. She took my hand lamely and although she was fighting hard to appear friendly, the reproaching veneer refused to peel from her face.

As she was placing her handbag on the coffee table, I was busy drawing my battle-lines. Without being told, I knew that her family must have undergone a harrowing experience and this I saw in her facial expressions. Having worked for a long time in the police force, I was aware of the trauma that the families of suspects went through. I knew if I was to make any significant inroads, then I had to make sure I won her over to my side.

"Madam, sorry for this unannounced visit but I hope you will bear with me," I said calmly.

She said nothing. She just sat calmly on the sofa, her repellent eyes digging into me like two arrows.

"I am here because of the kidnap incident involving your husband," I went on unceremoniously.

Her face drastically grew tight and this time she did not attempt to hide the hatred in her eyes.

"What do you want from me!" she snapped. "I have told you everything you wanted to know!"

That told me that I was walking in a mine-infested field

and I had to watch where I placed my feet. I fought hard to make my face appear calm and friendly, hoping to disarm her with my gentle looks.

"I am not here for that, madam. I want something else," I said politely.

She opened her handbag, fished out a clean handkerchief and went ahead to wipe away her tears. I hadn't expected her to break down this fast but considering the weighty case at hand, I understood.

After a short spell of silence, she faced me and softly asked me what I wanted.

I knew time had come to play my first card.

"Madam, I know it's hard for you to understand but I am here as a friend and I am conducting my own investigations to net the real culprits. I happen to know someone who knew your husband very well. This person swears that your husband couldn't have pulled this job. I and a group of friends are working to see whether we can get the necessary proof to exonerate him."

She gazed at the floor for a while, then looked up and asked, "Who are you?"

Her tone, though hard sounded welcoming and this told me that I had hit my first break.

I went ahead and told her that I was a detective attached to the Directorate of Criminal Investigation and that I was working on a private basis to net the real masterminds of the kidnapping.

She shifted her eyes to the floor and placed one of her palms on her cheek in a sorrowful gesture. I gave her time for, even though she had changed, there was still a chance that she could throw me out if I made a false move.

"Before this thing happened, this house was always full

of people," she began. "Then all of a sudden, it became deserted, like a graveyard. No one wants to be associated with us. My family is now isolated and even some of my relatives treat me as if I am a leper." Her tears were now flowing freely and I decided that it would not be polite to interrupt her. In a way, I thought she was crying for sympathy and I knew if I played along this line, I would win her confidence.

"The police keep hovering over us like vultures and we barely have space to breathe. When it happened, they came and ransacked the house, almost tearing it into pieces. When I asked them what they were searching for, they slapped me and told me that they were searching for the ransom money. They harassed me, claiming that I knew where my husband was hiding. It is now too much to bear."

"But the newspapers reported that no ransom was paid!" I pointed out.

"What newspapers report is one thing and the reality another," she answered sullenly.

"Has you husband ever called you since it happened?" I asked.

Her red eyes went round in surprise and she shook her head.

"He has not called. I wish you know how much I would want him to call just to know that he is alive. I have tried with all his best friends and his most trusted confidants but none has heard from him."

Her crying had now ceased, although I could tell from her eyes that she was a very troubled woman. I decided to change tack just to confirm a couple of facts.

"How were the working conditions in your husband's place of work? Did he tell you of any problem he may have been undergoing?"

"My husband was my best friend and my confidant," she said. "He never did anything behind my back and he would share everything with me. The job was well paying and he always brought home the pay package and he would involve me in the family budget planning. I knew he used to earn some extra money as bonus because at times, he would work beyond the normal hours. He always told me that he was well treated in his place of work. That is all I can tell you."

That confirmed Jackline's claim that the chauffeur could never betray Tracy. I swallowed some air and prepared myself as time had come for me to play my first jolly.

Looking intently into her eyes and with my voice hard but gentle, I leaned forward towards her and asked, "Madam, do you think your husband really helped to kidnap the general's wife?"

She first looked at me in a blinkless stare, gazed at the floor then lifted up her head and shook it saying, "This is next to impossible and I can swear by my late father. On this fateful day, he had called me in the morning confirming that he would be driving here the next day so that we could go and visit our daughter in school. He called me again during lunch and asked me to inform my brother that he was ready to close a land deal they had been working on. He asked me to instruct my brother to bring the seller to our home the next day in the evening. That was the last time I heard my husband's voice. The next thing I heard was that the police were looking for him in connection with the kidnap."

I probed her face looking for any give-away signs but I found none. Having dealt with professional pretenders, I knew that you don't just give a clean sheet to a witness just because he or she plays sad. I had seen witnesses who wailed their innocence even when they had guilt hidden in their pockets.

"Then why has he gone into hiding?" I asked just to show her that she had not bought me yet.
She gave me a strange look and smiled, saying, "You speak as if you don't live in this country. If the police can rough me up knowing that I am innocent, what do you think they would do to my husband if they lay their hands on him?"

I gave her full marks for this. Although I didn't tell her this, I knew that once her husband resurfaced, he would walk into a harrowing experience. From the look of things, in the court of public opinion, he had already been tried, found guilty and all that remained was his execution.

I decided that I had had enough of her. I produced a pen and wrote my cell phone number for her.

"Madam, I am now convinced your husband hasn't pulled this job but we need his collaboration if we have to portray him as clean. In case he calls, give him my number and tell him to call me. I will see to it that he gets protection and that he goes through a fair trial if need be."

As I gave her the paper, I begged her not to say any word about our meeting to anyone.
She took the paper, stared at it, then broke into another session of weeping.

"I know my husband couldn't have done this thing," she said amidst her sobs. "All I want to know is where he is and if he is still alive."
I patted her shoulder and promised to do anything to bring the real kidnappers to book, then I walked out, leaving her in tears.

* * *

I set my sunglasses straight and entered the lobby of Gossip club. I was gasping for breath after having muscled my way through the crowds, which were agitated due to the street runs that were going on between the hawkers and the city *askaris.* These kinds of street battles were a common phenomenon in the evenings since the hawkers normally invaded the pavements in a bid to earn themselves a last shilling for their daily bread. I was one of the people who hated these cat-and-mouse games that usually threw the city into a stampede but on this particular evening, the melee was a blessing. I wanted to make sure no one followed me. With such a pandemonium, I had a perfect opportunity to camouflage myself and throw off-track any would-be tail.

I had boldly persevered with the nerve-wrecking stretching traffic jam on Dinka Road, knowing very well that whoever was following me was still with me. It was a bit dark and I could not see very well due to the lights of the other cars behind me but I knew that somewhere in the long tail of cars, the white car was still there. While the other drivers hooted and cursed, I sent my mind working and began formulating a fool proof plan to throw them off-track. When I reached Hangani round about, I suddenly carried out a daredevil and reckless manoeuver, changed my direction and raced down Hangani road. The other drivers braked, hooted and insulted me but I didn't care.

I knew my pals in the white car had seen me but I also knew it would take them a couple of minutes before they caught up with me and that to me was enough. When I reached Hangani Police Station, I entered the station and drove slowly towards the quarters. I knew the place very well since I once lived there when I was working in the crime department. Most of the tenants knew me and I hoped that I would'nt meet any known face. I parked my car in front of a block where I knew one of my friends lived, picked up my satchel and locked the car. I then walked hurriedly to a smaller gate that led to the rear which we normally called *panya* route, for it was merely a hole in the fence and landed on Circus Avenue. I then flagged down an overcrowded matatu and headed towards the city centre.

As the matatu cruised towards the city centre I nodded to myself and smiled, mocking whoever had been following me. Well, I murmured to myself, this last move would warn them that they were not dealing with a toddler.

The loud music coming from the jukebox filled the bar and made me feel a bit nervous, though I liked the song. It had been long since I had listened to this song.

'You were my eyes when I couldn't see. You were my legs when I couldn't walk.'

This song made my heart snap for it was one of Sarah's favourite songs and I used to sing it to her whenever I wanted to tease her. I settled down and sipped my beer, watching the spirited revellers and listening to the music. The club was packed to capacity and this served me well because I would not have wanted anyone to notice me. Time flew past and I kept my mind busy watching the surroundings and bidding my time. I had already fashioned my plan and the only thing that was remaining was to identify the prey. I surveyed the barmaids keenly. They were all dressed in a beautiful uniform – a white blouse and a black pair of trousers and they had name tags sticking on their breast pockets. They were all beautiful creatures with nice figures to look at. It was not easy to choose between any two of them but one of them had a name that struck me: Sue.

I beckoned to her and told her that I wanted another beer. I then removed a one-thousand shillings note and handed it to her. After some few minutes, she came back with the beer and the change. Time had come for me to break the ground. I picked up the money but I made sure I left a one hundred note on the tray.

"That is for the sweet name that you carry on your breast," I said charmingly, making sure I gave the best smile from my collection.

She looked at her own name, which was pinned on her right breast pocket, smiled broadly exposing her white dentures then walked away.

I idly sent down my beer as I put the final touches of my plan. I had to cross-check all the details, even the minute ones before I put them into play. I was sure that if I made a false move I would spoil everything and for this, I kept my mind busy. Though I knew that my plan relied heavily on luck, I was sure if it worked, I would not leave this club empty. I called Sue and ordered another beer and slipped her another hundred.

"Is it still for the sweet name?"she asked with a chuckle, giving me a smile too benevolent.

I saw my chance and took it.

"To be sincere I would not mind to know whether the breast covered by the name is sweet too," I said, giving her a mischievous twinkle.

She smiled shyly, patted my shoulder and said something that I was not expecting. "I have to go now. If you are a patient man and you really want to know, my shift ends at eleven o'clock."

This was too good to listen to and I made sure I followed it before the fire died. "Well, if I am still waiting for the return of Jesus, I don't see why I should not wait for three hours, sweet Sue," I said, giving one of my best smiles.

She had swallowed it hook, line and sinker, faster than I thought she would.

I did wait for her and although the wait was long, it served to help me arrange my cards and study the battlefield in advance. Finally, her shift over, she went to the changing room, discarded her uniform and changed into an evening dress.

"You look like a beauty pageant candidate," I teased her. "Now I know that my wait was worth it."

She smiled again then led me out of the bar. We went down the stairs, with her in front of me. I produced my sunglasses and wore them again. I would have hated to step into the streets with a bare face. Though I had lost my tail, I was not underrating whoever was following me. When we reached the ground floor, I let Sue take a few steps, then I followed. I didn't want to give the idea that we were together. The girl who took care of the reception eyed me curiously but that didn't bother me.

When we stepped into the almost deserted street, I was glad to find that there was a taxi next to the entrance waiting for a customer. I talked to the driver and instructed him where he was to take us.

One hour later, I was closing the door of a room at Love Nest Motel while Sue was sitting on the bed.

Chapter 5

I had chosen Love Nest Motel partly because it was out of the city centre and partly because I wanted to impress her. If my plan had to work, I had to make sure that she knew that she was dealing with a modest person. If I expected her to play ball, then I had to make sure I convinced her that I was a harmless person.

I went to the bathroom and took a shower. While the warm water soaked my tired frame, my mind was overwhelmed by wild thoughts. I wasn't sure whether she knew something, but the choices on the tray were few. I had to cross my fingers and make a trial. The thought that she may not know nothing scared me, for that meant time and money wasted on a wild goose chase.

When I came out of the bathroom, a towel tied around my loins, she was lying on the bed dressed only in her inner garments. I looked at her beautiful curves, her chocolate tanned skin and her breasts that now stood firm and defiant and I felt a lurch inside my chest. Looking at her smooth body and her beautiful curves, I guessed that she was between twenty and twenty-five years of age. She looked so beautiful and desirable that I almost changed the plans I had made. Since Sarah had died, I had fought hard not to touch another woman and now the sexual starvation was beginning to weigh on me. Now that I had a beautiful woman within reach, my blood got hot and I almost cracked but I forcefully fought off the temptations. I sat down on the edge of the bed, removed a cigarette, lit up and smoked in silence for about one minute.

I had decided that I would not be wasting any time. Convinced that money could buy anything, I knew what awaited me. Well, I was here to buy information, so I saw no need to employ delaying tactics.

"I beg you to forgive me, Sue," I started. "I brought you here because I want to buy some information from you." I paused, fished out three one-thousand-shillings notes and placed them on the bed next to her.

"A few days ago, a journalist was killed at your place of work. I know you were on duty on that night so I guess you can help me with some valuable information."

It was like touching a sleeping tiger. She hurriedly sat up, reached for her clothes and began to dress, saying angrily, "That ninety-nine per cent of the men are false is known even by termites but I must admit that I was not expecting this from you. Well, they say all that glitters is not gold."

I reached for her and held her hand firmly but gently. I then turned her head with my other hand so that we looked at each other. Her eyes were ablaze with hatred and if they were bullets I would not have left that room alive. "Sue, please listen to me. I need help and perhaps I can only get it from you," I pleaded.

She gazed at me loathesomely for what seemed like ages, then shifted her eyes and fixed them on the bed. After a brief silence, she asked, "Who are you? You don't look like a cop."

"I am just a desperate man who wants to know who killed his brother. Yes, I am a policeman but I am a good policeman, so be at ease."

She sneered at me then forced a smile and that could only mean she didn't want to do that.

"You are a good policeman! If there exists something like a good policeman, then I am the Virgin Mary."

I said nothing. Once again, the ugly tag that we policemen carried around our necks was returning to haunt me. Though I hated it, like the others I had learnt to live with it.

"I leave the judgement to you. All I want to know is who killed my brother and why. I beg you to help me if you can."

She wiped off the remaining drops of tears, remained silent for a moment, then said, "I don't know who killed him or why he was killed but all I am sure is that Milly didn't do it."

I knew I had hit my first break.

I walked to the table that lay in the corner of the room, lifted up the handset of the phone that lay on it and called the bar. I ordered two beers, dropped the receiver and walked back to the bed. I lit a cigarette and smoked in silence while waiting for the waiter to deliver the order. After a couple of minutes, the waiter knocked at the door and I went to receive the two beers.

I opened one of the beers and poured myself some.

"I would like a drink too," she said.

She was no longer sitting on the bed. She had pushed her clothes back to where they were and she was now lying on the bed. This told me that I had finally managed to win her over to my side.

We sat next to one another sipping the beer in silence. When I could bear it no more, I turned to her, saying, "So your friend was the last person to see Larry alive?"

"That is the version of the cops but to me the last person to see him was the person who killed him."

She had finally managed to compose herself and the way she was talking told me that she was ready to spill the beans

All I had to do was to steer her like a professional and in this, I was an old hand.

"What do you mean by this?"

She took a long gulp then set her glass on the floor. "On the evening your brother was killed, Milly had been with me the whole day. It was mid-month and business was bad. Your brother had been sitting there the whole afternoon drinking and smoking. He wore a very impatient face and it was not difficult to guess that he was waiting for someone."

"Did anyone join him?" I asked impatiently.

She shook her head. "No. Two girls tried to make a move on him but he repulsed them. He just sat there reading his newspaper and looking very agitated. He would glance at his watch every five minutes and curse. At around nine o'clock, he started calling. He kept calling but it seemed like the person on the other end was not in a mood to answer him. At around 22:00 hours, he seemed to have given up. He ordered three beers and it seemed as if he wanted to drown his frustrations in beer. That is when Milly made a pass on him."

"Who is Milly?"

She ignored my question and went on, "Most of us know when a man has been let down and that is when we make the hawk-dive. He fell for Milly and some minutes later, he clicked his fingers for her and soon they were drinking together, chatting and laughing as if they had known each other for ages. They drunk together till half past ten, then he went down to the reception and hired a room. He then came to the bar and ordered four more beers. Milly gave me a wink before they left then they headed to the room. One hour later, Milly came to the bar, handed me a one-thousand-shilling note, gave me a wink and bade me goodnight. I asked her nothing for I immediately knew that she had struck gold.

My shift was almost ending so I went to the changing room, changed and headed home."

I was now alert, like an aroused viper.

"Something doesn't add up here," I said without hiding my apprehension. "You mean he paid her and remained in the room alone?"

Again she shook her head. "No, he hadn't paid her, she had robbed him. That is how it works"

I narrowed my eyes and stared at her inquisitively. "Can you please fill me in?"

She picked up her glass, took another long sip then set it on the floor.

"You said you are a policeman but I must say you look very innocent for that job. If you are not well versed on how things work around here, then you are in the wrong profession. Most of the girls you see hanging around night clubs are armed with very lethal drugs. They prey on the victim and when he gets distracted they drop some drug in his drink. By the time the victim regains his senses, they are far and safe, enjoying the loot."

I was now breathing heavily for I could see that I was gaining ground. I filled the two glasses to the brim, picked mine and took a sip. "Something doesn't fall into place here, Sue. Larry had been fed an over-dose. How do you explain this?"

She eyed me pleadingly saying, "You will have to believe me. Milly couldn't do this, it was not her line."

"Okay. Perhaps we say that she applied an overdose without wanting to and it turned out to be fatal?"

"That is improbable. Milly, like all the others, knows the rule of the game. The drug she uses is only strong enough to knock off somebody for a couple of hours. Besides, if she had done this, she would not have dropped by to see me before vanishing."

I believed her but I needed more before I could draw the final picture. "That can only mean that someone else entered the room after Milly had left?"

She looked at me and nodded. "Yes and you can bet this to your last cent. What makes me feel this is the way things went is that I chose to believe the version of the man who saw the body first and not the version the police fed to the press."

My eyes grew round in alarm.

"I don't follow you," I said hoarsely.

"The man who entered the room first swears that there was a rope around your brother's neck, meaning that he had been strangled to death. The police later dismissed this as hearsay and insisted that the postmortem had shown that he had been drugged. That was the version they fed to the press."

I was now sweating profusely. I had all along suspected that the pathologist was hiding something, but I wasn't expecting to pick such a precious clue.

We remained silent for a while until I came in again.

"You told me that Larry had a briefcase with him. Did she take that too?"

"No, she only took the money and this I am sure because when she came to bid me farewell, she had nothing."

"What about the phone?"

Again she shook her head. "Second-hand phones are too hot to handle these days. A friend of mine bought a very expensive phone at a throwaway price. A week later, the cops knocked at her door. Little did she know that the phone she had bought belonged to a man who had been killed during a robbery. Although she jumped the robbery with violence charge by leading the cops to the man who had sold him the phone, she is in jail serving a ten-year stretch for handling stolen goods. No one wants to be traced out through a stolen phone and Milly is no exception."

Although I had covered some considerable mileage, still something was missing and I knew if I pressed on I could dig up something.

"Have you spoken to her since it happened?"

She seemed to hesitate then perhaps convinced that I was harmless she gave me the answer.

"Yes, I have. The morning the newspapers carried the story, she called me and swore by her mother that she hadn't killed that man. She told me that she had not taken anything else from him except the money, ten thousand shillings."

"Do you know where she is hiding?"

"No, I don't and this is the truth. All I know is that she is somewhere safe. That is all I can tell you."

I did a quick review of what I had gathered and realised with a sinking feeling that I did not have any hard facts to warrant the compiling of any conclusive evidence. All that I had gathered was that Milly had not killed Larry but that was according to Sue. To the police, Milly was still the villain in the piece. I decided to change tack and see what would come out.

"Tell me about Larry. Was it the first time he was coming to Gossip club?" I asked her.

She shook her head. "No. This was the second time I was seeing him at the club."

"Why are you so sure?"

"He was in the company of a woman who looked like she used money to wipe her nose, somebody of the upper caste and that made me pick him out easily."

My heart skipped a beat. Why, I couldn't tell.

"Can you explain?"

"A day before your brother was found dead, he came to the club and ordered a beer. Again he was alone and he kept reading his newspaper. I formed an impression that he was waiting for someone, for he kept calling. Thirty minutes later, he was joined by this woman. They didn't seem to know one another very well and they kept conversing in low tones as if they were sharing a secret. After about thirty minutes, the woman picked up her handbag and walked out."

"Why did you say that this woman looked as if she didn't fit in the class of the club?"

She licked her soft lips while at the same time shaking her head in a gesture of surety. "She was too sophisticated and looked every inch a member of the top crust, like someone who belonged to the royalty or was married to royalty. She had expensive jewelry and a close look at her handbag revealed that it was made of very expensive game skin. Generally, she behaved as if she didn't want to be recognised and that is what made me conclude that she was out of place - like a fish out of water."

My blood was now hot with boiling excitement while my heart was racing.

"Can you give me the description of this woman and make it as detailed as you can?"

She closed her eyes and scratched her head in an attempt to dig deep into her memory. After a while, she said, "I could say she was between thirty and thirty-five years. She had a beautiful bright face with brilliant round eyes, average height and her figure looked well maintained. Apart from the jewelry, she wore an expensive dress and black pointed shoes. I didn't see her eyes because she had dark glasses on all the time."

"And the hair?"

"On that I can't help much. Although her hair looked good, you only needed to look at her keenly to realise that she was wearing a wig. That is why I said she looked like someone who wanted to make sure that no one remembered her."

I was now not listening to her. I quickly reached for my satchel and fetched out one of my newspaper cuttings. It was the photo of Tracy that had appeared on the obituary pages of one newspaper. I showed her the photo without taking my eyes off her face. "Could this be the woman?"

She studied the photo keenly then her eyes lit up. "Yes, it's her. If you put a pair of dark glasses before her eyes and a nice wig on her head, that makes it her. Who is she?"

"You are sure it's her?" I asked, excitement boiling in me the way magma burns inside a volcano.

She nodded in affirmation.

I was now fidgeting as if the bed was infested with black ants. I folded the newspaper page and placed it in the satchel then reached out for my cigarette pack and selected one.

I had covered the first milestone.

I smoked in silence, watching the thick curls of smoke and deep in thought. I was now sure that I had covered the first milestone but I felt that I needed some time alone so that I could reorganise my cards.

I could hardly believe what I had heard.

So Larry had met Tracy before he was killed!

I just need to get a good journalist and we fly to paradise.

If Tracy had met Larry, then it could only mean that she had some very precious information to sell and that meant that their murders were cogged together.

I took a quick glance at my watch and sighed. Time had come for me to call it a day.

I zipped my satchel then turned to her. "Please keep

this interview a secret and in case Milly calls, tell her to call me. Tell her that I am ready to see to it that she gets off the hook as long as her testimony is true. I promise to hire a good lawyer for her so that she is not molested and I will make sure she gets a fair hearing. Okay?"

She eyed me strangely, then moved her head up and down to mean that she had heard and understood.

I pulled out my pen and my notebook, scribbled down my number and handed her the paper.

"In case she calls, give her this and tell her to trust me. I can't promise anything but I guess it won't be difficult to pull her out of it. If it's a frame, it will be easy to beat so long as she collaborates."

She took the chit and viewed it the way you would view a farewell note from a dying friend then reluctantly put it inside her bag.

After taking her phone number, I lifted up my tired frame and went ahead to dress up, aware that she had her eyes on me all the time. When I was fully dressed up, I looked at her lovingly, just to convey the message that I was sorry for having let her down. I could see a strange sparkle in her eye and that could only mean that she was exasperated. I produced my wallet but before I could open it she asked me, "Mr Good policeman, are you married?"

An electric shock tore through my bowels and I looked at her curiously. "Why did you ask that question?"

She looked at me and smiled; a charming smile that almost disarmed me. When she didn't answer, I went on and answered her.

"Yes, I was but I lost my entire family in the genocide: my wife and my two sons."

She cupped her mouth in horror, rose up and placed her

tender hand on my shoulder saying, "I am sorry."
Now that I was through, I picked up the money and offered it to her but she declined to take it.

"I have never seen a policeman offering money so I will give it back to you as an offering. I have seen that you are ready to go great lengths to see justice done and that confirms that you are a good policeman."

I didn't want to press her so I put the money back and pocketed my wallet, then I thanked her and after thanking her, I walked out of the room.

* * *

After leaving the Love Nest, I had taken a taxi to Hangani Police Station and picked up my car. As I sank the ignition key, I couldn't help a grin when I thought about my followers. Well, if they finally managed to trace my car, then they must be still hovering around thinking that I was visiting a friend in the police line. As I drove away, I didn't bother to look over my shoulders: I had already accomplished the part that needed to be free from any roving eye. I drove straight home and when I opened my house, I walked to the fridge and fetched a beer. I started drinking while at the same time thinking about the case as I tried to knit the pieces together. I dozed off and by the time I woke up, it was almost dawn. I had left the sofa and staggered to my bedroom, dropping my tired body on the bed as if it was a log.

After taking a shower, I shook off the hangover and decided that I was fit enough to start working. I fetched my satchel, some blank sheets of paper and a pen and I sat down to work. I studied the case the way a scientist would study a specimen, putting down all the clues and hunches on paper. I went through the few facts I had in hand with a fine tooth brush checking and cross-checking them while at the same time comparing them to the suspicions that were building up in my mind. From the look of things, it was clear that Tracy's kidnap and subsequent murder and Larry's killing were interwoven. I tied up Jackline's killing too; she was cleared because someone was hell-bent on frustrating my investigations.

Having tackled the chauffeur, time was now ripe to turn my attention to the dead DJ.

Many people believe that dead men tell no tales but I believe that in the last steps of the dead you can get tales. I believed that the DJ could have known what secret information Tracy was holding. I decided to dig around his grave just to see if I could get some skeletons. I went into my bedroom and dressed casually in a pair of blue jeans, a polo shirt and sports shoes. I counted my money just to make sure that I had enough to see me through the day then I walked to the bus stop and boarded a matatu to town. As the matatu cruised towards the city centre, my mind wandered down memory lane and I remembered a funny episode that shared some similarities to the case I was handling.

A man had travelled from Umeru to the city to collect his hard-earned pension. According to the the hotel workers, he had appeared in the evening and booked himself a room so that he could travel to Umeru the following day. He had spent the night alone and when morning came, he went upstairs and ordered some breakfast. According to one of the waiters, one of the girls who was seated in the bar made a gesture to him and he in turn invited her to join him. They got chatting and after some minutes, the man ordered two beers and the pair walked back to the man's room, obviously to have a good time. Thirty minutes later, the hotel workers were treated to the most bizarre and comical drama. A pot-bellied man, stark naked, dashed out of the room, ran berserk downstairs and headed to the streets. There was a condom sticking on his dead penis and he looked like one possessed by demons. The mob in the streets tried to apprehend him thinking that he was a mad man and when they finally managed to pin him down, he claimed that he was searching for a woman who had robbed him in his hotel room. I was in the company of a colleague doing the beat when we saw a mob surrounding someone. Thinking that it was case of mob-justice, we dug through the crowd to rescue the victim. When he saw us, he immediately shouted, "*Afande!* You have to help me trace this woman! I can remember her if I see her again!"

We took him with us and led him to Kati Police Station and that is where we got to the bottom of the whole story. According to him, the girl had accompanied him to the room and they had both undressed. The woman had opened one of the beers and filled the two glasses. The man had gone to the toilet and when he came back, he had taken a sip from his glass. He then told the girl that he didn't have a condom but the girl saved the day by telling him that she had one in her handbag. The woman even offered to fix the condom herself then started caressing him lovingly. That was the last thing he could remember. When he stumbled back to his senses, he found the woman missing and his entire life's savings gone.

We did not need to interrogate him further to know that he had fallen victim to the usual tricks of the twilight girls. Of course the woman had spiked his drink when he had gone to the toilet. We sympathised with him although a good number of us could not resist a smile. Finally, we carried an impromptu fundraising to help him travel back to Umeru. One of our colleagues donated a shirt and a trouser and while giving them to him, he told him, *"Mzee rudi nyumbani lakini kumbuka jogoo wa shamba hawiki mjini* - old man go back home but remember that a village cock cannot crow in the city."

My first stop was at Mambo Leo. I wanted to hear from the editor if he had stumbled onto something of value.

"I don't want to commit myself Sherriff but there is something that may interest you," he told me.

My dying hope received a shot in the arm. Any clue at this point was valuable.

"This comes from one of my reliable informers. He told me that he has a reason to believe that Larry had been snooping on the events leading to the murder of Bob Smart. My informer insists that this is why Larry was killed."

My mouth went dry and I cursed myself for not having having looked at the case from this angle. I felt ashamed not to have remembered that the last time I had talked to Larry, he was heading to Smart's funeral.

"My informer tells me that he is still digging up and in case he comes across something precious, he will let me know."

I wanted to ask him the name of the informer but I knew that this was akin to asking for the sun. Newspapers never betray their sources. I was tempted to confide in him what I had found out the night before but again I braked. I thought it wise to leave that for the opportune time, when I was sure I had all the works in the bag.

"Thank you, Editor," I said rising up. "In case you get something, you know where to find me."

I was back in the streets and was walking idly towards the heart of the city. After walking for a while, I remembered what I had gone through the previous day. I started looking behind my shoulders just to be sure if I had company or not. I memorised the features of three or four men that I saw behind me and kept walking on. I stopped next to a newspaper vendor and ordered for a newspaper. I then opened it and began perusing through taking all the time in the world. After some minutes, I folded the paper and started walking along the street. After walking for about a hundred metres, I turned my head expertly and looked behind my shoulders.

Two of the four faces that I had memorised were still with me. Their smartness and cool demeanor told me that they could not be common cops. I would have turned my head again but I didn't want them to know that I had discovered that they were following me. I thought of what to do with them for I needed some free space. Finally, I decided to play some games with them, hoping that they would get bored and leave me alone.

How wrong I was!

I entered a popular bookshop and started surveying the bookshelves, making it look like I was searching for something in particular. I finally stopped next to the thriller section and started going through the collection of fiction stories. I selected one and I started perusing through it. I never at one time looked behind my shoulders. As a trained detective I knew all the tricks in the book and I was well versed on how to deal with a tail. You keep taking him round and this stretches his patience to near breaking point, leaving him seething with anger.

After about twenty minutes, I dropped my head then peeped with the corner of my eye.

He was there in the far end, a magazine in his hands with his back facing towards me.

Although he was not looking at me, I knew he was aware that I was still inside the bookshop.

This to me rang out like a warning shot; I was dealing with professionals, not amateurs and that meant I would not be having them off my back too soon. I looked around the bookshop but I did not catch a sight of his comrade. I looked at him again, taking in all the details, now that I was sure he couldn't know that I was watching him. He had a neatly pressed suit but that did not tell me anything. His brim hat and dark glasses told me nothing either but one detail almost made my heart grind to a stop. I again looked at him from top to bottom until my eyes settled on his shoes. They were gleam and shone like a mirror and this almost made me drop dead for now I finally knew whom I was dealing with.

I did not need to consult a crystal ball to know that I was now under the searchlight of the national intelligence agency.

In the police inner circles, we called them the 'shoe shine boys', in whispers of course. They were held in awe for they were the ears and eyes of the establishment. They were at the same time viewed with envy for unlike the other members of the police service, their pay-packet was heavy and they had a lot of incentives. They were always smartly dressed and shining shoes and dark glasses were their trade mark.

My whole body shuddered and my hair almost stood up in fear.

Although I had never worked in that department, I knew that the men there only involved themselves with matters that touched on national security. This meant that I was meddling with highly sensitive matters and that is why I had merited the attention of the national spy agents. Although I was rattled and felt unsure of myself, I had picked up a precious clue which changed the physiognomy of the entire case.

In a flash, I remembered what Jackline had said. *You either give me a legal divorce or this gets into the wrong hands!* These were Tracy's words. The words she had used to bring her husband on his knees. Could it be that what Tracy had been holding was something that touched on state security?

I was now sure that the general was the man who was frustrating my efforts. You don't just secure the services of the country's secret service unless you are a big shot in the security department and the only person who could do this was either the big man who ruled Ndiambo-land or the country's top cop. This could only mean that whatever information Tracy held had enough value to warrant the case to be treated as a matter of national security. Having discovered this, I felt a bit relaxed for now I knew who my adversary was. I picked a book, walked to the counter and paid for it. As I waited for the teller to give me my balance, I looked behind my back and noticed that my man had shifted his position. I threw my eyes around and caught sight of him. He was in the storybook section and he still had his back towards me. I picked up my change and briskly walked out of the bookshop.

When I stepped in the pavement, the first thing I did was to survey the vicinity. I looked up the street but I did not see him yet. At the back of my mind I knew he was somewhere watching me. I looked down street and my eyes stopped at a shoe shine stand.

He had just finished having his shoes brushed and he was now paying for the service. I hummed to myself and walked up the street.

As I waded through the busy crowds, my mind was busy and alert. I was thinking of a plan to throw these boys off track but none was coming. I had heard a lot of stories about them and I knew I was challenging them in their own game. They were trained for this kind of job, meaning that I had to burn the midnight oil if I was to lose them. I did not bother to look behind my back, although I knew they were still with me. I looked at my watch and discovered that I still had ample time. That meant that I could afford to play games with them and still have extra time to do what I wanted.

I walked into a cyber café and paid for two hours, then opened my email account and started going through my mail account but careful not to lose contact with what happened at the door.

Then he came in.

Unlike his friend who had been with me in the book shop, he was slightly short but stout and also wore a brim hat. He settled on his chair some few spaces away from me and got busy. The fact that they had swapped places told me that they were not underrating me. They knew that I was a cop and they were not taking chances.

I did not want to look at him for I would not have wanted to alert him. After reading all my messages, I opened the Google page and started navigating idly.

When the clock struck 16:00 hours, I rose up and walked out without looking at my friend. As I walked downstairs, I thought of his mate out there in the streets and sighed anxiously.

Although I knew he was waiting for me, I knew I had to do anything to lose him, for it was necessary that no one followed me where I was going this evening.

I stepped into the streets and looked around. The pavements were now milling with people so it was not easy to spot him. I waited and took my time, though I knew that I had to act fast before the man in the café glued himself to me. My chance came in the form of a Matatu which was heaving with passengers. Though the Matatu was groaning under the weight of the passengers who were packed like bags, the tout was hanging from the door and shouting that there was still room for one more. I hated boarding overloaded Matatus, but this evening, it was a godsend. I boarded the Matatu without caring to ask where it was headed to and thanked the stars when the driver sped off without waiting.

The first part had worked.

Halfway through the journey, I paid for my fare and alighted, then I took another Matatu to South Gate. As the Matatu cruised towards South Gate, I thought of my two friends hovering somewhere like cats waiting for a mouse and I smiled to myself. "Serves them right," I murmured to myself.

Chapter 6

THE PASSION BOX, as it was called, looked every inch the joint that could host a popular DJ whose death was newsworthy enough to draw the attention of the media. They had an elegant and spacious bar with a big dancing floor in the middle. The soothing music that came from the juke box kept me company and the sizeable number of patrons helped make me feel at ease. I had ordered a beer and settled down to read the fiction book I had picked up in the bookshop as I thought about the case.

As I sipped my beer and held my book, I realised with a shameful feeling that I neither knew why I was here nor where to begin. The subject who could have answered my question was six feet under the ground and I did not know anyone here. I was just about to give up and walk out when I thought of a plan. I didn't fancy it working but it could give me something. I pulled out my phone and dialled the editor's number then waited. I listened to the *brrbrr* sound and I was ashamed to notice that my hand was sweating. After a couple of seconds, the editor's voice came over the line.

"Yes?"

"Hello mate. I am at the Passion Box and I need your cover. What do you say about that?" I asked rapidly without giving him any details.

I could hear his heavy breathing and that could only mean he was foxed. "What is it, Sherriff?" he finally asked.

"Sorry, I can't explain anything now. I am working on something, something that could have a link with Larry's murder."

I heard him gasp. I knew that once I mentioned Larry's name, I would get full attention.

"How can I help?"

"Well, I am a journalist who works for Mambo-Leo and I want to cover the story of a popular DJ who worked here just in case the management calls you for confirmation."

His sigh of relief was audible even from the other end. "You can bank on me, pal. Good luck."

I switched off my phone then called one of the waiters who looked idle. I introduced myself, then I told him I wanted to talk to the manager. After probing me for a while, he motioned me to follow him.

We went up the stairs and stopped next to a big mahogany door. He rapped twice and a growling voice told him to enter. He then turned the handle and ushered me in.

The manager, a man in his late thirties and who looked bossy, was reluctant to talk to me at first when he learnt that I was a journalist but when I mentioned that I wanted to carry an article on DJ Cool in the weekend magazine, he drastically dropped his repellent attitude and his brown face turned appealing. I didn't know how to explain this sudden change but I guess he must have thought that an article on the slain DJ would be good publicity and could boost the popularity of his joint.

"Business is doing very badly these days but when we had Cool with us, things were different," he said while pouring me a soft drink.

"I know," I said with feigned concern. "I used to frequent this joint some time ago and I loved his job. I am sorry that his life ended this way."

He shook his head in a gesture of remorse while at the same time biting his lips. Then he said, "Cool was a good comrade-in-arms-with many wonderful qualities but like everyone else, he had his failings and one of them was that he could not keep his zip up. It's a pity he couldn't keep off women."

Though this is what interested me, I had to pretend that it didn't interest me since I didn't want to stir his suspicions. "I know but that is secondary. We have to dwell on his good qualities and leave the rest to God for judgment," I said cunningly.

I produced my notebook and a pen and selected a clean page.

"Let's have your name for a start?"

"You can call me Dave. I am the manager."

The first part of our interview dwelt on Cool the man and his talents as a disc jockey. It was entitled *From Congo with Love.* In it, we talked of how he used to pull the crowds and how he could even fire up the dead with his raps. We talked of a selfless person who had crossed borders just in the interest of sharing his music talents. We talked about a personality whose presence would be missed by all music lovers. We ended up with a call to the authorities to fix the security so that rampant crime may not continue robbing the society of its precious gems.

It was a perfect act and by the time I placed a full stop, I felt proud of myself. I looked at our final note, 'DJ cool is gone, but his spirit lives on in the hearts of music lovers' and I fought hard to resist a chuckle.

"Thank you very much, Mr Editor. I am sure this is an epitaph worthy of a great friend," he told me when we had concluded. As I was interviewing him, I had made sure I mentioned Passion Box a couple of times for I knew that this was all that interested him. I closed my notebook and sipped my drink.

Time had come for me to do what had brought me here.

"Now that we have finished the official part, we can now talk about his private life. Of course we won't publish that for it would not be polite to talk bad about the dead," I said to set the ball rolling.

He laughed mildly with the air of a very contented man.

"That forms part of the popular lies we tell at funerals. As they say, when the people die, we bury their bad things with them but keep the good things with ourselves and we talk about them."

"You told me that he couldn't keep off women?"

He passed his tongue over his thin lips and without looking at me said, "Yes, and that was his Achilles heel. As a DJ, he was very popular with the girls. Unfortunately, apart from having it around with any girl, he also fell very easily to love-hungry moneyed women and that I guess was his undoing."

"So you can agree with the story of the police; that his death was linked to his Casanova defects?'

"Don't quote me but that's not the way I see it, although I bet that the story of a love triangle cannot be completely written off."

"Is there any particular woman?"

He shook his head. "That I can't tell because Cool was a cool man even in his underground operations."

I knew I had reached a dead end although I still hadn't got anything interesting. I was tempted to give him Tracy's description, hoping that he had seen her but discretion told me that this would be taking the risk too far since it could end up provoking ripples.

"Where did Cool live?" I asked, just to see whether I could prolong the talk.

"Here in the club. He was one of our few workers who resided here full time."

"And you didn't find anything in his room that could point to his death?"

His facial expression changed and he held his chin in his palm in a gesture of sorrow. "That was the first place the police raided when he was identified. They ripped the apartment apart, carrying everything. From letters, videos, flash disks even photos. They carried away even his laptop and they are yet to return anything. When I complained, they told me off and said that they needed the stuff to trace his killers.

I immediately smelt a rat. The police had done the same with Larry's office and home and that formed another pattern. Without consulting an oracle I guessed why the DJ had been killed and what his killers were looking for, but this I did not tell him.

"How did the police identify his body since according to the newspapers, his face had been burned beyond recognition?"

He caressed his head then leaned forward and said, "This is what makes me buy the love triangle story. His friends easily identified him through a trademark chain around his neck and a ring with the initials DJC. The person who killed him had made sure that he threw his documents next to the burnt shell so that he could be identified."

"Do you have any of his photos?"

Again he shook his head. "The police took those too but I guess I could be having one in his personal file that I keep in the filing cabinet."

He walked to a chest of drawers, pulled out one and fished out a thin file and removed a small passport size photograph, which he handed over to me.

"This is all that I have but I could get talking to the other workers and see whether someone might have a bigger one."

I thanked him heartedly and requested that in case he found it, he should send it to the editor of Mambo-Leo before Saturday. After promising that we would do everything to feature the DJ's story, I rose up and walked downstairs to the bar.

When I stepped inside the bar, the first thing I did was to move my eyes around.

He was seated at the far end, a cigarette burning on his lips and busy reading a newspaper. Unlike in the bookshop, his eyes were not bare; he had covered them with a pair of dark glasses. Although he was bending his face, I knew he was looking at me behind the dark glasses. While I took my former seat, I could not help wondering how he had found me out. My movement from the cyber café was so fast that unless he had boarded the same *matatu*, he didn't stand a dog's chance to follow me. Slowly, it dawned on me that he must have had a car parked next to the café, waiting for me.

Well, the score stood at one-nil and this made me feel annoyed. I decided to throw caution to the wind and bare the things. I took out my notebook and made a short note. Before I folded it, I looked at what I had written and smiled.

'I appreciate your company. Thank you.'

He could as well belong to the league of the shoe-shine boys but I had to make him know that I was not ready to cave in to cowardly intimidations and that if they wanted to wage a battle against me, they had to know that I would not take it lying face down. I placed the folded note on the table then I called a waiter and ordered for two beers. When the waiter returned with the order, I picked one of the beers and then handed him the note I had made.

"Take this beer to that man over there, then give him this note," I instructed the waiter.

In my long career as a cop, I knew that there was nothing as irritating as a prey driving you nervous. Of course the note carried a tacit message. I wanted them to know that I knew who they were and that their tailings were not amusing me. I knew they would change tack but I wanted them to know that I would be ready for them when that time came.

I followed the waiter as he placed the beer on my tail's table. I saw him put a question to the waiter, probably asking where the beer was coming from and the latter handed to him the note. He unfolded it slowly, read the message then he asked another question and the waiter turned around and pointed towards me.

The sudden change of his face almost made me fall from my chair with laughter. I smiled at him broadly then lifted up my arm and gave him a sarcastic wave. He half-heartedly waved back then returned to his newspaper.

The die was now cast. Satisfied that I had sent the message home, I left my beer untouched and walked out of the club.

I reached my estate at around 20:00 hours. My mind was drumming as if there was a swarm of bees inside. The *matatu* cancer that I hated had made sure that what was remaining to drive me nuts was done. Shouts, foul air, loud music and emergency brakes, all that comes with the *matatu* madness. People cursed and complained but the crew didn't care; to them, complaints were just but a mere storm in a teacup.

Halfway through the journey, my phone beeped and I pulled it out to read the message. The words I read almost made my heart grid to a halt.

You either stop what you are doing or buy yourself a coffin. The choice is yours.

I stared at the message and felt my spirits waning. I have to accept that even though I had been frustrated, I hadn't felt threatened at least up to this point but now things were taking a different shape.

Was it a hoax? A cowardly joker trying to scare me away? This I highly doubted.

I alighted from the *matatu* and took a short walk to my house. The threat I had received had peeled away some of my courage and I found myself looking behind my shoulders after every two metres. A strange car was parked just next to my gate and without knowing why, I felt my legs vibrate. Though waves of fear and doubts kept tearing through my stomach, I decided to ignore the car but when I caught sight of the glowing end of a cigarette burning inside the car, I flinched. I touched my breast pocket to feel for my gun but I realised that I hadn't carried it with me. I must say that I almost turned back but the curiosity to know who was waiting for me kept me on my feet. When I was some yards away from my gate, the front door of the car opened and a thickset man stepped out. I had no problem recognising him and that made me relax.

"Good evening, Sherriff?"

"Good evening, commandant," I replied.

"I have been waiting for you since seven o'clock and I was almost giving up," he said in friendly note.

"Then I am here," I replied with a note of disinterest.

"What is it?"

He cleared his throat in an attempt to hide his embarrassment.

"General wants to see you. He sent me to fetch you."

General again! The last person I would have wanted to meet after what I had gone through!

"What does the general want?" I asked for the sake of it. I knew that he would have no ready answer but I had to ask the question all the same.

"That you have to ask him," he replied curtly. The friendly note in his voice had now vanished.

I decided not to argue. I wanted to ask him why the general had not called me on my phone but I stopped in my tracks. I knew he would not have an answer to that.

Now that I knew who the caller was, I found myself relaxing and I regained my breath.

"I oblige but I hope you wouldn't mind if I took a quick shower. I am feeling damp with sweat and I guess this would not be good for the general's appetite."

He laughed. An irritating laughter that I knew was forced. I didn't blame him for that. In a way, he must have noticed that I would have willingly done without this visit if I had a choice.

I pushed open my gate, walked to my front door and sank in the key. I walked to my bedroom and even as I undressed I could not help wondering why the general wanted to see me. I had no doubt that he had a part in the act and that left me foxed even more. I had been frustrated, tailed and even threatened.

Why this new development?

Twenty minutes later, I was clean and fully dressed. I harnessed my gun, picked up a heavy jacket and joined the commandant in the car.

"Sorry for keeping you waiting," I said as he started the car. "The general seems to prefer night to day so he has to put up with the inconveniences that come along with this."

He said nothing although he released a smile. A long wicked smile that told me that perhaps he knew what awaited me.

"You mean the general didn't tell you why he wants to see me?" I said after a brief silence.

He didn't even bother to look at me. He just kept his eyes fixed on the traffic, as if he had not heard my question. After a lengthy silence, he turned to me and grinned.

"In my long career as a policeman, I have committed many mistakes but insubordination has never appeared on my charge sheet."

I decided to let it rest at that.

* * *

He was seated on the sofa, a glass of whisky on the table before him as a cigar burned evenly on an ashtray next to the glass. He didn't look like a man who had just come out of mourning a dead wife. His face looked expressionless and I noticed that he had lost his friendly aura making his glittering eyes look rough and aggressive. Unlike in our first meeting when he made it look like it was meeting between friends, the kind of face – hard and repulsive – I was seeing now told me that this was a meeting between a boss and his junior.
He invited me to have a seat and I sank into the sofa facing him. The commandant did not sit down. He remained standing, assuming a very servile poise that made him resemble a dog waiting for the master's whistle.
During the journey, as the commandant cursed and snaked through the traffic, I was busy arranging my cards. I wasn't sure whether I was being summoned because the commandant had complained about my interference or to be asked to stop my investigations. Since I didn't want to be caught flatfooted, I deemed it necessary to prepare plan A and B. I would first wait to see the direction of the waves before I chose which plan to put into action. I sat facing him, waiting for him to walk the talk. He didn't seem to be in a

hurry and this drove me jittery with impatience, for I wanted to know what awaited me.

"I thank you for what you did for me, Sherriff," he said fixing his eyes on me while his blank face was bereft of any warm candour. "That was a terrible fix out of which you pulled me and I don't know what I would have done without you." He paused, stared at the glistening content in the glass then turned towards me. I could see that he had discarded his diplomatic demeanor and his face now looked hard and scaring.

"In spite of your help, I have to tell you that your work is finished," he ended flatly.

I frowned, without any attempt to hide my surprise. What he had said was aimed at telling me that someone had kept him updated about my personal moves.

"Though I don't doubt your capability, I am convinced that the commandant who is handling the investigations of my wife's murder is up to the task and can manage on his own. We don't need volunteers."

I normally managed to control my anger for, when I get close to my boiling point, I always feel like slicing my belly, getting out my liver and chewing it. Anger welled up in me for a couple of things. One, I didn't like his brusque language. By branding me a volunteer, he wanted to tell me that I didn't know my profession. I remembered when I was in college and they told me that I was called to duty so long as it involved maintaining law and order. Secondly, I would have wanted to tell him that his wife's kidnapping and murder would not have interested me if I hadn't discovered that it had something to do with the killing of my friend. Nevertheless, I did manage to contain myself even though I needed an iron effort to do that.

"I don't follow you, Sir," I said, the pretense in my voice obvious even to the pictures that were hanging on the wall. He looked at me curtly and gave me a small sneer just to tell me that he had seen through my trick.

"I have heard that you have been a very busy man of late, in spite of the fact that you are still on leave. This shows a strong sense of duty, but I propose that you stop your private investigations and leave the job to competent people," he said, pointing towards the commandant, who was still firmly on his feet.

I let that one ride although it gave a chance to know where I stood. Now that I knew the motive of the summons, I decided to end my hibernation and since he had given me one of his cards, I decided to reciprocate by giving him one too.

"I have no objection to this Sir, but I would want to know up to what point you want me to stop my investigations. True, I have to accept that the case involving your wife's kidnap and murder would interest anyone who has a passion to investigate. It would be interesting to discover why the events of this kidnap were altered and the mystery surrounding her death treated like a state secret."

He looked at me the way you would look at somebody who had killed your brother and the expression of disgust in his eyes was ugly to look at.

"Private investigations are unconstitutional in this country," he went on ignoring me. "It is true that you are a policeman but no one has assigned you this case, not to forget that it doesn't fall in your jurisdiction."

I was now tired of his threats. Now that I was sure he was in league with those who were punching holes into my efforts and deflating my ambitions, I needed to know why this was being done. I decided to give him another card, if only to flush him out from his cover.

"I see your point but that does not mean I agree with you," I said, this time ignoring the 'sir'. Time had come for us to deal like equals. "The facts available are very juicy and tempting. First, your wife is kidnapped and her body is found dangling in a half-built house. The next day, the charred remains of her lover are found in a burnt shell. Some days later, a hitman clears your house servant who happened to be one of your wife's closest confidants as I was interviewing her. These dramatic twin-events are sauce to any investigator. Don't you think so?"

He regarded me meanly for a spell of time, lifted up his glass and swallowed some whisky. He then turned to the commandant and ordered him to excuse us and the latter obeyed promptly. I was quick to notice the grudging look he gave me before walking out.

When the commandant was gone, the general selected a cigar and lit up. Strange, but I noticed that his face had turned a bit humane after his sidekick was gone. I was not a fool to fall for this kind of childish tricks. I knew that beneath the fake friendly veneer lay a boiling volcano waiting to erupt.

Looking at him, I knew that the sparring was over and time to exchange real jabs had come. I drew in a deep breath and waited for him to make the first move. He refilled his glass and it amused me to see that his hand was trembling. He asked me whether I wanted a drink but I declined. Now that the war had been declared, I had to make sure I kept my mind focused.

"They have told me what happened to your life, how you lost your family in the genocide," he started. "I pitied you especially after I looked at your colourful curriculum vitae, the accolades and medals you have picked along the way and the good reports from your seniors. It would be a shame for someone who has given so much to his country to mess up everything just because of being thoughtless."

I was now lost but I decided to wait and see where he was headed to.

"I know you are confused as to why I am telling you this and why I have called you here," he went on. "I have been a policeman for the better part of my adult life. I fought hard to maintain law and order in this country, defending her sovereignty and making sure that all the citizens feel happy to live here. I have run the police service for a decade and this means I have the necessary credentials and acumen to run this country."

"Run the country?" I asked with a note of surprise. I had to fight hard to accompany this question with a chuckle of sarcasm.

"Yes. I have decided to run for president in the next elections. Public opinion and good-will are indispensible talismans if one wants to run for public office. I know you will blame me for having attempted to hush the events surrounding my wife's death but you have to agree with me that if I had bared everything, this would not have augured well with my public rating. A police general who collaborates with kidnappers so as to save his wife is bound to start on the wrong foot if he runs for president. It is for this that I choose to personally ask you to stop the investigations."

I didn't need to screen him to know that he was hiding something but at least he had given me some ground on which to put my feet. Now that he had created a fake friendly environment, I decided to take advantage and sacrifice one of my aces. I had been yearning to give it to him just to know where exactly he stood. For the few times we had met, I had noticed that he wasn't very daft and that meant if I was to lure him to come out of his bunker, I had to bait him with something tempting.

"I have nothing to say about your presidential ambitions, but I will tell you why I can't afford to stop my investigations," I began, making my voice as hard as it was firm. "A day before your wife was killed, she had met a prominent journalist who happens to be my friend in a popular club somewhere in the city. Twenty-four hours after meeting your wife, this journalist was found dead in his hotel room in what bears all the clues of a homicide. Twelve hours later, your wife is kidnapped and she is found dead. The dead journalist happens to be a very close friend of mine and I want to find out who killed him. I am sorry for the loss of your wife general but I must tell you that her death does not interest me. All that interests me is to discover the laces that tie together her death to the killing of my friend."

I saw his face tighten and I knew he was fighting hard to cover his anger. Things were playing my way and I was slowly pulling him out of his lair. I had played it cool, leaving out anything to do with the secret information; the key to the whole mystery. I also didn't mention the DJ, although this was an intentional omission, an ace I knew I would play at the opportune time.

"My wife, besides being an irritant and worthless baggage, was a cheating whore," he said painfully without looking my way. He was now behaving like an actor on stage doing a soliloquy, which told me that I was beginning to get onto his nerves.

"Although I loved her, I cannot sacrifice all that I have built because of her. Your friend, I understand, was a two-penny reporter and hadn't you leaked to him that information about the pyramid scheme, he would never have found a base on which to launch his career. Now, do you want to tell me that we should sacrifice our future at the altar of two worthless people who are now rotting corpses under the earth?"

I felt like connecting a fist to his stout neck but I managed to contain myself. I could now see clearly where he was headed to and that set me aflame with anger. When I saw that he still had more to say, I decided to let him finish before I began unleashing my missiles.

"I am ready to help you rebuild your shattered life, Sherriff. The police superintendent is retiring next week and we have not yet groomed an heir to this coveted position. How would you feel if I told you that you are the most suited person to step into his big shoes?"

There it was.

I had all along been guessing that he would try to bribe me to stop my investigations, but I was not expecting him to do it in such a foolish way. I remained silent for a while just to fool him into thinking that I was reflecting over his mouth-watering offer. What he didn't know was that I was looking for a chink in his armour.

"Every man has a price, so they say," I said, giving him a wry smile. "I presume that this lucrative offer is tied to the condition that I stop the investigations, isn't it?"

He made a face and lifted his glass saying, "What is the use of continuing with investigations that will bear no fruits while your life continues lying in debris? The choice is yours."

I swallowed the thinly veiled threat and kept quiet. I had now gathered enough cannon fodder but I needed something more.

"What if I turn down your offer and I forge ahead to conclude my investigations? What will happen?"

It was trap question, aimed at smoking him out fully from his lair. I wanted him to know that I had seen through his trick and he had to stop the acting and come out clean. In this way, I would know exactly where he stood.

He regarded me for a length of time, perhaps not understanding why I was still stubborn, made a face with his lips then said: "Let us presume you refuse that offer. I lost five million shillings in the name of a ransom that bore no fruit, how much do you think I would be ready to lose if only to realise a life-long dream?

Again he threw my mind off-track. I didn't know where he was heading but what he said next not only left me baffled but it also told me the length he was ready to go to buy me off.

"Sherriff, what would you say if I offered you two million shillings?"

I could hardly believe my ears.

"To honour your job offer or to stop the investigations?" I asked curiously, narrowing my eyes.

He ignored my question, turned his head and began admiring the gigantic presidential portrait that hung on the wall. He then turned towards me and said, "If you want, I am ready to raise the offer to three million shillings."

My anger was now slowly mounting and I knew that it wouldn't be long before it reached the apex. By attempting to bribe me, he was prescribing sycophancy to me and a place in the line of his flower girls. What he didn't know is that I was a battle-hardened warrior who could not bring himself to stoop that low. I decided that I had had enough of him.

Now that I had known that he was the hidden Mr X who was removing wind from my sails, I decided time had come for us to put the cards on the table. I would engage him in an open game although I had already decided that my jolly would remain close to my chest. I stood up from where I was seated and faced him courageously.

"Thank you for your offer General, but I will not take it. If you have nothing else to say, I will excuse myself," I said, making my voice sound hard, like forged iron.

"Five million shillings, Sherriff!"

That told me that he was not yet ready to throw in the towel but I was ready for that.

"Stop this!" I shouted without wanting to. I was now goaded beyond endurance and since push had come to shove and the daggers were already drawn, I didn't want to show him that I could chicken out.

"Listen to me, Mr President-to-be," I said in a low but audible voice. "When I walked in here, I didn't know where to place you in this filthy puzzle, now I do. Someone of your calibre does not just offer five million for nothing, unless he wants to cover up something smelly that is giving him sleepless nights. I didn't know you were privy to the events that led to your wife's kidnapping and subsequent killing, now I do. I also wasn't sure whether you were aware of the links between your wife's death and Larry's killing, now I do. I may not be holding all the weapons but be sure I leave this palace with extra cannon-fodder." I paused, fished out a cigarette and went ahead to light it without asking for his permission. I pulled in a couple of puffs then turned to him again.
"I don't care about your wife and why she was killed. Indeed, if you had not called me to deliver the ransom, I would not have poked my nose into this affair. All I want to know is what her killing had to do with my friend's death. Larry may have been a two-penny reporter as you said, but he was my friend and I am ready to face all the blazing guns in this planet if this means discovering who killed him."

"Seven million shillings!"
He was now getting into my skin. If he thought that I was a strong believer in that when money talks, truth keeps quiet,

then what I said next must have left him utterly frustrated.

"Not even a billion!" I growled, then I moved close to him and with my eyes growing out of the sockets and my words coming through clenched teeth, I said, "Seven million is a lot of money General, but it is not enough to shield your name from a national scandal, perhaps a billion but don't offer it to me because I will not take it."

I could now smell his fear and panic and that told me that this was the correct moment to deliver the killer punch.

"What are you scared of General? That the scandal-loving Ndiambo-land public comes to know that your wife was cheating on you and that you organised for her to be liquidated? That a prominent reporter had a secret tete-a-tete with your wife before the journalist was found dead? That a popular DJ whose charred remains were later found in a shell was having a clandestine affair with the wife of the country's top officer? Well, offers or no offers, millions or no millions, intimidations or no intimidations, I am forging ahead in this epic battle. I don't know who between us will have the last laugh but you can bet to your last cent that I am going to give it a good try."

I crushed my cigarette on the ashtray and faced him loathesomely. Looking at him, I could see that my knockout blow had sunk, although I was not very sure for how long he would remain on the floor.

"I guess I have to go now. Don't bother to call your flunkey, I will find my way back home on my own."

With that I turned around and started walking towards the door. The silence I left behind was horrendous.

Chapter 7

I HAD LEFT THE General's palace with a million doubts and painful anger gnawing my stomach and I had gone straight into hiding. In spite of my bravado, I knew I had stirred the hornet's nest and the consequences would follow. It is because of this that I decided that going back to my apartment would be ill advised so I decided to change my address until the heat died down.

My choice of a hideout was a cosy hotel, deluxe and up to class, the kind where security is watertight and where chances of playing funny games is next to naught. Every car that enters is noted and you can't be booked unless you produce your identity card or passport. The place is flooded with CCTV cameras not to mention the guards at the gate and at the lobby. Time of checking in and time of checking out is noted in a big book and that meant that whoever was dreaming of fixing me would have to work overtime. I fancied that this would be a perfect hole to spend my first night as a fugitive before I chose a worthy hiding place.

While I swallowed my beer, I started thinking that perhaps I had done a mistake by crossing the red tape. "Should I have waited longer before exposing my cards?" I wondered. Well, I said to myself, I had already crossed the Rubicon and there was no other option but to march forward. Having made this decision, I stopped thinking about the case and started worrying about the general. A quick glance at my crystal ball was enough to convince me that I was up against a dangerous adversary. Neither did I need anyone to tell me that he owned the force lock, stock and barrel and that meant I had a paper-thin chance of pulling the rug from under his feet. In a way, I thanked the gods that I had managed to keep my jolly hidden up to the end. Amidst my outbursts and show of bravado, I had made sure that I kept the part touching on the blackmail in the vaults. I was keen to make it look like I knew nothing about his wife's attempt to blackmail him. I knew that if he came to know that I knew about some secret information that his wife was using against him, this would change the chessboard, making him come after me like a shot and this would leave me with limited space. Now that he thought I didn't know this, I thought, he would relax and lower his guard offering me a chance to floor him.

As the night wore on, I thought of nothing else apart from the case. I racked my mind and turned my brains over and over again, yet I found no clear answer. I had just begun dozing off when my phone squealed. A shudder tore through me and my heart missed a couple of beats. I was growing scared of the phone.

Half-heartedly, I picked the phone.

I heaved in a deep breath when I recognised the voice of Larry's widow.

"Sorry for calling you this late but I thought it was important. I was packing Larry's clothes when I came across something queer in one of his coat pockets. There are newspaper cuttings of all the articles dwelling on the killing of Bob Smart. I thought I should tell you," she said.

I stood still, my mouth dry, the muscles in my legs weakening and my heart pounding against my side. Finally, with the last effort of a dying man, I managed to thank her and wished her goodnight.

* * *

We all called him Shylock, for it was to him that we went when we needed soft loans. He was the brain behind the idea that it was good for us to form a kind of a savings society. We all thought that it was a brilliant idea and we decided to give it a try. Since a police savings society could not be allowed by law, we decided to choose a person to be keeping the money and Shylock was tailor-cut for the job. Besides being a teetotaler, he was a strict churchgoer and above all a family man of high standing. Owing to the above, we found him to be the best guardian of our 'sweat,' as we called our savings. The idea turned out to be a brilliant idea and as time went on, it started to bear fruits. We would all contribute and then those of us who needed loans would apply. Many a time, it helped us to pull out of financial crises. It came in hand especially when we had funerals or weddings. Some people even took soft loans to pay school fees for their children. After giving it a try, we finally decided that the idea had passed the test and we were all ready to construct it to greater heights.

Ask me to show you a clean, incorruptible and committed policeman and I will show you Shylock. He was an iconic policeman; a paragon of virtue and above all a man who, like Caesar's wife, was beyond reproach and whose moral probity could not be matched. He was a man who believed in leading from the front, one of the few men who showed an untainted dedication to his job as a police officer and who we all took as our role model. Above all, he was one of the very few who was proud of his career and believed in our motto, *equal service to all.* While most of us were police officers because fate had forced us into it, Shylock was a policeman because he loved the job. When we wanted to tease him, we called him the saintly policeman.

I met him when I was working in the crime department and by then he was an inspector. He struck me as a good person and was easy to get along with. He was a strict churchman and a devoted Christian; a man whose moral fibre was intact. This is why when Sarah and I decided to get married, I invited him and his wife Sherry to be our best couple. His wife and Sarah became very close and this helped cement the relationship between the two families. My wife liked singing and since Shylock was also a member of the parish choir, our paths kept crossing.

Then came the terrorist bomb attack that rocked Ndiambo-land city. This was the only time I saw Shylock withered and broken. He had lost his brother and sister in-law in the tragedy and that meant that besides his own family, he now had his brother's children to take care of. Although we all rallied around him, helping him to rise up and tie the pieces until he recovered, it was his strong personal will and unshakable faith that finally saw him through. Like the biblical Job, he stoically refused to be swayed by the devil and his trials and it was not long before his life was back on track.

After the terror attack, the authorities decided to set up an anti-terror police unit and they appointed Shylock to head it and lay its foundation. He went to Israel for a six-month course and when he came back he helped to mid-wife the anti-terror police unit and within a year, the brutally efficient 'guardian angels,' as the squad was code-named, was one of the most respected elite units of the police service, adding yet another feather to his already over-filled hat. After I talked to Larry's widow, it dawned on me that there was something that I was ignoring. Bob Smart had now been mentioned twice, yet I had not followed this lead. Could be it was because Smart had been killed when I was away and I had not followed the case very well. It was because of this that I decided I had to talk to Shylock. Above all, with the passing of time, it was becoming clear to me that working as a lone ranger was not only dangerous, but could also lead to nothing hence I needed a formidable ally.

I drove to his estate without alerting him and when I parked my car outside his gate, I was happy to see his car parked in front of the house and that told me he hadn't left for duty yet. I pushed open the gate then went up to the door and rapped it with my knuckles.

After a few seconds, the door swung open and his ever-smiling wife, still dressed in her nightdress received me.

"Hello Sherriff? What a sweet surprise!"

I took her hand and pressed it tenderly.

"Hello. I hope I am not too late for breakfast," I quipped. She smiled and ushered me in.

Bang! Bang! A voice came from behind. "If you move a nerve you are dead!" I turned my head and smiled when I caught sight of Shylock's youngest son who had been hiding behind the door holding a toy gun and pointing it at me like one of those cowboys that you see in the Far West films.

"There are so many thieves out there! So many bad men! But Daddy shoots them bang! bang!" he went on aping a police officer.

"Kiddy, please stop this," his mother roared. "How many times have I told you that you should stop this game?"

The boy lowered his toy gun, grinned then came to greet me. This was the way he usually received visitors when they came to see Shylock. Though I never liked this game, I always admired the boy. Right now, he made me remember my eldest son; children who always believed in their fathers and their strength. I caressed his head lovingly as I shook his hand.

"I know you want to talk to Daddy. He is dressing up and should be ready soon," the boy told me, then scampered to the kitchen.

Shylock was a tall man with an admirable physique. With his round brown face and ever-trimmed hair, he looked every inch the kind of man any woman would fall for head-over-heels. He was always neat for he always wanted to give the police force a good image.

"Good morning, your highness?" I greeted him, using the nickname we used while teasing him for his exemplary neatness. "Are you going to mount a guard of honour or something?"

He patted my shoulder and smiled. "When you talk like that I know you have come for a loan."

We both sat on the sofa and enjoyed the usual morning pleasantries. We hadn't met since I had got over my mourning period, although he was one of the people who stood by me during the dark period and I drew most of the strength to carry on from him.

"Sherriff, you look like someone who has been fed to a mincer," he told me after a while. "Is this visit casual or official?"

I drew in a heavy breath and caressed my unshaven chin as I thought of how to begin. Since the case had molested my mind enough, I decided that there was no time to waste eddying around.

"Mate, I want to talk to you," I said in a serious tone. He smacked his lips, hoisted himself up and motioned to me to follow him.

That is why we loved Shylock. You got into his house, spoke a couple of words and within a minute he could tell what you wanted. By choosing to talk in a private place, he must have guessed that whatever I wanted to talk about was burning and not meant for many ears. We walked out of the kitchen door and landed in a small garden where there was a table and some lounge chairs. The morning was a bit chilly and although I was not dressed warmly, I did not feel the cold. What I had in my heart and head was enough to drive away any cold.

"What is eating the other, Sherriff?" he asked, his voice hard and his eyes intent.

There was no time to waste. I went ahead and spilled everything from the beginning to the end. I began with Larry's death and how I had smelt the odour of foul play. I then told him of how the general had summoned me to deliver the ransom and how I had detected monkey business in his wife's murder. I recounted how Jackline had been assassinated and how I had travelled to the home of the missing chauffeur. Finally, I gave him a blow-to-blow account about the conversation I had held with Sue and how the shoe shine boys followed me up to Passion Box. When I finally told him how the general had tried to bribe me by dangling a prize carrot so that I stop the investigations and his subsequent threat, he opened his mouth in horror without wanting to.

"That's the picture, Shylock. I want you to tell me about Bob Smart's killing. The Editor thinks that it is cogged to Larry's murder."

He blew out his cheeks, dipped his hand in the pocket, fished out a pen and a paper and started doing what he liked most: doodling.

After drawing a couple of nothings, he faced me with curious eyes saying, "I will give you what the newspapers said before I tell you what I think. Smart was carjacked and his dead body was found some hours later riddled with bullets. At face value it seems like a simple case of car-jacking but to me, there is more than meets the eye in this story."

I was now alert and did not interrupt him.

"Viewed with the naked eye, it may seem what the papers said was true. Smart's gun was missing and so were his wallet and documents but I refused to swallow this story. If it was a case of carjacking, why then did they have to spray his car with bullets? Wasn't one bullet enough? Smart was one of my closest confidants and if there was any threat on his life, I would have been the first person to know. What made me start having ideas about his death was the fact that he was to return under my command the next day."

"When was he transferred from your squad?" I asked in surprise.

"He had never been transferred. Some months ago when the post-genocide brouhaha was dying out and the last embers of the genocide were still smoldering, I received an unusual call from General. He ordered me that he wanted to have Bob Smart at his disposal for some time so that he could head a very special mission. When I asked him what the mission was, he declined to tell me. So Smart went away and I never heard from him again. From what I gathered, he was based in the headquarters and he was reporting directly to General and that was enough to warn me to keep my snout off. Two weeks ago, I received a call from Smart. He sounded jovial, like he was happy that whatever he had been doing was over. He told me that he was finally free and hence would report under me the next day. The way he was talking told me that he was a very happy man and that could only mean that whatever General had told him to do was not all cake and ale. That was the last I heard from him. The next day, I saw his bullet-riddled car in the papers."

He removed his handkerchief and mopped his face then went on, "There was nothing on him that could have given anyone a clue. His gun, his cell phone and his wallet were gone. A perfect set-up to convince anyone that this was just an ordinary case of carjacking but to me, this set-up was begging for answers. I decided to follow it up and this led me to the commandant, who I was told was the man handling the case. The commandant told me that they had found nothing that could lead to suspicions of foul play so they were just treating it as a robbery."

I almost interrupted him and I had to put up a relentless fight to control myself.

The commandant again! The man who had divine luck! Always in the right place at the right time!

"I decided to have a look at Smart's house in a bid to pick up something but when I got there, his girlfriend whom I knew very well told me that the police had already come and carried away his files. That is when I started smelling a rat. I went to the headquarters and asked to see the office which Smart had been occupying but I found that it had been assigned to the accounts department. I asked them if they had found any computer but they told me that the office was bare when they moved in.

I decided to do investigations about the other men who had been working with him but no one was ready to give me even a single name. I was told that the outfit had closed shop after the mission was over and all the other men had been deployed to other departments. That is when I decided that I had to dig deep until I discovered what Smart had been working on and who his comrades were. The only man who could shed light on this was General himself hence I booked an appointment with him. I am still waiting up to date."

He folded the paper that was now filled with doodles, placed the pen on it then with a voice below his breath said,

"This is an assassination, Sherriff. Don't accuse me of reading too many novels but only men who have meddled in matters of state security die like Smart."

We both dropped into a deep pit of silence for a moment. My suspicions had now gone berserk although I lacked the words to frame my thoughts. When the general and the commandant had bumped into the scene, I found myself believing in Shylock's suspicions though that is the far I got. Well, I decided to concentrate on my case and leave him to sort out his own.

"I don't know what to do Shylock," I said, breaking the long silence. "It is true that I am foxed but I have a feeling that if I can manage to lay my hands on the prostitute and the missing chauffeur, I could crack this one."

To my surprise, he stopped me with a wave of the hand.

"This is easier said than done Sheriff. They say fish rots from the head and that is true. If what you are saying is true then I would advise you to tread slowly for the last thing I would want is to see you committing a sin of hubris."

I made as if to talk but he stopped me. "If I were you I would think twice before challenging an elephant to a farting contest. With this kind of set-up, I bet it's better to shelve your zeal and let prudence take charge."

I could hold myself no more. "You are not telling me that I should stop on my tracks, are you?" I asked him without hiding my surprise.

He ignored me and went on, this time pointing at me with his finger. "Pipe down and listen to me. You know very well that I am a strong believer of justice. I believe that you are doing this because you want to see justice done for Larry. I too would do anything to see justice done for Bob Smart but this is the far we can get. Something tells me that

General is deeply involved in this affair and that means that the barriers ahead are high and spiked hence, I propose we coil and let things be."

Although this was not what I expected from him, I bought his line of thinking. True, I would have wanted to tell him that I was not expecting him to give up this easy but discretion told me that this would be uncalled for.

"I tell you this because of what you and I know. To the public, it is an open secret that our police service is no better than a militia group. Thugs for hire run by warlords. You and I would like to correct this but our hands are tied. We have neither the muscle nor an armoury worthy writing home about. Of course you can ignore my advice and go on but do you know what will happen? With the odds against you and an empty war chest, the knight in the shining armour will come down crushing from his horse."

I drew in a heavy breath and clasped my hands. I found my hopes waning for I knew what he was saying was true. However, I decided to make a last-ditch effort for even though my hopes had whittled down, there was still a small flicker of optimism.

"What if I manage to track down the chauffeur? Do you think I can get far?"

He shook his head in a gesture of frustration. "*Equal service to all,* that is what is on paper but you and I know that it's bullshit when we get to the situation on the ground. It is true courage is a virtue but caution is a golden virtue. When a man enters into a cave of vipers blindfolded, that is not courage Sherriff, it's foolishness. This is a mountain too high and too dangerous to scale. I propose that you borrow a leaf from me, shelve your ambitions and let this case go just like I did with Bob Smart."

I remained silent for a while and chewed his words over.

I did not need to look at his face twice to know that any attempt to fight on would end up irritating him and this I would not have wanted to do hence I decided to change the course of the discourse.

"Well pal, I may not agree with you fully but I accept that it's the reasonable way to go. I had hoped that this was the last case I would tie before quitting but now it seems I have to eat my humble pie and call it a day."

From his eyes, I could see that he was lost, obviously unable to see where I was headed to and since I was not in a mood to drive him nuts with anxiety, I unceremoniously dropped the bombshell.

"Shylock, I have decided to resign from the force."

He cupped his mouth, leaned towards me and whispered loudly, "What?"

I hid my face. I did not want him to see that my decision was driven by frustration and dejection.

"I know you will not understand but I have neither the will nor the motivation to go on. I am not doing this due to the fear of the general but so many things have happened that have dampened my spirit thus I believe the best thing to do is to call it a day and search for greener pastures."

A brief silence followed and I knew he was preparing himself to convince me to turn back on my decision.

"Listen Sherriff," he said in a fatherly voice. "You have just crawled out of a terrible tunnel. You lost your family and now you have lost your friend but I believe that you have all what it needs to pick up the pieces and rebuild your life. I too have travelled this road, when I lost my brother and my sister-in-law in the bomb blast. All you need is to give time a chance to heal the wounds."

I remained silent for I had already exhausted my arguing

reservoir and I knew that if I continued being adamant he would continue making rigorous attempts at making me to change my mind. I decided to be crafty. Since I would have hated to tell him that he was fighting a losing battle, I decided to give him something that would make him slow down, at least for this moment.

"I understand you," I said, keeping my voice low such that I hid my crafty intentions. "I guess I will shelve the decision for a while and reflect about it."

That did it. His face beamed with joy and I could almost smell his aura of gratitude. Looking at him, he looked like a hunter who had just shot down a quarry and this filled me with a feeling of remorse. I knew it would hurt him if he came to know that I had resigned behind his back but this didn't worry me then. Now that my hopes had taken a nosedive, all I wanted was to go back to my house and savour my loneliness.

We both stood up and shook hands.

"It's long since we invited you for supper," he said as he saw me off. "If you have time you can show up today in the evening and share a meal with us."

I politely declined his offer for I wanted to be alone and recover my lost energy before I presented my resignation letter the next day.

CHAPTER 8

I DROVE TO MY house and settled down to reorganise my mind. Now that I had made my final decision, I felt light and unusually at peace. I did not need to hide myself anymore or to keep looking behind my shoulders; I was now as free as a bird. It was the first time I was experiencing this kind of feeling since I had lost my family. It was as if I was a new man. I went to my table and collected the notes and the newspaper cuttings I had made about the case and placed them in a brown envelope. My intention was to burn them as a symbolic gesture that my old life was over and I was ready to usher in a new era but I decided that I would do this in the evening. I then shed off my jacket and started to clean the house. I whistled merrily as I worked and when the clock struck mid-day, I had moved away a good chunk of the workload. I then cooked myself a simple meal and after I had eaten, I decided to lie down and catch some sleep.

I must have slept for about an hour when the squeal of my telephone woke me up. I would have ignored the call but the persistent ringing was getting into my skin so I decided to answer. I reached for my phone, gazed at the private number and cursed. I pressed the button to stop the ringing, cursed again and placed the phone where it was before. With the strange events of the past days still fresh in my mind, I was done with private calls. Ever since the general had called me in that fateful night, I was beginning to get wary of private callers.

I had barely finished placing my head on the pillow when the phone squealed again. I cursed loudly and wrestled with the idea of switching off the phone but I finally decided to take the call.

"Yes?" I growled without wanting to.

The caller said nothing but I thought I heard some strange noise; like someone was gasping for breath.

"Can I help you?" I came in again this time grudgingly.

"Is it the Sherriff?" a feminine voice said.

I detected a tone of fear in the voice and this made my heart skip a beat.

"Yes, it's me. Who are you?" I said in my normal voice while hoisting my legs from the bed. A strange silence came over the line but I could still hear her uneven breathing. My heart was now thumping and I was fighting hard not to repeat the question.

"My name is Milly," she finally said. "I am the woman who was with your friend the night before he was killed."

If a bomb had exploded next to me, I wouldn't have been more startled than this. I felt a vacuous feeling in the pit of my stomach and my hand started shaking. I pressed the phone firmly on my ear but when I attempted to speak, my words choked me. It was as if a piece of cloth had been stuffed down my throat.

"I did not kill your friend but I know who did it," she went on. She seemed to speak in separated words, as if she was reading from a script and the edge of fear over her voice was touchable.

"Who did it?" I croaked.

She fell into another moment of nagging silence but her breathing was still audible and that told me that she was still there.

"If you want to know who killed your friend, come to Soweto at exactly 19:30 hours and come alone. Please be careful that no one follows you, she said. "Walk down Mtwapa lane and when you get to the end, you will find a half-finished storey building. Walk upstairs and knock at the third door. I will be waiting."

Her words sent a prickle of excitement shooting up my spine and my mind went in a whirl.

"Who did it?" I asked again in a voice that sounded strange even to me.

She remained silent although I could still hear her faint breathing. I repeated the question for a third time but the ting ting sound from the other end told me that she had disconnected. I stared at the phone as if it was a scorpion then slowly placed it on the table and sighed heavily.

I am the woman who was with your friend the night he was killed.

These words banged against my cranium and resonated to all the systems of my body. It was not difficult to knit together the pieces. Sue must have done her part and that could only mean that she was calling me from her hideout. I paced around my bedroom weighing the options on the choice tray. I knew there was no way she would have called me unless she held the key that could unlock the door of the mystery surrounding Larry's death.

I didn't kill your friend but I know who did it.

These words rejuvenated my dying morale and seemed to work magic in me. My wilting hopes blossomed back to life, sweeping away all the fears and my weakening enthusiasm received a new lease of life. All doubts melted like ice under the sun and I felt like someone had injected me with the blood of an ambitious lion. The new turn of events emboldened me and in a niche of time, the general's threats, my impending resignation and Shylock's pieces of advice faded into oblivion and became distant memories.

I had to go!

I glanced at my watch and nodded to myself. There was ample time for me to prepare myself. I was used to long waits but none could match this one. Time seemed to crawl at a snail's speed and I lost count of the times I had looked at my watch. I went to the kitchen and prepared some Scrambled eggs just to kill time yet even this failed to push the hour hand. Seconds seemed like minutes and minutes like hours. It was like waiting for the second coming of Jesus.

At 16:00 hours, I waddled into the bedroom and took a quick shower. I then slid in a pair of jeans, a polo shirt and casual shoes. Though I was sweating profusely due to the anxiety, I picked up a heavy jacket, just to hide my holstered gun. Finally, the clock hit 17:00 hours and I knew it was time to move. I picked my gun, checked it and dropped it into my shoulder holster. I then switched off my phone and decided to leave it in the house. I was not ready to be disturbed by any caller just this night. Finally, I picked up my cigarettes, glanced at my watch again and walked out of my house. A few minutes later, I was muscling myself through the nagging evening traffic with my heart drowning in hope and my mind submerged in youthful optimism.

* * *

Show me a place where danger sits on the throne like it does in Soweto and I will keep off from it for the rest of my life. This is a kingdom where the devil calls the shots and evil dances during the day. Think of illicit beer dens, drug peddlers, muggers, brothels and rogue police officers and you get the true picture of Soweto. In Soweto, pay someone to bring you a human head and it is delivered within half an hour with a smile painted on it and with the mouth still mumbling words. Park your car in Soweto without paying some sentry and ten minutes later, it is resting on stones minus all the wheels. If you are the kind that worships coming home in the wee hours, do it in Soweto and if you escape to be beaten up to death then you must be having a very alert guardian angel. Those who know the place well know the rule of the game; incase you come from work late, just walk to one of the 'thugs for hire' dens and you will be escorted home by goons for a fee because without them you can't get far. As one of my cousins once told me, "Boy, to live here, you need a manual."

It was not very difficult to pick out Mtwapa lane. It lay on the edge of the estate where residential areas were sparsely distributed. I drove through the dusty potholed road closely surveying the buildings in the semi darkness searching for a half-finished house.

I caught sight of none. Could it be that I had been sent on a wild goose chase?

I quickly pushed the thought behind my mind and kept driving on, this time in a snail's pace. I threw my eyes far ahead and I noticed that I could not see the end of the lane.

Then, a warning signal, the kind I never ignored, lit up in my mind. I felt that I could be walking into a trap, so I thought it wise to park my car and walk the rest of the distance.

I pulled over to the verge and parked. After locking my car, I looked around furtively and once I was sure there were no suspicious eyes around, I started walking down the lane. Both sides of the lane were lined up with newly built houses, a sign that this was a new extension of the estate or a new residential area that was sprouting up. The voices of children playing, the crying of the babies and the shouts of mothers calling their children home gave solace to my heart for it meant that this was not a hotspot like the rest of the estate. I caught sight of a half-finished house and I stopped in my tracks. Could this be it?

I remembered that she had told me that the house was a two-storey building and that it lay in the far end of the lane.

I heaved in some fresh night air and kept walking on. The lane suddenly darkened and I realised that I was walking in a stretch that was very poorly lit. Even the houses I could see were lit with lamps, meaning that there was no connection to electricity. The place now looked hideous and I found myself wondering whether I was taking the risk too far. Nevertheless, I kept walking, although I now kept looking furtively behind my shoulders. I had hardly walked for 100 metres when I caught sight of it. My heart skipped a beat and I found myself touching my gun if only to draw some extra confidence.

It was the last building and even in the darkness, I could see that it was a two-storey building. The end of the lane was covered by tall elephant grass and there were sparsely distributed shrubs right ahead. It was a lone house and when I glimpsed behind it, I saw something that looked like an open field. I walked ahead until I stopped right in front of it. My eyes toured around the deserted building and its scaring vicinity and I was assailed by a wave of doubts. There was not even a single flicker of light; no trace of movement and that threw my mind in a spin of suspicion. Was she really there? At face value, the house looked every inch a place where a fugitive would use as a hideout but this helped little in whittling down my fear. I looked around me and once I was sure I was alone, I drew out my small flashlight that I never left behind, lit it and swung the thin beam around.

There was a mountain of sand in front of the house and

long grass in the flanks. The drive that led to the entrance was hard and covered with weed and it seemed as if no building activity had been going on for days. I looked behind me then I started to walk towards the entrance. The entrance had no door and even from the outside, I could see the heaps of sand and concrete that littered the floor. I pulled out my gun and walked inside in a tiptoe. The stuffy air made me feel uncomfortable and I kept hoping that a cough or a sneeze did not come calling lest it betrayed my presence. The half-finished floor was hard and littered with an assortment of building materials. I swung my flashlight around and I caught sight of the stairway.

Gun in one hand and a flashlight in the other, I went up the staircase like a ghost until I reached the second floor. The second floor was a replica of the first one. The floor was hard, the walls were rough and there was a line of rooms without doors. I toured the corridor with my flashlight until I was sure there was no soul in sight. She had said she would be in the last room but she had not specified whether the room was in the left or in the right. I stood fixedly trying to untangle the dilemma and finally I opted to go right. I tip-toed until I caught sight of the wall opposite then I halted. Again I surveyed the rooms and picked up something odd. Unlike the other rooms, the last room had a door. This made me suspect that she must be in there.

I walked softly towards the door but before I could knock, something happened that sent all my muscles tightening and my hair standing. I felt my stomach go hollow and a feeling of fear gripped me. I had a strange feeling that I was not alone in this ghostly place. I tightened my grip on the gun, pulled back the safety catch and curled my finger around the trigger. Before I could turn around, something happened that sent the blood in my veins freezing.

A heavy kick landed on my hand that was holding the gun-making me press the trigger without wanting to. The deafening sound of gunfire almost made my head explode and before I could regain my balance, a strong weight crashed against me sending both the gun and my flashlight flying from my hands. A strong arm went around my neck and I felt the thick fingers as they sought my throat. I joined my two hands together and elbowed him in the ribs. I heard him groan; I repeated the act. The grip around my neck slackened but he still had me against the wall. With difficulty, I made a half turn and aimed a short blow at his stomach. Although it hit the target, it lacked the necessary weight to make an impact. I elbowed him again, this time leaning all my weight and this got his hand away from my neck and he ringed my waist. I saw my chance and took it. I went on my knee in a flash and shoved him forward with all my strength. The thudding sound of his head as it connected against the wall sounded like music to my ears. I lifted myself up and threw him behind. Although I did not manage to throw him to the floor, the slackening grip around my waist told me that I had him where I wanted him. I knew that I had to act fast before he regained his balance, I swerved around like a mad bull and unleashed a punch. I brushed his ear and this helped me to know where his face was. Before I could unleash the second blow, a blow thudded against my chest, driving the air out of my lungs, but this was not enough to floor me. I decided to wait for him at the same time struggling to see his features. My eyes were yet to be accustomed to the darkness and this made the set-up look nasty.

He came towards me like a mad bull but I was ready for him. I shifted my position slightly, then unleashed one of my killer punches. I caught him on the jaw and although I didn't fell him, the sound he made with his feet told me that I had sent him staggering. My eyes were now accustomed to the darkness and I could see the vague outline of his massive build. I went for him but he lifted up a kick sending me staggering backwards. Before I could regain my foothold, he came over to me with elephantine fury and ringed his right hand around my neck again but this time he wasn't that lucky for I didn't have my back towards him. I felt his thick fingers as they searched for my jugular and I knew that if he beat me to it I would be dead meat. I punched him on his stomach but he held on. I supported one of my legs against the wall then heaved and drove him crushing against the opposite wall. I then took a step behind, packed my left blow with all my strength and unleashed it. He made an attempt to dodge but his move came too late. The blow connected to his nose sending him staggering backwards and before he could regain his senses, I half turned and kicked him on the chest finally sending him sprawling on the floor.

I could see him in a kind of a silhouette while he raised his massive body and I knew I had to act fast. I wasn't sure if he had a gun or not and I didn't want to risk being caught in a surprise. I saw him leap for a flying tackle and my mind moved fast. I sank on one knee, collected him on my shoulders and flung him heavily to the ground. I then quickly disengaged myself and waited for his next move.

Then something strange happened. The assailant raised himself but instead of charging towards me, he turned and ran into the darkness. I listened to his heavy thuds as he ran down the stairs and disappeared to the ground floor but I was too stunned to follow him. I couldn't understand why he had chickened out so quickly. Perhaps, I thought, he had realised that nailing me would not be a downhill task hence he had decided to bolt while there was still a chance.

I dusted myself then fetched my cigarette lighter and switched it on. I looked around the floor until I found my gun and my flashlight. I dropped the lighter into my pocket and swung the beam of my flash light around. After what had happened, I realised that I would not be having those boys off my back so soon hence I had to be careful lest some hidden soul took a fancy on me. I knew I was risking sticking to this place and I had to get away fast before another surprise attack came calling. I wasn't sure but it was possible that someone had heard the shot and had already alerted the law. I was just about to get moving when I heard something that sent my blood freezing. The noise of a weak groan, like someone was gasping for life hit my ears. I quickly moved my flashlight around but I saw nothing. The place now felt haunted and I found myself getting almost shivering with fear. Then the groan came again, this time sounding like a deep mournful cry of an animal in deep pain. I moved my flashlight around again and I let it rest against the only door that there was. I looked at it keenly and I noticed that it was slightly open. Before I could decide what to do, the groan came again and this time it was accompanied by a faint thud. Driven by curiosity, I decided to enter and see what there was inside.

I held my gun at the ready and pushed open the door with the tip of my shoe then I gum-shoed into the dark room and shone my flashlight around. What I saw drove my mouth dry and made me hold my breath. She was sitting on the bare floor leaning her back against the rough wall. Her head was half tilted with her eyes facing the roof in a sightless stare. Her hands were tied behind her back and she was stark naked. She was full of fresh wounds all over her body, which told me she must have undergone a lot of torture. Although there was a trickle of blood running down from her mouth, she gave an impression of someone who was still alive. I quickly moved towards her to see if I could save her but then she started moving sideways until she crashed to the floor. I knew without touching her that she was gone. I rested my flashlight on her face and studied her dead face.

She had a brown face, a long neck and jet-black hair. I noticed that her cheeks had bulged unusually and when I studied her keenly, I noticed that she had a piece of cloth stuffed inside her mouth. I grimaced while I looked at the rest of her features. In spite of her mottled look, her well cut figure, fleshy thighs and beautiful legs made me think that she was too young to die. I bent and touched her neck; her body was still warm meaning that if I had been a trifle quicker, I would have found her alive. My mind worked fast while I tried to think of what could have happened. From the look of things, they must have traced her out and brought her here. Her fingers, which had now turned into hooks and the dark smudges around her neck told me that she must have been strangled to death. The torture marks I saw on her body reminded me of the torture marks I had seen on Tracy's body. Slowly the truth formed itself and I now could see things clearly. You don't torture someone like this unless you are extracting some very valuable information and I did not need to consult a guru to know what this valuable information was.

But why did they force her to call me?

I didn't waste my time on this for I knew that with time I would have the answer. I shifted my light from her and surveyed the rest of the room. There was no furniture and the floor was littered with cigarette butts, which told me that the room must have hosted a couple of men. I drove my flashlight around and something in the far corner grabbed my attention. I walked softly towards the corner just to satisfy my curiosity. I did not need to look at the old leather briefcase twice to know that it was the usual briefcase that Larry always carried around with him. I bent on one knee, placed the gun on the floor and opened the briefcase. I lit the inside with my flashlight and studied the contents. There was a laptop, a digital camera, a cell phone and a small notebook.

With my blood boiling with excitement and my heart pounding, I gazed at the contents the way an archeologist would gaze at a prize fossil and wondered if I had finally cracked the case. Then I heard something that made me panic, the only way a deer will panic when it hears the roar of a lion.

Since I had entered the room, my only companions had been the deep silence, my audible breathing, and the dead corpse lying on the floor. Thus, when the sound of a siren hit my ears, it sounded like a rock that had dropped into a calm millpond. My heart sunk to my loins and I looked searchingly, the way a rat would look for the nearest route of escape when cornered. The volume of the siren kept growing louder and that could only mean one thing; a police car was approaching at a fast speed and I did not need to think twice to know where it was heading.

Well, put yourself in my shoes. The police general has already given you a warning to lay off a case and to make his warning sink, he made sure that he sends it home accompanied by a threat. His spanner boys are heading to a scene of crime where you are present and where an important witness is lying dead with incriminating exhibits of a slain journalist next to her. I don't know about you but as my late friend Larry would say, only someone who has porridge in the head would wait to be nabbed in this kind of set-up. I moved my eyes hither and thither the way a trapped rat would do while looking for an escape route then without thinking, I picked up my gun, grabbed the briefcase and burst out of the room like a charging buffalo. I hurriedly went down the stairs and by the time I reached the door, the siren was howling some three hundred metres away. Like a caged animal, I smelt blood. Quick reasoning told me that if I run anywhere near the road, I would run right into them. That left me the rear whose map I didn't have. Without wasting time, I dashed to the rear and stretched my legs.

When the situation calls for running, I can run. Though many years had passed since I had participated in a marathon, the embers of my athletic prowess and the memories of the good old days when I used to bag medals at will were yet to be completely extinguished. After rounding the house, I jumped over a shallow ditch and sprinted towards the open field. I knew I had to put a considerable distance between those boys and me lest I earned myself a bullet behind my back.

I started off across the open field at not perhaps my best speed, but close to it. The siren grew louder and with it my legs moved like oiled pistons. When the howling of the siren ceased, I had already put a safe distance between me and the scene of crime but that was not enough to stop me from running. Against an open field and the moonlight shining, I knew that I would be easy prey to spot hence I did not look behind. I heard a car grid to a halt and I knew this was the time for the final spurt. I was beginning to pant and my legs were now aching but I still managed to stretch what was remaining in my reservoir of energy until I covered another hundred metres. When I connected to an alley, I stopped running and began walking. I was still panting and I was worried that this could draw some suspicions in case I met someone. Luckily, the alley was deserted even though it was lined up with residential houses.

I walked on until I reached the junction that connected to Mtwapa lane. I could not risk showing myself just yet hence, I peeped expertly up the lane before taking a chance.

My car was still there, where I had left it. Other people had parked their cars behind and in front of my car. Human traffic along the lane had increased and this was godsend since I needed to camouflage. I gazed further up the lane and I caught sight of the blue light of the siren which was still flashing but there was no police officer in sight. That could only mean that they were still inside the house and that it would take time before they began combing the area.

It was time to move. I quickly entered my car, made a U -turn and sent the car cruising towards the city. The clock was hitting 20:00 hours when I brought the car to a halt in front of my gate. I left the engine running and hurriedly opened my gate. I then brought my car in closed the gate and walked hurriedly to my front door, the briefcase in my hand.

While I drove back to the city, I was drowning in a mixture of doubts, fear and anxiety. I could not figure out the shape things would assume after this showdown. I was sure that sooner than later they would come looking for me although I knew this would take some time. Now that their trap had aborted, they first needed to go back to the drawing board and reorganise their strategy, so I thought. However, behind my back I knew that surprise was always lurking in the shadows and that meant that I had to begin seeking for some secret weapons. I contemplated calling Shylock and spilling the beans but I thought this would be premature. Calling my lawyer was out of question until I knew what they had on me. Finally, I decided that the best thing to do was to wait for them to make the first move before I decided how to counter attack.

Before this happened, I had to know where I stood and that meant I had to race against time. I hurriedly walked to the bedroom and placed the briefcase on my bed. I frantically searched for my laptop cable and when I found it, I opened the briefcase, fetched out Larry's laptop and connected it to the cable. I then connected the cable to the socket and waited with bated breath. As I waited, I decided to begin scrolling in the other gadgets. I took the digital camera and switched it on. I found it strange that in spite of the time that had passed, the battery was still powerful. I scrolled through the archives but to my dismay, I did not find even a single photo. I picked up the expensive cellphone and switched it on too. Like the camera, its battery was still charged. I only needed to scroll through for some minutes to realise that what I was holding was a shell. Like the camera, the memory had been wiped clean and there was not a single call registered. The contacts list had also been wiped clean and that meant that whoever had come before me had done a good job.

I set the two gadgets aside and rested all my hopes on the laptop. I moved the mouse of the computer and clicked on the files but there was no single file in sight. After a trial that lasted for three minutes, I had to accept the naked truth. They had beaten me to it.

All the files had been erased and most of the programmes were empty. I banged the table with my fist and cursed loudly. The chessboard had changed and I had to understand where the new change would lead.

Could it be that Sue had lied to me and that Milly had taken Larry's briefcase besides the money? This I found to be improbable. If they had come after Milly had drugged and robbed the victim as Sue had claimed, then they must have gone after her thinking she had taken what they were looking for. It was after I put the torture in the picture that the fog started to drift away. They would not have tortured her unless they wanted something from her. I was beginning to think of the next line of action when someone knocked on my door. I felt my heartt skip a beat and before I could rise up from the chair, the person knocked again, this time persistently and in an odd way; like he was telling me that I had to open and open fast. I quickly disconnected the computer and stuffed it under the mattress, then grabbed the cell phone and the camera and stuffed them inside the pocket of one of my jackets, which was hanging in the wardrobe. As the persistent knocks continued, I looked around just to see if there was anything that could give me away and satisfied that everything looked in order, I walked to my living room.

I stood in front of the door and before I opened I asked, "Who is it?"

"It's the police! Open!" a harsh voice growled. Although the fear had dwindled, I was still feeling unsure. By introducing themselves, they wanted to send the message that the hide -and-seek game was over. I pulled open a part of my curtain just to be sure and peered through the window. There was an unmarked prowl car parked next to my gate and I could even see the outline of the driver as he smoked. I drew in some air, turned the key and swung the door open.

They were four of them, all dressed in plain clothes. They were all mean-looking and beefy with blank faces that betrayed no emotions. All these notwithstanding, I faced them with feigned calmness.

"Yes?" I uttered with a croaking voice.

"Can we come inside," one of them who seemed to be the leader uttered while gazing at me intently. I found it strange that they did not bother to introduce themselves and this could only mean that they knew this was a war between friends. Without saying anything, I stepped aside and let them pass. They all filed in silently and while I was closing the door, the unexpected attack came. I was not expecting the sudden move thus the scuffle was very brief. After a short while, they had me handcuffed and seated on a sofa.

"Sorry Sherriff, but it couldn't be helped. We have orders to bring you in and we had to do it the way the boss likes it," said the leader. I knew it was an ironic apology but that didn't worry me. I was worried by the new change of scene.

"Do you have a warrant of arrest?" I asked for the sake of it, just to show them that I still had some guts left. They all laughed in a strange way that betrayed sarcasm. Then the leader said, "I have heard of your fame as a sleuth but I didn't know you speak foreign languages too."

"Can I then make a telephone call to a friend," I insisted, ignoring his irony. Although I knew I could not get this, I wanted them to know that I was down but not out. No one answered me and that confirmed my thoughts. While I sat there, I had a good chance to study their faces. Three of the faces looked alien but the face of the leader was familiar. I probed into my memory until I fished him out. I only needed to put a pair of dark glasses before his eyes and a brim hat on his head to know who he was: One of the men who had been trailing me the day before and who had been with me in the cyber café.

"Take him to the station!" he ordered, pointing at me.

One of the men came to me with a black scarf and blindfolded me. He held me by the jacket, sent me on my feet and herded me outside. No one told me but I knew why they were remaining behind: my house would have to undergo a thorough search. While my guide shoved me in the backseat of the prowl car, my mind went to the notes I had been making and which were still lying on the study table and my mouth went dry with fear.

Chapter 9

The drive to the station was chilling and nerve-wrecking. I was at pain to know where they were taking me, owing to the blindfold. As we kept meandering around, I knew that my end had come. I knew that this kind of treatment was only reserved for political delinquents and this was enough to tell me that things had really reached the boiling point. I was sure they were acting on orders from above and that was enough to convince me that my life was now hanging on the edge of a precipice. The sounds of the hooting cars and the shouts of the touts as they called for passengers told me that we were still in the city. At a certain point, the noise lessened and all I could hear was the zooming of other cars and the noise of the engines. My body began becoming numb since I was sandwiched between two beefy men. After about half an hour, the car increased speed and I knew that now we must have shook off the traffic and that we were headed to the final destination. After a ten-minute drive, the driver reduced the speed.

I placed my handcuffed hands on my blindfolded eyes and said a prayer. I felt the car swerve and then it grid to a halt. I felt a trickle of cold sweat run down my spine.

I could still hear some noise of the passing traffic and this gave me some reassurance. I heard a creaking sound and I knew someone was opening the gate. The driver sent the car ahead in a slow speed and after covering a dozen yards; he brought the car to a halt and cut down the engine. I heard the back door open and one of the beefy men who was seated next to me stepped out. A gush of cold air hit against me as I waited breathlessly. The other man ordered me to get out and helped by pushing me out through the open door. The beefy man who had stepped out first grabbed me and herded me ahead. I walked like a ringed bull towards a destination I did not know. At a certain point the sound of my footsteps changed as the surface of the ground changed. I felt some warmth and that meant we had entered a house. I could hear some inaudible voices, probably coming from some closed rooms. After making a couple of curves and turns, he stopped me and I heard some noise of an opening door. I was again herded inside and then something seemed to lift me up. I knew I was inside a lift that was taking me up a tall building. The lift came to a halt and again I was led outside. After a short walk, the noise of an opening door told me that we had entered another room. My escort pushed me forward and after a few steps, he made me stop then pushed me into a chair.

A profound silence, broken only by my uneven breathing reigned inside the warm room. I could feel his presence next to me and I knew he was waiting for someone. A couple of minutes elapsed and I heard the door open followed by some footsteps. I heard someone pull back a chair and I knew the hour of reckoning had come.

"Remove the blindfold!" a hard voice ordered.

I could feel his massive hands behind my head as he undid the blindfold. A strong light hit my eyes and I had to blink a couple of times before my eyes got accustomed. When I had fully regained my eyesight, I gazed around just to know where I was. It was a medium-sized room with a table and some empty chairs. The walls were painted white and they were bare. I thought it strange that nothing was hanging from the walls, not even a calendar. There was not even a single window although the room was airy owing to the gigantic fan, which acted as the air conditioner.

Although I had never been here before, I knew immediately that I was in the headquarters of the national intelligence agency.

I felt a chill crawl up my spine. The game had now changed and instead of fighting General, I now had the state in the opposite side. That I was being treated like an enemy of the state was something that told me that what was being sought for had immense value. For sure, I knew I was in for a tough grilling but I hoped they would save me the torture.

I lifted up my face and faced the man who was seated on the chair and my heart took a leap. It was my lucky boy, the commandant. He riveted his eyes on my face and I did the same to him. For a brief moment, we stared at each other like two perennial adversaries until he nodded contentedly and released a sheepish smile. Turning to the man standing next to me, he growled, "Get out!" The man obeyed instantly and walked out and from the way he moved, I could tell that he wanted to make the noise of his footsteps as low as possible. When the door closed, he turned to me, this time a treacherous smile on his face and said, "You didn't think you could get away with it Sherriff, did you?" I remained silent for I didn't know what he meant.

"She may have killed your friend but revenge killing is taking the law into your own hands, making it a crime." If I still didn't have the handcuffs clipped on my hands, I swear I would have torn him into pieces. I was so annoyed that when I started speaking, my voice was vibrating with anger.

"You can't pin it on me!" I hissed. "She was dead before I walked in and that you know!" He grinned at me with triumph and tapped the table with his knuckles, then looked at me threateningly, saying, "That is what you think but once you listen to our dossier on this case, you will willingly confess to four murders."

The door opened and the man who had headed the operation of my arrest came in. He was holding a briefcase in one hand and a gun placed inside a plastic bag in the other. I did not need anyone to tell me what had happened. The briefcase belonged to Larry and the gun was mine meaning that my house had undergone a thorough search. I remembered the notes I had been making over the case and I wondered whether they had found that too. The new arrival placed the briefcase on the table, opened it and removed the contents. The laptop, the digital camera, Larry's phones and my gun were now packed inside transparent plastic bags, the way one packs valuable exhibits found in a crime scene.

"Where did you get these from?" the commandant asked in feigned surprise. I knew he had the answer and this made me almost smile. If he was the man running this show, it meant he was lying.

"In his house, Sir," the new arrival said, pointing to me, his face beaming with satisfaction. The commandant sneered at me then nodded to the new arrival (whom I later learnt was a sergeant) to sit down. He looked towards me with a smile of triumph and echoed, "Well mate, this drives in the last nail on your coffin. These exhibits were mined from your house and that makes our task even easier. This is how the story will read: A prostitute kills a prominent journalist and steals some of his equipment. One of the slain journalist's closest friends who happens to be a professional detective decides to take the thing in his own hands. He tracks down the prostitute and avenges his friend's killing. Unluckily, someone spots him getting to the building where the woman was found dead and alerts the law. The rest you know. Sounds cool Sherriff, doesn't it?"

He paused, pointed to the equipment that lay on the table and said in a low voice, "Sherriff, this is what the prosecution calls hard evidence. I have never doubted your qualities as a police officer but I would want to see you convincing the prosecution that a naughty goblin carried these things to your house."

I was now like a confused player inside an alien game whose game-plan he didn't have hence I decided to exercise patience just to see where he was heading to. My patience paid dividends faster than I was expecting. He probed me for a while, wore a smile and even managed to make his hard face look friendly.

"There is another way of settling this thing, Sherriff," he said in an unusually calm voice. "If you want we can put a stone over this story."

"How?"

He drew in a deep breath then leaned forward and said, "There was some valuable information inside those gadgets, which we want to lay our hands on. We believe you siphoned them out before we pounced on you. The deal is simple; you give us the information, we set you free."

I had to fight hard to suppress a smile. *So there it was!* By saying this, he had committed a big error. First he had let me know that his weapon of coercion was breaking and that made me earn a couple of aces and a jolly. Secondly, and this was my jolly, he had made me discover why they were holding me. I made a review of the case and I discovered that they must be after some information and that explained why they had tortured Milly. Having failed to find anything on her, they must have thought that I had something. Finally, he had confirmed that Larry had been killed because of some information someone wanted to recover from him. Having tied up this, I decided to create a false climate of negotiation just to see whether I could fully flush him out.

"Now that you have given room to negotiation, can you tell your side-kick to remove these bracelets, my hands are getting numb," I said calmly.

I saw the sergeant's face tighten with anger and I knew that my jab had attained its objective. To blow them out of their cover, I had to make them know they were not dealing with a coward.

"Remove those handcuffs!" the commandant roared. The sergeant coiled, rose up and unlocked the handcuffs. I caressed my wrists and stretched my hands taking all my time.

"Well?" he quipped impatiently. I was now in a tricky position but I knew I had to stick to the rules if I was to maintain my advantage. If he thought I would reciprocate his kind gesture, then what I said next must have left him incensed to the core.

"Commandant," I began, my voice as cold as frozen ice. "You and I know that these gadgets were in somebody's hands before I got to them. Yes, I carried them to my house, I will give you credit for that but there was nothing in them. Whoever had found them first had already beaten me to it."

He looked at me curtly and said, "So you have no problem if we proceed in building up a case against you?" By jumping the gun, he was telling me that the gloves were now off and final showdown was not very far. I decided to show him one of my aces before I dropped my jolly.

"I would want to see how you will go ahead mounting one," I said with a scoff. "You don't even have a single witness to make your lies stand."

"That's what you think, you bastard!" he half-shouted, his face aflame with fury. This is exactly what I wanted. As long as I managed to keep him in fury, I was sure he would drop his guard and offer me some space to fire my missiles.

"We have your fingerprints on the briefcase and in all these gadgets. The doctor carrying out the autopsy will confirm that she died some minutes after you were seen entering the building. Well Mr magic worker, if you think you can beat all these, then consider yourself a potential material for a mental asylum."

I could not write him off completely for I know what he was saying though an uphill task was not entirely impossible knowing how the corridors of justice operated. Hence, I decided time was now ripe for me to slam my jolly against his face just only to drive my point home.

"Tell me commandant," I said unshaken. "Is the general losing confidence in his men and he has decided to shift the goal posts?"

The sergeant who had all along remained in silence gasped audibly, the only way a very petrified man would gasp. The commandant slowly rose from his chair, his tempered eyes goring into mine, his mouth hanging half open in awe. He rested his hands on the table and asked in a loud whisper: "What have you just said?"

"You heard me loud and clear commandant," I replied, firmly throwing all the caution to the winds. "Some days ago, the general sent you to get me and when we got into his house, he dangled a hefty bribe in my face if I accepted not to meddle with this case. When I told him off, he sent me away with a gift of ten kilos of threat over my head. Some days ago, this sergeant together with another of your sniffer dogs spent the whole day tailing me. Is it that you are running short of arms, or ideas or both? Well, you guys go ahead and hurl me to court and you will regret the damage."

Then the unexpected happened. As quick as lightening, with anger scribbled all over his face, the commandant rose from his seat and furiously headed towards me. I immediately knew he was coming to attack me and with my adrenaline shooting to the peak, I found myself standing up and heading towards him. I didn't know what I wanted to do. Perhaps I wanted to get hold of his neck and squeeze the life out of him. I was all but getting on him when a booming voice brought me to a stall.

"Halt!"

I froze then slowly I turned my head and caught sight of the sergeant, who was now standing some two metres away from me, his raised gun pointing at my head.

"Sit down, Sherriff! Don't make another stupid move!" he roared.

The three of us remained in a frozen position then the commandant came over to me and thrust his blood filled ugly face near mine. His throbbing veins now looked like small serpents and I could smell both his anger and his after-shave.

"You wanted to hit me Sherriff, isn't it? Well, go ahead and hit me!" he growled seething with rage, his mouth foaming with bottled anger. I stared at his blood-congested face and I was tempted to hang a blow on his jaw and send him sprawling to the floor but I managed to contain myself though with extra effort. I knew if I hit him I would play right into their trap hence I decided to beat a tactful retreat He looked at me loathsomely then turned to the sergeant and bellowed, "Throw this fool in a cell before I kill him! By tomorrow we should have enough evidence to pin it on him."

* * *

I sat calmly in the cold cell and analysed the sudden turn of events. That they had thrown me in a solitary cell was a blessing for now I had ample space to know where I stood. This arrest shocked me but I also found it to be providential. The commandant had provided me with the final answer that helped to fill the glaring lacuna that had been tormenting me. I was now sure that Larry's death was hooked to some information that Tracy wanted to pass over to him or had already passed over to him. I figured it out that this was the information they were hunting for. They must have thought that Milly had taken it and when they traced her out and found nothing, they must have decided that perhaps the only person who could be having it was I.

But what was it?

After a lengthy pondering without finding an answer, I decided to consider another hypothesis. I looked at the string of events and I noticed a pattern. Anyone who had gone near the fireplace or anyone who was deemed to have known something about this case was gone. It began with Larry, then Tracy and the DJ, then Jackline, Milly and now me. Looking at the shape of things, I concluded that the chauffeur too must be six feet under too and if he was not, then he was being shielded.

I stopped worrying about the dead and shifted my attention to the fate that awaited me. Though I knew they could easily make real the threat to wipe me out, I hoped they fell for my bluff. I cursed myself for not having thought of calling Shylock or the Editor, the only formidable allies who would have helped pull me out of this mire. I hadn't lost hope yet, but I was now sure that a threat on my life was hanging over me like the sword of Damocles. That they had made Milly call me spoke volumes and now that they had me all for themselves, nothing could stop them from dispatching me to my tomb. They had not booked me in the occurrence book and this only helped increase my fears that I was finally their mercy. If they got rid of me, I would join the long list of 'the missing without trace' and this I now knew was possible. I sighed heavily and resigned myself to fate.

The cold in the cell began to bite and I thanked the heavens that they hadn't made me remove my shoes or taken my jacket. The darkness in the cell now grew thicker and I suddenly remembered my small flashlight. I dipped my hand in the pocket and sighed with relief when I felt it next to my wallet. I fished it out and switched it. Though the light was not very strong, it gave me company and I hoped it would last till morning.

I was still buried in my thoughts when I heard the sound of a key turning. Then the door creaked and I quickly switched off my tiny flashlight and dipped it into my pocket then waited. The door opened and a strong light flooded the room rendering me blind. Someone was violently pushed into the cell then the door closed as quickly as it had opened. In the darkness, the new arrival, unaware that there was another soul in the cell stumbled against me almost knocking me down.

"Careful mate," I said politely. "I know you can't see me but you better know that you have company."

He apologised then sat down next to me and dropped into a silence. I could hear his fast breathing and the noise of his skin as he scratched it continuously. Then he started coughing, a pathetic cough that left me wondering if he had TB. When he stopped coughing, he started aping the sound of the guitar with his mouth, then he would sing.

Tititirititi! The law is an ass! He sang in a kind of rap tune. I made no comment though I found it funny.

Tititiririririti, the law is made for small people, he went on. Still I said nothing. I thought he was drunk although there was no trace of alcohol fumes in the cell.

Tititiriririti! The law is like a cobweb, the small flies get caught while the big ones break through. I could not resist a chuckle though the wisdom withheld in the anecdote struck me. He then broke into a song, much to my surprise. He sang about the irony of the law, about the police and the brutality of life in solitary confinement.

"Mate, what is the meaning of all these?" I asked, still chuckling.

"A song that will be a hit-song if I ever leave this hovel," he replied. I immediately noticed his odd accent. He spoke English with a deep Franco-phone accent, like a foreigner. I said nothing. Having worked as a policeman, I had seen some people fall in lunacy due to the loneliness of the cell.

"It's good to have company after six days of living like a lone buffalo," he said after a brief silence. I frowned in the darkness without saying anything. When one is held in solitary confinement for more than three days, this could only mean that he or she was a very special prisoner; like a political dissident.

"Sorry if I am talking too much," he said in an apologetic tone. "I know that you may need some silence so that you can think. Does my yapping disturb you?"

I said it didn't and that got him talking.

"Life can sometimes be unfair," he said sorrowfully. "At times I wonder if the gods have a score to settle with me."

The darkness was now becoming unbearable and I wasn't sure whether it was safe to produce my flashlight with a stranger in the cell. I battled with the fear until I decided that he was a safe man. I removed my flashlight and switched it on for besides getting rid of the nagging darkness, I also wanted to catch a glimpse of him. I glanced at him in the semi-darkness and I immediately noticed that he had a very athletic physique. His head was round and clean-shaven while his biceps told me that he was a fan of the gym. When he saw the light, he immediately turned his head in surprise.

"Hey mate! How did you manage to sneak this one in?" he asked in a whisper.

I smiled mildly. "I didn't sneak it. A lazy police officer slept on his job."

He patted my shoulder.

"We must thank the heavens. To have light in a cell is like having manna raining from the skies. Could there be a chance that he missed your cigarettes too?" he pressed on. When he mentioned cigarettes, a strong urge to smoke grabbed me like a strong spirit. I hadn't smoked for more than three hours since I had other things to worry about. My hand went to my shirt pocket and I almost shot through the roof with joy when discovered that the packet of cigarettes was still with me.

"It seems that the gods are on our side," I said, pulling out the packet. I felt for my rear pocket where I normally kept my lighter and sighed with relief when I touched it. I offered him a cigarette and we both lit up. We smoked in silence then he turned to me. "Who are you? I have never heard of anyone with a *carte-blanche* to enter a police cell with shoes, a lighter, a flashlight and cigarettes. Who are you?"

"Forget about my identity but if you insist, you can call me Santa Claus," I replied jokingly. He laughed lightly while inhaling more smoke.

"Why did you become a tenant of the state," I asked him.

With nothing else to do, I guessed chatting would come in handy. He shook his head in a gesture of regret.
"It's a long story and since we have nothing else to do except talk, I will furnish you with it."

He crushed his cigarette end on the floor, scratched his feet again and began telling his story. He told me that five years earlier, there had been a regime change in his country. The bickering and wrangles between the incoming leadership had torn the country apart leading to an explosion of a bloody civil war. One day, the rebel soldiers descended on his village and what followed was a chilling bloodbath. They wantonly slaughtered any soul in sight including his parents. He managed to escape by a whisker and dodged through the bush for days. When he reached Isiru, a kind truck driver hid him in his lorry and sneaked him into a neighbouring country.
"I stuck in Kalimpala for one year, moving from nightclub to nightclub hawking my music talent. A good friend who worked in the capital of the neighbouring Ndiambo-land noted my exceptional talent and told me that he was ready to help me to move there. He managed to sneak me through the border though we had to part with a hefty bribe. I reached the city and I immediately found a job in a nightclub as a guitarist though I didn't have the necessary papers. My friend worked through thin and thin until he got me the papers though again, we had to spend a fortune in the name of a bribe."

"Is that why you are in?"

"No, I am in for my hot balls," he said with a chuckle.

"You mean you are in for rape?"

He laughed again, this time patting my shoulder.

"No. Although I have hot balls, I am not a beast."

He asked me for another cigarette and I gave it to him.
"Having hot balls is a tragedy but when hot-balls meet hot-pants the result is a catastrophe and that is my case."
I was not following him keenly. I just listened to him because I found what he was saying to be interesting.
"My music career blossomed and gave me bread and a roof over my head. Then I landed myself a nice job in a popular nightclub as a disco jockey and I quit singing. All was set for rosy times ahead until I met this hot-panted woman."
He stubbed his cigarette, coughed softly then went on.
"She was a good lay but the most interesting part was that she was rolling in dough. The icing on the cake arrived some months later when she gave me a car for a birthday present. To me, the set up was perfect but I hadn't reckoned that she would fall in love with me."
"You mean you didn't love her?"
He shook his head. "All I wanted was fun and the money. Then suddenly she started having new ideas and started talking about marriage. That is when I started getting wary of the set-up. I would have ditched her then but I decided to take my time and siphon out more money from her before ditching her. Little did I know that this would turn out to be my undoing."

Another brief silence followed.

"Seven days ago, I received a call from her. As usual, I knew she wanted some dose. She told me that she would be sending her chauffeur to pick me as she always did. When night came,

I left the nightclub and as usual I found the usual car waiting for me but alas, when I opened the door, she was not there. In her place was now seated a mean-looking man who had his gun pointed to me. I felt my mind go wild but before I could even scream, I felt the cold feel of a gun muzzle digging into my spine and a stern voice behind me told me to board the car. Out-numbered and outsmarted, I had no choice but to play ball."

He coughed again and asked for another cigarette. The air inside the cell was now getting stuffy and I was tempted to deny him the cigarette. Nevertheless, I yielded to my good will and gave it to him.

"In the beginning I thought they were thugs although their demeanor made me doubt this. They were four of them, two in the front seat and two behind. After a short drive, they stopped the car and asked me for my car keys. I gave them the car keys and the keys to my apartment. They then frisked me and took all my documents including my foreigner's identity card and my wallet. One of them dialled a number and spoke in a language that I could not understand. When he finished, he took all my documents with him and stepped out. One man who had been sitting in front came behind and dug his gun in my rib while his companion blindfolded me. I heard another car stop just next to us and when I heard the bang of a closing door, I knew that the man who had been with us had boarded that car. They sent the car rolling and I found myself shivering with fear. I didn't know who they were and I didn't know where they were taking me. The truth of their identity was unveiled some ten minutes later. One of the men instructed the driver to turn left and when the latter answered *ndiyo afande,* I knew I was in the hands of the law although I didn't know why."

He inhaled some more smoke, held it in his mouth for a while then sent it out.

"Since I came to the city, I had always made sure I kept a clean sheet. Save for the illicit affairs with rich women, I had never found myself in cross hairs with the law hence I was now at pains to understand why they had arrested me. Then I remembered that I had got my papers in a clandestine way and I wasn't sure if they had sniffed this one out. Since I couldn't tell whether this was the bone of contention, I decided to wait."

He inhaled in some more smoke, stared at the red tip of his half smoked cigarette intently before picking up again.

"Finally, I found myself in a brightly-lit room in the company of four men, all of us seated around a table. One of them who looked as if he was the boss asked me why I was in the country illegally. I told him that my documents were legitimate and that earned me the heaviest slap I have ever received. The next question gave me a hint of why I was in trouble. The same man asked me why I was messing around with other people's wives and that finally told me that my hot balls had finally landed me in trouble. Without warning, I was stripped, whipped and kicked all over my body. My balls, which were now cold like a piece of wet iron, were squeezed to submission, leaving me writhing in agony. When they were through with me, they threw me in a water-logged cell, naked and gasping for my dear life."

He asked for another cigarette but this time I boldly told him that we risked suffocating ourselves.

"'This cell is very small. It's better we smoke one person at a time in intervals." He did not insist and he just went on with his story.

"After one hour, they came for me again but this time only one man interrogated me. He apologised deeply for the brutal treatment I had received and promised to take action on the perpetrators. He told me that he would offer me protection if I told him what he wanted. He told me that one of the women I had been messing around with had been killed and he wanted to know from me who had killed her. That drove my blood cold. I confessed that I had messed around with a dozen of women hence I was in pain to know which one of them had been dead. I told him I could only believe him if he gave me the name. He did not tell me the name but he told me that before this woman was killed, she stole something precious from their boss and that they believed she had handed it over to me. "If you give it back to us," he told me, "we will see to it that this thing is pushed under the carpet but if you don't, we will pin her murder on you." I told him that I knew of no murdered woman and I had not received anything from any woman. That made him go mad with fury. He called back the four torturers and they picked up from where they had left."

I was now not listening to him for my mind was running full throttle. When he had mentioned about a woman and something precious, alarm bells started ringing all over my body.

Could it be a coincidence?

Before I could ask him anything, he was already on with the story.

"They tortured me until I could scream no more. They now kept asking me where the things that my lover had given me were hidden. They then asked me why I kept forcing the wife of their boss to ask for a divorce. When they got nothing from me, they frog-marched me back to the horrible cell and locked me in." I could hardly wait for him to finish! *It can't just be a coincidence!* I kept murmuring to myself. Without warning, I studied his face with my flashlight and in a loud whisper I asked, "What is your name?"

He narrowed his eyes, perhaps wondering why I had suddenly started to look interested.

"Why should my name interest you?"

"Never mind! Just tell me your name!" I hissed.

He blew his cheeks, caressed his chin and fell silent. I was just on the verge of pestering him again when he turned to me and said in a Low voice, "My real name is Regis but I have a string of aliases. To those who love the Congolese jigs, I am Dombolo but to my closest friends, I am BMW."

"BMW..? The car..?" He laughed lightly. "Not the car. BMW: Beer, music and women, the emblem of my life but to my fans, I am DJ Cool."

CHAPTER 10

I SAT TRANSFIXED LIKE a carved statue, my awe-struck eyes staring fixedly at him. I was now breathing very fast and I was sure he could listen to the beats of my thudding heart. He moved his face close to mine, stared at me with eyes of wonder and asked, "Mate, what's biting you?"

I did not answer him. My sleuth mind had already taken over. *There was no way they could have put us together unless they had laid a trap!* I stood up hurriedly and emptied my pockets. There was only my wallet and the cigarette packet. I stopped and whispered to his ear, a very low whisper. "Cool, please stand up and search your pockets."

"Why all this," he asked in amazement. "Don't ask questions, just search your pockets!" I hissed. He did not insist anymore. He went through all his pockets and found nothing.

I now turned my attention to the four walls. I toured them with my flashlight and found nothing yet my mind kept telling me that there had to be. I went further up and my flashlight rested on a single widow some three meters up. My last hope. I went back to his ear and whispered again, keeping my voice as low as possible. "Cool, I want you to kneel down and I will step on your shoulders. My hands have to get to that window up there. I am not very heavy so you will manage."

Even in the semi darkness, I saw his face turn from surprise then to real fear. He now wore a very puzzled face but this I understood.

"Santa Claus or whoever you are, are you planning an escape?"

"Cut the questions and do what I have asked," I hissed impatiently. "There will be time for that."

That shut him up. He went on his knees and I mounted on his shoulders. He then heaved himself up and lifted me until I reached the window. I held the cold iron bar with one hand and with my heart now thumping; I moved my hand along the small floor of the window. When my hand reached the end, I felt something metallic. While I carefully closed my fingers around it, I was now burning with excitement and I thought I could fall.

We sat down on the floor of the cell and watched the tiny tape recorder. It was still running and that meant we had escaped thinly. I pressed the stop button and while I pulled out the small tape, I could hardly resist a smile. Either these boys were underrating me or they were taking me for a dimwit, I thought. I had seen this kind of tape a million times when I was working in the crime department and it was one of the finest tricks in the book. I remembered my days in the crime department when I couldn't get a confession from the criminals or a case turned foxy. I would dump the suspects together in a cell then plant a tape. They would then talk amongst themselves at times organising their defense or at times quarrelling and blaming the other for the hitch. From their talks, the suspects ended up giving themselves away because some of their talks helped me pick up some valuable clues and counter-check the facts. Well, it was a close shave, this I accepted but if they thought I could fall for such an old trick, then they were yet to see the best of me.

I viewed the tape with curious eyes, resisting the urge to crush it. It slowly dawned on me that whatever the information they were after was very precious, to the point that they were ready to travel to Hades if that meant retrieving it. The more I thought about it, the more I was dying to know what it was. When my mind grew calm, I slowly discovered that the man who held the key to this mystery was the man who had returned from the dead: DJ Cool.

I was busy planning for the best line of attack when he pulled me out of my thoughts.

"Santa Claus, tell me what is happening. Who planted this tape and who are you?"

Although I knew I had to handle him in a crafty way, I was now aware that time was not on our side. Though I didn't want to throw him into panic, reason told me that I had everything to gain by laying my cards on the table. I replaced the tape in the recorder, placed it on the floor then faced him calmly.

"Sorry for keeping you in the dark but soon you will understand why I had to do it. When they brought you in, I couldn't fancy that we were facing the same jury and for the same charges. Now tell me, this woman you were flirting around with, is her name Tracy?"

He leaned towards me, his eyes almost bulging out of the sockets. "Yes. How do you know?"

"And you are DJ Cool who used to play at Passion Box, aren't you?"

"Yes, that's me. But who the hell are you and how do you know me?" He whispered loudly. I nodded with a chuckle then placed my hand on his shoulder and said, "Then welcome back to the world of the living. Now I can say with certainty that dead men do indeed tell tales."

"What do you mean by this?" he asked while grabbing my arm in a firm grip. I brooded for a while not knowing how to tell it to him. I was yearning to spill the beans but I wasn't sure whether he would believe me.

"My name is Sherriff and I am a policeman," I finally said owning up. What I had feared happened. His immediate reaction left me helpless. He instantly got to his feet and stood over me the way Muhammad Ali stood over the fallen George Foreman in the famous rumble in the jungle.

"I knew it!" he said in a menacing tone. "I knew they had planted you here so that you can flush me out! That explains why you had the flashlight and cigarettes!"

"Please calm down and listen," I pleaded. "It's not what you are thinking."

"I am saying no word to you," he said while sitting down far away from me. "I should have thought twice before letting loose my mouth."

Now that this way had failed, I knew I had to seek refuge in the psychological approach. In a way I had understood him but his reaction had given me a golden clue; he couldn't have reacted that way if he wasn't the man who held the key to the puzzle.

"You have just come out from false grave Cool and if you don't listen to me, you will go down again but this time to a real grave."

He said nothing. He just scratched his bare feet then placed folded his arms.

I forced myself and moved close to him then spent the next minute imploring him and cajoling him to co-operate. He listened to me without interrupting but the clicking sound he kept making with his tongue told me that convincing him would be a tall order

"Believe me, mate. We are cogged in this together and unless we join hands, we have a paper-thin chance of sliding out of it."

He covered his face with his hands for a couple of minutes then asked me for a cigarette.

I hurriedly gave it to him and gave him all his time. He drew in a couple of puffs without saying a word but I noticed with a sinking feeling that he kept regarding me suspiciously. After a short while, he crushed his half smoked stick, placed it on the floor and turned to me.

"I don't know how much of my trust I should yield to you but I will wait to hear your side of the story before I tell mine." I knew I had reached my first break. I went ahead and fashioned him with all the events. From the morning Larry was killed then to Tracy's kidnap and later murder. I told him about Jackline and how she was assassinated then how the general had tried to thwart my efforts of unearthing the mystery. I recounted to him how I had made my visit to the Passion Box and how the shoeshine boys had tailed me. I told him how I had been hooked in the murder of Milly then my arrest and interrogation. As I talked, I saw his face loosen and that meant that he was softening.

"From the look of things, these guys are after something and they will not rest until they lay their hands on it," I said. "Woe unto us if they lay their hands on it before we do. It is our only key to freedom."

He said nothing. He just stared blankly at the semi darkness but the way he was breathing told me I had won him over. Thus, I mused, time was ripe to make my million-dollar question.

"DJ Cool," I started in a sibilant and cajoling voice. "I could be wrong but I guess that the person who is holding this key is you."

He looked at me straight in the face for a brief moment then smacked his lips. He then placed his hand on my mouth and said. "Sherriff, I don't know how you intend to pull me out of this but I hope I can trust you. Yes, you are right. There is something I am holding back. I don't know whether it's this key you are talking about but believe me it's what is keeping me alive. I knew that if I told them, they would certainly kill me but as long as I had it, they wouldn't dare kill me."

I admired him for his power in discretion. I had also concluded the same; they were not ready to clear the possible leads until they laid their hands on the wares.

"If what you told me is true, then I would hate to die a second time so I will tell it to you." I leaned towards him and opened my ears full.

"It all began a week ago," he began. "Tracy came to me wearing a beaming face and bubbling with unusual enthusiasm. I could see she was excited to the toes and I was eager to know why. When we reached our usual love nest, she handed me a small package saying, "Darling, guard this with your life for it is the key to paradise, the bridge to our happy times ahead." I didn't understand her but I didn't press on for I was burning to have her. I placed the small package in a drawer and went back to her. To my amazement, she sent me back saying, "Put that package in the safest place where not even God himself can find it." Thus I went back, fetched the package and put it in the safest place I knew and from the look of things; I guess it is still there. I went back to her and after we had made love, I asked her what was in the package. She caressed my chest lovingly and said, "A key that opens the door to happy times. All we need is to get a good journalist then you and I will fly to paradise and live like angels for eternity."

Again, I did not understand but from what you have told me I can get the full picture. But is it true she is dead?"

"Yes she is," I said flatly. "I was the first person to see her corpse."

I heard him draw in a long shuddering breath but I didn't give him time to recover from his grief.

"What is inside the package?" I asked eagerly.

He was now burying his head in his knees with his hands over his head. After a brief moment, he lifted up his face. "I know you will not believe me but I don't know what it is. I never thought about it again nor gone back to look at it. Two days after this, the police got me." He answered.

My heart was now racing. I knew that the clock was ticking and I had to act fast before we got time barred.

"Where is this package?" I asked impatiently.

He drew in a deep breath then turned his eyes towards me. "Before I tell you this, I want to know what you are planning to do."

It hurt me to lie to him but I had no option. 'Never tell the truth where a lie can do better' Larry always told me and right now I had no choice but to follow this maxim.

"Before the police got me, I had called a trusted friend and alerted him that the police were after me. I told him where to go and what to do in case he missed me. I am sure he is already busy and by tomorrow he will have traced me. Once I get out, I promise to do everything to pull you out but to do this I need a weapon in my hand and the only formidable weapon is this package," I said, making my voice as convincing as possible.

"I don't follow you," he said with a tremor.

"What you said is true; they will not dare make a lethal move until they get this package and that is our trump card. My idea is to get it before they do then use it as a weapon to bargain for your life. It's that simple."

"What if your friend doesn't trace you?"

"He will, believe me. Once the news get to the public that I am missing, they will have no choice but to produce me in court and since they don't have charges against me, they will be forced to release me."

I pointed to the tape recorder and went on. "With this toy, they hoped to nab us. They thought that once they put us together we would squeal but thank the saints that I was one step ahead in my thinking, otherwise they would have smoked us out. Come morning and they will discover that their trick has snapped wrong hence they will have no choice but to set me free."

I picked up the tape, regarded it then showed it to him saying, "Cool, we don't have time on our side. If these guys come to check on this gadget, they will sound our death knell."

He finally caved in. He slithered towards me then spoke to my ear in a low voice.

"Go to Passion Box and walk upstairs. You will find a big room that acts as the store. It is a dusty room filled with broken-down musical instruments and old furniture. This is what acted as our love-nest. Amongst the instruments there is an old medium percussion drum. You can't miss it because there is a sticker of Bob Marley on its side. The top is fastened with bolts. You will need a pair of pliers to open it. It has a false bottom. Inside there, there is my false passport, two golden rings and two golden chains. I had saved them as surprise gift to my fiancée. The package is together with them."

"You are sure no one could have entered there?"

He shook his head then spat on the floor. "No one goes there. It is a kind of warehouse to dump old things. Only the manager and the head waiter knew that I was using it as a love nest."

"Did Tracy see you putting it there?"

"No, she didn't. It's my most guarded secret. Not even my fiancée knows."

I believed him. Now that I had all I wanted, my mind was working like a computer and new ideas were flowing in faster than I could cope. I knew that even if I managed to get out I would not keep them off my back hence I was not leaving anything to chance. There was still one more detail to bag in before I began tying up the whole thing and I had to get it before time ran out.

"Tell me Cool, do you have someone whom you can trust; someone who can die for you and someone you can also die for?"

"Come again?" he asked frowning his face.

"We are not yet out of the woods yet," I told him. "Even if I get out, I am sure I will have these hounds on my trail day and night. One false move may send the whole plan in smoke. It is for this that we need a close confidant; someone who can go for the package and bring it to me. Once I have it in my hands, the rest will be easy."

He nodded in a gesture of affirmation.

"Getting someone who can die for you in this world is rare, but thank heavens I have one," he said without hesitating.

"Who is it?"

"Her name is Hilda, my fiancée. I had already finalised my plans to marry her. Then I stumbled on Tracy and I decided to postpone everything and pick the ripe cherries first. I have met many women in my life but she is the only one who can walk through fire for me."

"How do I get her?"

"If showing yourself in public is as dangerous as you say, then you better call her. Her number is 823124024. Will you remember it?" I made him repeat the number as I glued it to my memory.

"I guess it's easy. The first three numerals are common to all then 12 for the disciples of Jesus, 40 for Ali Baba and the forty thieves then 24 like the hours of the day. Did I get it?"

He laughed and patted my shoulder. "You have a sharp mind."

I now had all the works but there remained one important task and I had to do it fast. I took the tape recorder and rewound it putting it at the start.

"Time has come for us to fool them," I told him. "We are putting this toy back to its place and once I come down we will just have a casual talk. You will ask me why I am in and I will tell you off. You will then go on with your music tales until I tell you that I need my sleep. You will keep yapping and I will keep ignoring you. If we manage to fool them, this will buy us more time. Is it clear?"

He said 'yes' with a chuckle.

I placed the recorder back to its place, pressed the on button then I came down. We put our act into play as we smoked. It was a perfect act and I guess had we taken it to Hollywood, it would have won a couple of Oscars. He was the first one to start dozing. My eyes were heavy with sleep and I would have wanted to catch a quick nap but the anxiety and the fear of tomorrow kept me awake.

It was nearing dawn and I was just about to succumb to the desire to sleep when the door slid opened and powerful flashlights lit up the cell. They splashed the light in my face and I could barely see anything. Three stout men threw themselves over me and pinned me to the floor. I thought they had come to finish me so I fought hard; pushing, kicking and heaving but nothing bore fruit. One of them landed a powerful blow on my neck while another one kicked my ribs in what felt like a mule kick. A wet cloth was stamped on my nose and I was hit by a pungent smell. My kicking and pushing became feeble as life ebbed out of me. The last thing I heard before I passed out were the frantic pleas of DJ Cool as he begged them to spare his life.

* * *

I don't know for how long I had been unconscious but when I opened up my eyes, the first thing I noticed was throbbing pain in my head; like someone had hit me with a sledge hammer. When I attempted to move my head, pain shot up my spine like an electric shock and this left me panting for my dear life. My body felt so numb and wasted. It was as If I had been run over by a bulldozer. I opened wide my eyes and tried to look around but only deep darkness greeted me. It took me a couple of minutes to fully regain my senses. It was then that I noticed where I was. When my eyes got accustomed to the darkness, I realised that I was lying somewhere in a bush. My eyes slowly picked up some shrubs and tall trees silhouetted in the dark horizon. There was the silence of a grave all around me, broken only by the rhythmic sounds of the crickets and the croaking of frogs somewhere.

I have never felt this lonely in my life. Luckily, the night was full of fireflies, which helped light the dark night and give me some company. I felt like I was running short of air and I tried to open my mouth. Something seemed to block my mouth and I could not lift my lips. It was then that I realised I was gagged. Fear and panic gripped me and I tried to move my hands but another rude shock awaited me: my hands were strongly fastened together behind my back with a strong adhesive tape. I tried to move my legs but what I felt shattered my hope. I tried to kick strongly but I soon resigned. Whoever had tied my legs together had done a good job.

I leave to those who have been to hell and back to tell their story but if hell is akin to what I went through, then I promise never to skip a church service for the rest of my life. Never before in my life had I felt so tormented, so scared. The panic and the fear settled in the bottom of my stomach like silt and however hard I tried to vomit it out, it remained defiant like a chronic disease. Here I was, immobile, with a throbbing headache and in darkness, with no sense of time and without any idea where I was. When the biting cold of dawn started piercing me like needles, my hell was complete.

My body was now beginning to get numb and this made me worried. A cold wind was now sweeping across, caressing me and leaving me cold to my nerves. I knew if I didn't make a movement, the whole of my body would freeze hence I mustered my remaining energy and managed to sit down. Suddenly, I heard a strange scream; a continuous eerie scream that tore through the silent night and ended in a nerve-wrecking diminuendo.

Both my heart and my mind stalled. I had grown up in a mountainous region just close to the great savannah hence this kind of scream was not new to me. I had grown up listening to the screams of the hyenas and I knew that where there were hyenas there were other dangerous animals and vultures. I also knew that a hyena, though a cowardly animal, would not hesitate to maul a tied-up person. Hyenas were dangerous for they moved in a clan and this told me that in case they sniffed me out, I would not stand a chance. Two more screams followed and I felt shock waves running all over my body. The cries were not very distant meaning that the more time crawled, the more I was prone to danger.

When the chirruping of the birds and the first rays of daylight came, my wilted hope received a new lease of life. With some light, I could now survey the scene and plan how to free myself. They had placed me on a grassy patch surrounded by huge trees. I roamed my eyes around hoping to catch sight of something that I could use. I saw none.

I was now panting like a trapped deer that has nothing to do but to wait for the mercy of the hunter. My whole body was beginning to get numb and I felt like I needed air. I wanted to scream, give out a loud cry hoping that a good Samaritan would hear me and come to my rescue but I had neither the courage nor the strength to do it.

I must have passed out or fallen asleep but the howling of what sounded like a dog was enough to make me regain my senses. The noise increased and I realised that it wasn't just one dog but many. I swallowed dry air and my nerves grew stone-cold. I wriggled, kicked and rolled but all these came to naught. In the meantime, the noise of the barking dogs grew in volume, meaning that they were getting closer and closer to where I was. Never in my life had I felt this helpless. I was trapped, with all routes of escape sealed. All I could do was to lie still and wait.

Soon, the dogs got to where I was. They all surrounded me, panting, sniffing and baring their canines. They were big and wolf-like dogs and their fierce eyes were enough to tell me that a slight move would be enough to get them devouring me. I became rigid and held my breath watching their fiery eyes. Then they whined and wagged their tails making way for their master.

He was a tall man with hard eyes and cold features. His hair was long and uncombed and he was dressed in a long coat and a traditional shuka. His rough face which bore some tattoos and his pierced earlobes were enough clues to tell me that he was an indigenous. In his hands, he held a bow and arrows. He stared down at me for what seemed like an eternity then he lifted up his shoulders. My sorry state must have convinced him that I was harmless for he bent down and removed the gag from my mouth.

Like a drowning man who had just been pulled out of water, I opened my mouth and fed my starving lungs with air. After a couple of seconds I gazed up to the 'good Samaritan' and thanked him. To my astonishment, he shook his head negatively. I switched from English to the national language but again he shook his head. This told me that he was a native. He spoke to me something that I could not understand, then he dug inside his dirty coat and pulled out a sword. He cut loose the tapes that had tied my hands and my legs then stood back still holding the sword.

I rose from the ground and sat down burying my face in my arms for a while. The feel of freedom was overwhelming and the gratitude was almost overflowing. After a while, I stood up and offered my hand to my liberator. He first eyed me suspiciously then reluctantly took it though his other hand still held the sword firmly just in case I pulled a surprise. Since we could not understand one another, I had to use gestures. I pointed to the ground then spread out my arms. He shook his head in affirmation then moved his eyes around. He then gestured me to follow him as he bent down and crawled under the creepers with his dogs in tow. He then stepped aside and pointed at a track. I could see some marks of footprints and that told me that this was the way my captors had used. I stretched my hand and offered it to him in gratitude. Again he took it and uttered some words that I did not comprehend but which I guessed could only mean 'good luck.' I bid him farewell and walked down the track.

Chapter 11

IT WAS A NARROW PATH, hard and covered by over-hanging creepers. I could see a couple of fresh footsteps and that told me that I had thought right. I stooped and hurriedly waded through and when I could stand upright, I trotted on the dark footpath aware that I was racing against time. After walking for about a kilometre, the path vomited me into a bigger road wide enough to accommodate a small car. It was a kind of a junction hence my mind was thrown into a dilemma. There were numerous tyre marks on the ground. This meant that more than two cars had passed there. I tried to study the marks to see whether I could tell to which direction the car had turned. The turning marks were many and they couldn't help me.

I cursed in frustration. I was now in the middle of a forest and there was a chance that I would either walk to the heart of the forest or find the exit. After five minutes of fighting with the dilemma, I decided to take a risk and chance with the right.

I walked hurriedly down the small road hoping to hear the sound of a car. Somewhere down the road, I came across a small stream and I stopped to wash my bruised face and hands, then using my hands, I quenched my thirst.

I had barely walked for three kilometers when I heard distant noise that brought me to a standstill. I listened keenly then I felt my hope take a leap.

It was a faint roar of a car engine. Gripped by a child-like excitement and in spite of the pain and the fatigue, I broke into a run and sprinted like a mad man. It is difficult to express what I felt when I heard the noise of a passing car, this time very close or when my eyes caught sight of the tarmac. It was something akin to a lone walker in the desert who suddenly comes across an oasis or a shipwrecked survivor who catches a dim sight of dry land. It was too good to be true.

Looking like a vagabond, dirty and haggard, I knew that only a very kind person would be willing to offer me a lift. Two cars passed by and although I frantically tried to flag them down, none of the drivers gave me an eye. The third car came and I tried my luck. This time, the driver thrust his head through the window and hurled some unprintable words towards me then sped away. Frustrated, I decided that I would rather begin walking than wait for an absolution that would never come. I began walking but before I could cover fifty meters, I heard a thundering roar behind me. I turned round and caught the glimpse of a lorry. I waved at it imploringly with both hands and to my relief, the driver started to slow down then brought the lorry to a halt just next to me.

Only two people were seated inside the cabin. The driver, who had pierced earlobes eyed me with kindness and asked, "Where are you going?"

"I am going to the city," I answered. By his accent, I could tell that he was indigenous. He regarded me for some time and I guessed that he was looking at my bruises and my haggard look. "What happened to you? You look like you were wrestling with a leopard?" he asked politely.

"No, I was car jacked," I lied. "The robbers left me tied in the forest for the whole night and I only managed to free myself this morning."

He nodded sorrowfully and I knew he had believed my explanation.

A minute later, I was seated in the cabin saying a silent prayer of thanksgiving while the driver pressed the gas pedal and headed to the city.

It was only after we had driven for some ten minutes that I started seeing features that told me that we were driving along Ngog road. After driving for about one hour, we got to the outskirts of the city and I told the driver to drop me at the Plainsview bus stop.

"Don't you want to go to the police station first," the lorry driver asked me as he brought the lorry to a halt.

"No. I will first change my clothes then I go to the station."

I thanked him whole-heartedly then briskly walked towards the estate. The road was filled with commuters, some heading to work and taking their children to school. No one cared to look at me and notice my bruised face and haggard looks.

* * *

When my sister opened the door, she looked at me with a horrified face and cupped her mouth. I guess the disheveled figure she saw before her reminded her more of scarecrow than her brother.

"What have they done to you!" she exclaimed.

I hurriedly pushed her aside and entered the house. I didn't want a nosey neighbour to get curious and start shooting questions.

My brother-in-law was coming from the bathroom; a towel tied around his loins and his reaction was not very different. He immediately stood back and his face turned pale.

"Bro, what has happened?" he asked in a groaning voice.

I knew I had neither the energy nor the time to explain everything to them so I told them the only thing that could help me grab their sympathy.

I told them to be calm because I was only doing my job and that made them relax. What I did not tell them is that I needed their house as the base of my operations but I knew time would come for that.

My sister served me with breakfast and after I had taken to my fill, I asked to have a shower. My sister who worked as a teacher was busy preparing their only child for school so only her husband was still with me.

I took a shower and he lent me a clean pair of trousers and a shirt. When I was fully dressed, I called him aside and explained the mess I was in. I had thought it wise to confide in him and not to my sister since I would have hated to sow seeds of panic.

"Listen, brother. I am in a terrible mess. Something to do with my job and I would not want my sister to know about it."

He started breathing fast though he maintained his face calm.

"It's nothing big but it could turn tricky and that is why I have chosen to come here and not to my house. I need help."

The alarm in his eyes vanished and he nodded in affirmation. I guess he softened when he realised that his house was the only place I could run to.

"What can I do for you Sherriff?"

"There is a very valuable witness that I have to contact and I dare not show my face in public hence the safest place to meet her is here. I then want you to lend me your cell phone."

"I guess you need some cash too?"

When he mentioned money, my hand immediately went to my back pocket and I realised that I still had my wallet with me intact. All my documents were there including the two thousand shillings. I told him that I had enough but he offered me two thousand shillings.

"I beg you not to tell my sister what is happening. In case she insists, just tell her I need rest." He scratched the top part of his head then turned around and walked out leaving me alone.

When he came back, I was already fully dressed. He handed me his cell phone saying, "You have the house for yourself. I have talked to my wife, there is no fuss."

Once again, I thanked him earnestly. Ten minutes later, husband and wife walked out and I had the house all to myself.

When he walked out, I gave the phone a blank stare and I had to resist the urge to call Shylock. I brushed the thought aside and decided that I would only call him once I had all the evidence in hand. I dialed Hilda's number and pressed the phone to my ear as if my life depended on it.

After a brief wait, a melodious voice answered the phone. I knew I had to play my cards well lest I found myself going back to the drawing board.

"Am I talking to Hilda?" I said, making my voice sound as courteous as I could.

"Yes, this is me. Who are you?"

I swallowed some saliva and hoped.

"I happen to be a close friend of DJ Cool," I responded. I heard her catch her breath and I crossed my fingers. I hoped she didn't bang the doors in my face because if she did, then I had to hunt her down to her house and that meant a waste of precious time. After a while, she came in again.

"Who are you?"

That was it. I only needed to listen to the note of repellence in her voice to know that I was treading on a mine-prone ground. Now that I had her, I had to play the next part with caution.

"You can call me Stanley. Cool had deposited some valuables with me. He told me that should anything happen to him, I should hand them over to you."

Another longish pause followed and I knew she was chewing it over. I noticed that my hand was sweating and I cursed myself for allowing nervousness to take the better of me. What she said next made me even more nervous.

"Regis has never mentioned your name. Besides, why did you take this long before calling?" The melody in her voice was now gone and the way she was now spitting her words told me that unless I made a smart move, her next words would be 'check-mate'.

"I am sorry that this thing happened while I was away. I only came to know about it today when I arrived this morning. My condolences miss."

The line went silent save for her soft breathing which told me that she was still on the line. Then I heard beeping sound. What I had feared had indeed happened. She had hung-up. I made three successive trials but I received no answer. I was now sweating with fear for I knew that without her I would have lost the contact I needed.

I dialed for the fourth time and this time she picked up. Before I could say anything she warned me, "If you keep disturbing me, I will pass your number to the police!" she snapped then disconnected.

I was now desperate. I knew I could do without her but with her, my mission would be easier so I decided to make one last attempt. I wrote her a quick short message packing it with imploring language then sent. I gave her a couple of minutes to digest the message then I called her.

"You must give me a hearing please," I beseeched, once she had picked the phone. "If you can't come here then tell me where I can meet you."

When I heard her draw in a deep breath, I thanked the stars. What she said next almost made me shoot through the roof with joy.

"Where can we meet?" Her voice, though not melodious like before, sounded friendly.

"I am at Tanga waiting for you. The estate is plainsview, house no. 234. I would prefer if you came alone."

I heard heavy breathing and that was enough to tell me that I hadn't bought her yet.

"Why should I come alone?" she asked suddenly.

I knew if I answered this one she would pin me so I dribbled it.

"I would rather if you took a taxi for I don't have much time. I will refund back the money."

She kept quiet again for a dozen of seconds. My heart was now drumming and I had a problem remaining on my feet.

"I will be there," she said, then disconnected the phone.

* * *

The last flicker of my hope was just about to get extinguished when the knock came. I sprung like someone who had accidentally sat on a hot stove and ran to open the door.

She was moderately tall with a dark skin. She had a pair of round seductive eyes, a thin mouth and filled up cheeks. She was smartly dressed in a navy blue skirt suit, a red blouse and red high-heeled shoes. A beaded necklace completed the rest.

"Hilda?" I greeted politely.

She showed me an enchanting forced smile that exposed

her milky denture then nodded.

I genuinely smiled back and opened the door for her. While I closed the door, I watched her catwalk to the sofa and I found myself getting mesmerised. While I joined her, I couldn't help wondering why she had never thought of challenging Naomi Cambell, the star model. I went to the kitchen, fetched a soft drink and poured some for her.

"I was almost losing hope," I said as I sat down.

"I thought you would never come."

She smiled again and lifted up her glass.

"What are these valuables that Regis left for me?"

She caught me off-side. I was not expecting her to come in this fast and this was enough to convince me that I had not yet fully convinced her. I knew I had no choice but to own up but I had to do it shrewdly.

"I guess he was the most precious valuable to you, wasn't he?" I asked fixing my undeterred eyes on her face.

She hid her face with her hands for a moment then uncovered them and said: "I would rather we don't talk about him. What is this that you have for me?"

"You are wrong, Hilda," I started, not risking moving my eyes from hers. "We have to talk about Cool because he told me that if I hope to save him, then I have to come to you."

She did not move an inch and that told me that she was still in the dark. I decided to hit the nail on the head. "I don't know whether you believe in miracles but at times there are some real things that happen that seem to be miracles."

This time she reacted by giving me a curt stare but I ignored this and went ahead to drop the bombshell.

"Hilda, I know this will be hard for you to believe but DJ Cool is alive, we met yesterday."

Her immediate reaction almost made me bolt. Her eyes grew enormous, her mouth opened agape and she looked like someone who had met a ghost in the dead of night. She supported her hands on her thighs and said, "Are you crazy? We buried him some days ago! I saw his coffin."

"Did you see his body?" I asked, cutting her short.

"Yes I did! Charred and black like coal, burnt beyond recognition!"

I shook my head emphatically and leaned towards her.

"Listen to me. Someone wise once said that not all the dead end up under the ground. Yes, you saw his body. You saw the coffin and his grave too but that was not him."

She looked at me in awe, her mouth still agape and in a hoarse whisper, she asked me who I was. I glanced at my watch for the millionth time and I noticed that time was running out. I had to hurry things if I hoped to work within the time-lines. I clasped my hands together and faced her.

"I want you to listen to me and I want you to understand. Cool is alive but his life is in danger and if you and I don't act fast we could both loose him," I said.

The horror in her face had not yet vanished and I could see that she was yearning to say something but that her words were choking her. I decided that there was no more time to waste. I first began by telling her who I was then I went ahead and fashioned her with the entire story without holding back anything. I recounted to her about the chain of murders and what linked these murders together. When I finished, I could almost touch the fear stamped on her beautiful face.

"Then whom did we bury?" Her voice was now raspy.

"Forget who it was!" I said in a whisper that sounded more of a shout. "That is someone else's worry. Our worry now is to get this mysterious package before they do. I am sure they have not yet harmed Cool but if they beat us to it, he will be done."

She kept silent for a while then started to pick her fingernails. The look of disinterest that I saw in her eyes dealt a blow to my hopes and I started wondering whether she would co-operate. She turned towards me and casually asked, " What do you want me to do?"

I lost no time for I had been waiting just for this moment.

"Take a taxi and go to Passion Box. Upstairs there is a room that acts as a store. You will find an assortment of broken down musical instruments and old furniture. Walk to the left side and you will notice a medium size percussion drum with a sticker of Bob Marley."

I fetched the pliers and gave them to her.

"The top of the drum is fastened with bolts. They are not hard and you can handle them. After you have removed the top, dip your hand in and feel for the board that separates the drum from the false bottom. Pull out everything there is in there and bring them back to me."

She first stared at the pliers then looked up at me and gave me a curt smile. She slowly placed down the pliers then pulled out her phone from her bag and pressed a button.

I flinched and my heart missed a beat but before I could ask her what she was doing, she pressed another key then replaced the cell phone in her bag and fixed a strange look on me. She regarded me briefly, gave me another blank smile from her selection then said, "Are you sure of what you are saying or will I find myself walking into a trap? Do you think it will work?"

My hope crept back and I sighed with relief. This meant that she was still with me.

"Everything will work fine, trust me. I have already talked

to the manager, he seemed a good friend."

Without knowing why I started doubting her. She did not seem to be in any hurry and she looked like she was waiting for someone.

"I guess you have to get moving. We are pressed for time."

For an answer she gave me a long smile, one coated with irony and blended with sarcasm while at the same time she shook her head.

"I don't know whether you are indeed a police officer but if you are you must be in the wrong profession. As a conman you would have been a disaster but as a second-rate actor you would have done better."

Something awful stirred in me and I felt like I had swallowed a dose of poison. I looked deep into her hard eyes and I read danger and treachery.

Had I picked the wrong person?

Before I could say anything, someone strongly and persistently knocked at the door.

My mouth ran dry and there was turbulence inside my stomach. I had the feeling of a trapped animal and with bewildered eyes; I instinctively looked at her suspiciously. To my dismay, she gave me a suspicious smile, the kind that Judas must have given to Jesus at the garden of Gethsemane. The second knock, which was now more insistent, drove me numb, lifeless and polarised in the brain. I knew if I didn't open the commotion would attract the attention of some undesirable cars so I half-heartedly walked to the door and turned the key.

I found myself facing the stoutest meanest man I have ever seen. He was tall, with a larger-than-life frame and his menacing muscles - that seemed as if they could squeeze water out of iron - made him something equal to one of those sumo wrestlers. His rhino-like neck and sunken eyes gave a voice to the energy bottled in his massive frame. He was wearing a leather jacket, a pair of skin-tight jeans and a pair of Mexican boots. He had a golden chain hanging around his thick neck while his clean-shaven head shone in the dim light.

"Yes," I managed to mutter though with a lot of difficulty. I was still half stunned and lost for words for I was yet to make out who this mysterious man was.

His mouth parted in a curt smile exposing a set of yellowish teeth while his small catlike eyes regarded me ominously.

"My girlfriend happened to enter through this door, said she was going to meet an old friend. I just wanted to make sure that she is fine," he said in a growling voice then grinned sheepishly while he lifted up his hand and touched his moustache exposing a thick set of fingers, all donning shiny rings. I said nothing for I was still tongue-tied. I was yet to understand what was happening hence I was short of ideas. On one hand, I was scared that this strange stand-off could invite some curious eyes but still I was not sure whether to let him in.

"Let him in, he is with me," said my visitor.

I understood everything. I remembered seeing her remove her phone and dial a number at one point during our conversation. I concluded that it must have been at that point that she had sent the S.O.S. Half-heartedly, I opened the door fully and stepped aside to let him pass.

When I joined them, he had already taken the seat next to her and was busy admiring the pictures hanging on the wall. With my heart still thudding, I sat down and waited for their next move. Without being told, I knew that somewhere I had messed up things though I didn't know how. She unzipped her handbag and fished out her lipstick then went ahead to smear her beautiful lips taking all the time that there was to take. When she finished, she capped the lipstick, replaced it in the bag then faced me with probing eyes.

"Please meet Kimbo my guardian angel. You will have to forgive me for this but once I furnish you with my side of the story, I am sure you will understand why I had to get myself a bodyguard so just bear with me," she started in a casual voice.

"I am yet to understand what you fellows want with me," she went on, her face suddenly turning stern. "I have been trailed, my house has been searched, I have received threats through my phone and now you call me here to feed me with the latest fashion of Oscar award winning cow and bull story!"

At this juncture, I felt that what was needed was the most cajoling and convincing speech made by a talented lawyer in front of an adamant jury; a brilliant emotional intervention like a last minute campaign speech – that would touch the rock-hard heart of this beauty queen and make her see the truth hidden in my desperate eyes. Unfortunately, I could not manage this for I was now desperate like a helpless prisoner facing a firing squad and who kept hoping that a miracle would happen and render all the guns inefficient.

"Hilda you have to…"

"No, I won't!" she blurted out, her angry eyes almost falling from the sockets. She eyed me briefly then a fake smile crossed her face. She went on.

"I knew that you people would not give me peace a day after the funeral. I returned home and I found my house turned upside down and everything else turned inside out. The books had been brought down from the shelves, the sofa cushions had been pulled out, the mattresses had been slashed. Whoever had done this had not left anything to chance, even the ceiling had been taken care of in a search that betrayed the hand of a professional. Then I started noticing strange people behind me. They followed me everywhere, in the supermarket, in the market, in the salon, everywhere including the social places! Then the threats started. Anonymous telephone calls became the refrain of my days. I have been threatened with arrest, I have been abused, and I have been intimidated. The reason behind all these is something that I am yet to discover."

She regarded me cunningly then gave me a smile, a small smile, vile and vicious that stirred fear in me. She leaned forward and glared at me loathsomely and I was surprised to notice that tears were now beginning to well in her eyes.

"What do you want from me and when will you ever give me peace?"

Tears were now beginning to roll down her cheeks.

"Please Hilda… I beg you…"

I was now trying to explain myself using my hands and at a certain point, I made as if to stand up and that put her bodyguard into motion.

For a man weighing like a jumbo, he surely could move first. He sprung on his feet with the speed of a trap and pushed me back to my chair. He then thrust a finger the size of a mini-banana in my direction saying, "You stay seated until she is through! If you make another move I will crush your skull into bits and pieces!"

This unexpected move caught me by surprise and I was left speechless. I sat down and watched his small twinkling eyes and listened to his fast breathing. I knew better than to challenge him so I kept my calm.

"Kimbo takes care of me and he knows his job so watch your manners," she said, this time her voice sounding composed. She picked up her handbag as if to indicate that the interview was over, gave me a forced smile saying, "I presume time is ripe for me to go away but before that I have a small message for you to deliver to your friends. Tell them Regis left me nothing of value except a broken heart. Tell them that my only crime was to have fallen in love with a man who could not let trouble alone."

She rose up and walked towards the door without bidding me farewell. Before opening the door, she turned to me and said, " Tell your friends that in case they have some scores to settle with Regis, then they can go and settle them with him at his grave."

After she had walked out, her bodyguard gave me a glaring look then made a gesture with his hands - as if he was squeezing clothes then in a hissing tone he said, "next time we get any trouble from you, I will wring you kaput!"

He then followed his client making sure that a banging door accompanied his exit.

Five minutes after the duo had walked out, I was still standing where they had left me stunned, bewildered and looking like a hen whose only chick had been scooped away by an evil hawk. My vision was blurred and my mind had already hit a gridlock. Like a walking corpse, I dragged my feet to the door and turned the key but even as I walked back, I could almost touch the words of the muscle man, which still lingered in room.

...I will wring you kaput!

I dropped into the sofa and buried my head in my arms like a desperate orphan.

Chapter 12

I stole my way through the door of Passion Box and headed straight to the loo. I needed a lonely place that could facilitate thinking and in the present circumstance, only the toilet could offer me this. I locked the door and sat on the toilet vase then dropped into a pensive mood and began to weigh my options.

After Hilda had left, I had fought off the desperation and hysteria that was gripping me and I decided that I had to go for the package myself. I knew that time was not on my side hence I quickly locked the house, called a taxi and headed to Passion Box.

My first option was to find my way to the store on my own and attempt to trace the wares 007 style. After weighing the option, I realised that I did not even have a map of the ground. Above all, the store might be locked and that meant more challenges. There was the risk that I would be nabbed as a robber bitching the whole mission. I explored the possibility of bribing one of the workers to sneak me inside the store but that meant more time was needed and this is what I was short of. I discarded this option although I did not completely write it off.

It is then that I remembered Dave the manager. I had completely forgotten about him after that encounter and now that I was in need of help, he stole his way back to my mind. I remembered that he had appeared to be an easygoing fellow who could swallow things rather easily. All I needed was to get to him and explain to him my predicament hoping that I could be a second time lucky. He had swallowed the journalist trick with ease, I hoped I would manage to make him play ball this time round. What if he asked me about the presumed story in the newspapers, what answer would I give?

That would be easy. I would only tell him that the story was in the editorial desk and would soon be in the print.

After I had banged my brains enough, I decided that I was ready. I drew some confidence by gulping down some fresh air, pulled out my cell-phone. I scrolled down in my memory section until I found his number. Again, I drew in a deep breath and pressed the dialing button. My anxious breathing accompanied the ringing. After two successful trials, he picked up the phone. Without wasting time, I went ahead and introduced myself just in case he had not looked at who the caller was. He had answered the phone with a growling unfriendly tone but the moment I mentioned my name, his tone changed and he sounded like a child who had just encountered Santa Claus in the middle of the year. I told him that I was headed to his office and he told me that he was ready to receive me.

I moved my eyes around the bar just to be sure that there were no probing eyes.

The bar was still deserted. I rose from my chair, buttoned my coat and headed to the stairs. He rose from his chair and offered me his hand while he wore a comely confident smile. "It's a pleasure to meet you again. I have been dutifully perusing the newspapers every day looking for an article over our fallen hero," he said, winking mischievously. This was a provocation, a reminder that I still owed him something but unknown to him he had given me a lifeline - a perfect beginning.

I rubbed my hands together just to gain confidence and hide my anxiety. I knew this was the most crucial moment and I had to arrange my cards well prior to beginning the game of wits. Once beaten twice shy. I had already failed once with Hilda. If I failed in this, I could as well call it quits.

"I know I owe you something, Dave, and in fact, the reason of my coming is connected to that," I began with a solemn tone painting my face with the colours of credibility. I knew I had to pull the best of my performance if I had to pull him to my side.

"I know it will be hard for you to understand but I am sure once you listen to the whole story you will bear with me," I went on, this time with a voice that was as subtle as it was cajoling. His face grew tight and I saw his eyes turn alert. This was the first warning sign.

"I work in the investigative department of our newspaper and I came to you because we were interested to dig out the mysterious death of the DJ Cool. We felt that the public needed to know the culprit who had stolen his life. That is why I came to you. I know you will hate me for coming as an undercover but once you consider the sensitivity of the murder, you will understand why this had to be done."

I noticed that his face had lost the friendly aura and he was beginning to probe me suspiciously. I knew I had got to the delicate stage.

"The day after I had visited you, we received an anonymous call. The caller insisted that he wanted to talk to the editor handling the DJ story and so our boss passed the call to me. The caller said he knew the hand behind the DJ's killing. He said the person was very powerful and dangerous and would kill him if he knew that, hc, the caller knew something about the murder. The informer claimed that there was concrete evidence to prove this. This evidence, according to him, was lying somewhere which only he knew."

I applied my natural talent of drama and allowed a considerable pause, partly to allow him time to digest that and partly to allow me prepare my next move.

"I asked him where this evidence was and he made me promise that I would blow the whistle once he led me to the secret. I gave him my word and he directed me where to find the evidence. That is why I have come to you."

He gasped loudly and I wondered whether I hadn't gone in too hard. His face had tightened and was visibly shaken and he was now very scared.

"What has this got to do with me?" he stammered. His face had already lost the friendly touch and I could tell without being told that I was dealing with the best coward there was. I knew I had to be careful. I gave him a reassuring smile and in the most comforting voice I said, "It has little to do with you except that you will be the man who will pave the way for the public to know who killed their icon. That is, if our informer is to be believed."

I had him draw a sharp breath and this meant that I had to move fast lest I gave him time to break down.

"Do you have a store where you preserve your junk and broken things?"

"Yes, we have," he answered in a loud whisper.

"DJ Cool sometimes used this room as his love nest, didn't he?"

His eyes grew wild and he hesitated. Although I could see the answer on his face, I could see that he was half-willing to give it to me.

"Speak out, Dave," I told him softly. "I will see to it that you remain in the clear so don't get worried."

He nodded then said yes. I sighed with relief. I was now almost there.

"This is the room that holds the mystery. According to the informer, Cool hid something here, something that will lead us straight to the killer's lair. All we need to do is to fetch this thing and we burst this case open."

He said nothing although I could see that his face had taken another dive into the waters of mystery. I started fearing that if I drove him hard he would crack so I decided that I had to be extra suave.

"What do you want me to do?"

I fought hard to hide my boiling excitement. "Kindly give me the key to this store then leave the rest to me."

He pulled open a drawer and fetched a key, which he handed over to me. I touched my pocket and felt for the pair of pliers. All I needed now was luck.

"Where is the store?" I asked.

"Take the stairs to the second floor. It is the last door on your left."

Without saying another word, I stood up, opened the door and walked out.

* * *

I closed the door behind me and gazed inside the dark room. The air was stuffy and choking due to the poor aeration. When my eyes grew accustomed to the darkness, I started making up some broken down furniture. I fished out my cell phone from my pocket and using it as a flashlight, I surveyed the walls until I found a switch. I pressed it and light sprung all over. My heartbeat increased and I moved my eyes around until they rested in the furthest corner.

There was a collection of broken down percussion drums all covered with dust. Moving like a moon walker, I started turning them around until I found what I was looking for.

When my eyes caught sight of the Bob Marley sticker, I felt something snap just below my heart. I was now sweating profusely and my breathing was now very fast. Using the back of my hand, I wiped the sweat from my face. I then produced the pair of pliers and started testing the bolts. Satisfied that all was in order and with my heart pounding against my chest and with adrenaline filling all the spaces in my body, I started unfastening the bolts. I hardly succeeded because my fingers were now shaking as if I was holding a pneumatic drill. I finally managed to uncover the top part of the drum and hence I dipped my hand in. My fingers touched the false bottom and I gulped down a deep sigh. DJ Cool was not lying after all.

I pushed the false bottom with the tips of my fingers and until I felt it turn. I pushed it aside and dipped my hand in then groped in the unseen abyss. My hand touched something that felt like an envelope. With sweat now flowing from all over my body and my heart pounding against my chest, I placed my fingers on the envelope and started pulling it out. Suddenly I heard a slight movement and blood froze in my veins. I felt a cold shiver ran down my back and my hand trembled vaguely almost knocking the drum. I slowly turned my head and what I saw sent my heart reeling with fear while I felt my legs melt under me.

He was wearing a long coat and a brim hat. His eyes were no longer covered by dark glasses so I had no problem recognising him. His ferocious eyes pierced me like two swords but this did not worry me. What made me worried was that in his right hand he was holding a .45 automatic and its barrel was pointing at my head. We both froze into the shape of trees while we did a silent battle with our eyes. No one had uttered a word and the store had become strangely and ominously silent, a silence broken only by our audible breathing.

It was the third time we were meeting. Our first close contact was at the bar in the Passion Box when I had sent him the provocative note. Then we had met in my house during my arrest, at the station and now here. I slowly let go the envelope and made as if to draw out my hand.

"Sherriff, if you make a stupid move I will blow off your brains!" he said in a growl making sure that he made himself heard while at the same time keeping his voice low.

I froze again, watching the way he was holding the gun. I knew I was dealing with a professional, someone who would shoot if constrained hence I decided that I had to watch my manners lest he shot me.

"If you don't know, this gun is silenced so don't try to pull a fast one," he went on. "I want you to bring your hand out of the drum and do it very slowly."
With him holding the whip hand, I had no choice but to dance to his tune.

He pulled back the safety catch and the metallic click of the gun provoked a snapping feeling inside my stomach. It was like the snapping of a tightened bow and it left a hollow feeling inside me. As I slowly pulled out my limp hand, I kept hoping that he didn't guess what was inside the drum although behind my back I knew that he knew that what was inside the drum was the treasure that he and I had been hunting. I cursed myself, cursed the demons of ill-luck and cursed Hilda. I could hardly believe that the whole mission was botched just as I was to get at its tail end.

"Put your hands on your head and move away from the drum," he ordered, this time making a step forward. I moved away from the drum hands on my head. I eyed the drum sorrowfully the way a lion would watch a kill that was being snatched from its jaws. His gun followed every movement I made, his finger around the trigger ready to shoot in case I made a false move.

When he was sure I was at a safe distance, he grinned at me triumphantly saying, "You thought you could win Sherriff, didn't you? You thought you are smart but not very. This game is now over."

I said nothing. He had caught me flat-footed and with no weapon on me. I wished I had a gun for if I had one, I would have attempted to distract him but without one, I was at his mercy. He fumbled into his pocket as if he was searching for something while he kept his eyes fixed on me. I thought that I had caught some movement - like someone was approaching the pillar – and just as I was about to dismiss it, a bulky figure of the man moved like a furious whirlwind and struck his back and hand. Like a flash of lightening, I threw myself to the ground and covered my head with my hands.

The metallic noise of the gun as it hit the floor and his groan sounded like one. I lifted up my eyes on time to catch the sight of my 'saviour' as he drove a powerful punch into the stomach of my rival. He released another loud groan then crushed to the floor as if he had been pole-axed.

I slowly rose from the floor and gazed at whoever had come in to save me. It was Kimbo, Hilda's bodyguard. He regarded me with his cat-like eyes then gave me a reassuring smile.

"So you are not as phoney as you look, after all," he said

with a grin. He then pointed to the floor saying, "You will want to pick up that rod lest someone else picks it up before you do then uses it to pin you against the wall again."

I bent down and picked the gun, eyed it curiously then lowered it. I was still breathing fast for I was yet to recover from the scare. There were so many questions I would have wanted to make but I was lost for words. He bent to the fallen figure below, touched his eyelid then nodded saying, "He is still counting the stars but he should be resurrecting soon."

He laughed softly then dipped his hands into his pockets and faced me.

"You are sure you have not killed him?" I queried, pointing to the lifeless body lying on the ground. "This log happens to be a star exhibit that I intend to use to convince the jury in some case that I have in court." Again he laughed.

"It's just a soft tap. I rarely apply my heavy-duty blow. When I do, they fall and stay dead but this one will be coming around soon."

I wanted to thank him for saving me, I wanted to ask him how he had sneaked into the scene and I wanted to ask him what he wanted to do next but I had no word for my mouth had suddenly ran dry.

"I kept telling her that maybe you were not a fake and that she should believe you but she could hear none of it. Then I told her that it was better to check on your story and she agreed to come with me and check on your story."

"Who?" I asked in a voice that sounded more of a groan. He looked at me, shook his head and said, "Hilda."

I understood why he had smiled and I almost laughed at myself. I was so lost that I could not even answer simple questions.

"When I found the door half open, I grew suspicious. Then

I listened and when I heard voices, I decided to come in unannounced. I tiptoed and found you two having a party. Then I realised that you were having the rough end of the bargain so I decided to step in and give you a hand."

I heard some footsteps and I lifted the gun but I lowered it when I saw who the intruders were; Dave and Hilda. Dave was leading and she was following behind. When Dave caught sight of the figure of a man lying on the floor, he looked at me with eyes that were submerged in mystery and seeing me holding a gun he asked, "What is happening around here? Who is this man?"

I knew that if I started explaining everything I would never stop so I decided to dribble the question.

"It's strange that in spite of his good nature DJ Cool happened to have many enemies. Well, he is one of them," I remarked subtly.

"Is he dead?" his voice betrayed a visibly shaken man.

"No, he is not. I know my job," said Kimbo.

Hilda stepped forward, smiled widely at her bodyguard, gave a friendly tap at Dave then faced me.

"I didn't think we would be meeting again. So it was not a hoax?"

"If it was then I am Michael Jackson." I did not smile.

Everyone watched me while I walked to the drum. I dipped my hand in the hollow space and fished out a medium sized brown envelope. I turned towards them then tapped the envelope with the tip of the gun saying, "This is what has been giving me sleepless nights for ages and now that I have it, I can do nothing than to thank all of you for your help."

Hilda walked over to me and held my hand. I looked into her eyes and I saw nothing else but thanks.

"I want the truth from you. Is it true that Regis is still alive," she asked in a loud whisper. I nodded.

"Yes, he is alive but he won't be alive for long unless you and I act fast. Are you with me now?"

Instead of answering me, she buried me in a long hug pressing her body against mine. After she had communicated her thanks, I pushed her away and turned to Kimbo.

"She and I will go to some place. I hope you have no objection.

He shrugged and motioned to the unconscious body. "What about this mess? Who is supposed to clean it up?"

My face lit up and I smacked my mouth. My mind was now working full throttle and I had answers to almost all the situations that cropped up. I gazed at the log lying on the floor and I grew anxious. He had been motionless for long and I started wondering if he still had warm blood flowing in him. I bent down and felt his pulse then turned to Kimbo.

"Are you sure you have not killed him? He is one of my precious exhibits."

He smiled then shook his head.

"Believe you me this log still has life in it. I know a dead body when I smell one." He retorted.

I motioned to the dazed Dave to come close then I whispered to him audibly: "I know it will be hard for you to understand but come tomorrow, you will have all the answers you need," I patted his shoulder. "This log lying here is one of the bad boys and like me he has been hunting for this evidence." I showed him the envelope then went on. "I need some free space if I have to burst this case so I would want you to hide him for me in some place until time is ripe to produce him."

I heard Dave draw in a sharp breath while Kimbo kept his face straight. I was beginning to love him for in spite of

everything he seemed to be very confident and at ease with everything and this told me that he could be a trusted ally. I turned to the shuddering Dave, ignored his fear and said, "Do you have a piece of rope?"
He nodded.

"Get it for me and get me an adhesive tape if you can."

He walked out before he could hear the rest of my words and I could see he was glad to excuse himself. When he was gone, I pulled Kimbo aside.

"I guess you know what is happening."
He nodded emphatically and I could see that he was very attentive and ready to collaborate.

"I will need you to stick here and watch this place while I wind up the rest of the show. I will take Hilda with me because I need her. Make sure no one comes near this man until you get a call from me."

Again he nodded then he turned to me and said, "Are you sure you can handle the rest by yourself? Sure you wouldn't do with some help?"

"I have that tied up so don't worry. Sure I will need help but I know where to get it."

Dave returned with a length of rope and Kimbo went ahead to bind the sergeant's hands and feet doing a good job of it. We then tapped his mouth and I helped hulk to drag him to a corner. I searched his pockets and found the two telephones, which I switched off then handed them over to Kimbo. I then gave him the captives gun saying, "I guess you will need this. Can you handle a gun?"

He chuckled, opened his jacket to expose a shoulder holster then added, "Guns are my life. That's why I am still alive."

I gave him the gun then I turned and placed my hand around Dave's shoulder and reassured him that all would be fine. I told him that if things worked according to plan, he would have his crowd-puller and that left him even more bewildered but this was not the time to fill him in. I told him that I was badly in need of a taxi and I asked him whether there was a good taxi driver he knew - one he could trust. He shook his head and said, "Judging from the look of things, I guess it's better not to trust anyone. I can drop you where you want with my car."

I silently congratulated him for his discretion. I had almost forgotten that the playground was now hot and mined.

We filed out of the store and after making sure that Dave had locked the door, I took Hilda's hand and led her down the stairs. I closed the door behind us and led her to the sitting room. Unlike her prior visit, this time there was an air of friendship and a feeling of solidarity. While Dave was driving us back to my sister's place, she apologised a million times for having doubted me. On my side, I was barely listening to her for I was wrestling with the idea of opening the mysterious envelope. When I was not doing this, I was busy looking behind just to see if I could spot any mysterious car following us.

We both sat down on the sofa and with trebling hands, I pulled out the envelope and we both stared at it with curious eyes as if it was a UFO. I was handling the envelope the way a high priest handles a golden bowl with an offering in it. I noticed with a feeling of shame that my fingers were trembling as I carefully tore the envelope at the top. I then turned it upside down and poured the contents on the table. We both stared at the various objects with the curiosity of a scientist. There was a passport, which I knew was false, two golden chains and two golden rings. But one thing stole my attention.

It was small box, the size of a cigarette packet and it

was sealed firmly with a tape. I went to the kitchen and came back with a knife then I went ahead to unseal it. When it was open, I dipped two of my trembling fingers inside and I felt the touch of something metallic. Slowly I drew the object out to see what it was. It was a flash disk.

I served her with a soft drink then I called my brother-in-law and asked him if he could send a laptop for me. I almost jumped with joy when he told me that there was one in his bedroom just next to the bed. Taking the flash disk with me, I walked to the bedroom and switched on the laptop. With bated breath, I waited for the computer to go through the usual process then when it got ready, I inserted the flash disk and waited. There was only one file that was entitled 'TOP SECRET'. I knew I was home. I pulled a chair and keenly started going through the contents. It took me thirty minutes to go through the whole file. I was now sweating profusely and shaking like one who had a strong fever. I am courageous yes, but I have to confess that at a certain moment, I almost stopped reading due to the fear that had gripped me. The photos, the film clips, the interviews, the confessions and hard facts I was reading were not meant for a layman's eyes. The last thing I saw before I closed the file was the signature: BOB SMART at the bottom of the page.

I heaved in a deep breath to shake off the panic that had gripped me for I knew I was toying around with a time bomb. Then I heard someone move behind me and turned my head instantly, the way a tiger will turn when aroused. That is when I realised that Hilda had joined me in the bedroom and she had been standing behind me. I smiled to hide the shame and turned quickly to wipe my face for I did not want her to see the fear in my face.

"How did Regis get entangled with these things?" I did not answer her though I had the answer. I pulled out my wallet, selected a one-thousand-shilling note and gave it to her.

"We are now racing against time. Go down to the shopping centre and you will find a mall. Look for a computer accessory shop and buy for me two empty flash disks."

She did not ask any questions. She just grabbed the money and dashed out leaving me alone to wrestle with my fear and panic.

After a couple of minutes, Hilda came back with the two flash disks and my heart was touched to see how she was soaked with sweat. She had been running around the whole morning and this truly convinced me that she could die for Cool. I sat down in front of the screen and went ahead to make two copies of the file. I put one of the copies together with a note in an envelope. After sealing it, I wrote a name and a phone number on top and handed the envelope to her. "I want you carry this envelope to the Editor of Mambo-Leo," I said, handing over the envelope to her. "His telephone number is on top. Call him and tell him you have an urgent message from Sherriff. You only need to mention my name and he will meet you pronto. Tell him if he doesn't hear from me by tomorrow, he should send this in the air waves and in the print media too." She dipped the envelope into her bag, zipped it up then turned to me again.

"Do you think Regis will come out of this ordeal alive?" Her eyes betrayed her sceptical feelings although she fought hard not to show it. I took her hand in mine and gave it a soft squeeze.

"I can't guarantee anything but chances are that he will. Now that we have beaten them, we hold the whip-hand and it's my guess that they can't risk harming him before they get it from us."

"How shall we know where they are holding him?" I already had a hunch but there was no time to share it with her.

"Let's cross bridges when we reach them," I said. "Just keep hoping for there is no night without a dawn."

She started walking towards the door but before turning the handle, she turned around and asked me whether I believed in God. When I said I did, she forced a smile and quipped, "Then say a prayer so that my dead man can come back to life." With that she walked out and closed the door.

I stood fixedly at the middle of the room, listening to the tam-tam sound of her shoes as she went down the stairs. When the sound faded, I dropped my tired frame on the sofa and got into deep thought. The weight of the information I had seen started to sink in my mind and I slowly began to see the gravity of things. What I had was enough to send the entire security machinery mobbing around me with fat cats baying for my blood. *But would I really make it?*

I realised I was developing cold feet but the thought that I was chickening out made me feel ashamed. I remembered my dead family, my friend Larry and the promises I had made to Cool and I found myself overcoming the fear and the panic and renewing my motivations. Finally, I managed to pull myself together and I decided that I was not ready to beat a retreat just when I was in the sunset of my mission. By now I was very exhausted and when I thought of the hectic night awaiting me, I decided that I had to do with a good sleep.

While I was lying on the sofa, I looked at my watch and thought of Hilda. I was sure that by now she was waiting for the editor in a secret place. In my mind, I could see the beaming face of the editor with his eyes glued to the screen as he watched what no eye should see and listened to what no ear should hear. I thought of DJ Cool sitting in the cold cell waiting for me to snatch him from the jaws of death. I was still thinking about him when I did finally manage to fall asleep.

Chapter 13

The streets were clammed with *matatus* picking and dropping commuters while the pavements were bursting with people who were waiting for transport home after a day of heavy work. Hawkers were busy calling for buyers, touts yelled and shouted, while shoppers jammed the supermarkets for a last minute session of buying. A *matatu* would stop and a crowd of people would swarm around it, pushing and elbowing just only to get a place. For the pickpockets, it was time to make hay while the sun shone. The cars honked, the people shouted and the loud music from the *matatus* drove people nuts. This was Ndiambo-land city; a tower of babel when evening came. Amidst this confusion, no one noticed a tall woman with a dyed wig and dark glasses. She was wearing a long flowered frock and low shoes. She carried a handbag. To many, she passed as any one of those *mamas* who were heading home to cater for their families after a full day at the office.

The disguise looked perfect and when I viewed my weird image in the mirror, I could hardly recognise myself. My sister's dress fitted me well since we shared the same height although she was a bit more fleshy than me. She had suggested that I use low-heeled shoes to alter my walking style a bit and the idea proved to be good. I had slept till four o'clock and after waking up and taking a shower, I regained my energy and felt relaxed. My sister had prepared for me an early supper and after I had devoured it, I sat down and started formulating my battle plan. When all was set, I bid my sister and my brother-in-law farewell. I had already given them the picture omitting the delicate details that would have made them beg me to call off the battle. I told them that the case I was handling was highly explosive and that it included rubbing some shoulders the wrong way hence putting my life at risk. I also told them that should they not hear from me the next morning, they should blow the whistle.

The crowded *matatu* cruised along Mwanza road, the loud music almost bursting our eardrums. I would have taken a taxi instead but I thought otherwise. After having worked in the police force for over a decade, only I knew how many police informers and members of the national intelligence masqueraded as taxi drivers. This was not a night of taking chances. After alighting from the *matatu*, I walked briskly along the pot-holed lane making sure that I maintained a uniform pace lest I drew attention. However, I kept looking behind my shoulders involuntarily. When I caught sight of Shylock's gate, I said another prayer, and when I reached the gate and saw his car parked in front of his door, I said another prayer in thanksgiving. If I had died this day, I mused, I would have gone straight to heaven for never in my life had I prayed this much in a single day.

For the umpteenth time, I looked behind my shoulders, then pushed the half-open gate and entered his compound. I don't know how many of you have ever met a person who was presumed dead then he or she suddenly appears at home unannounced. Well, you need to have seen the face of Shylock's wife to get an idea of what an experience it is.

After I had knocked the door, she came, opened the door and immediatcly frowned when she saw that the caller was a woman.

"Yes, can I help you?" she asked while studying my face. I could hardly resist a smile. Well, since it was an acting night, I decided to let the play run full.

"Is Shylock in?"

She hesitated then her eyes moved from my head to my toe. "Yes, he is. Who are you?"

I almost burst with laughter when I looked at the way she was standing by the door covering every space as if she feared that I would attempt to burst in. I decided time had come to cut the acting. I removed my dark glasses saying, "Forget who I am, Mama Kiddy, I have to talk to Shylock and it's urgent." She gazed at me, looked at my dress then at my face. When she recognised me, she opened the door wide and made way for me.

I had already got rid of the wig and I was placing my handbag on the table when she joined me. She stared at me curiously cupping her mouth.

"Sherriff, what has gone wrong? Have you gone crazy?" she asked hoarsely.

"No, I haven't. I just wanted to see how I would look in a woman's attire. Is your husband in?" I asked sarcastically.

Well, I guess I took the acting too far for she took it for real. She came towards me, her eyes full of pity and placed a sympathetic hand on my shoulder. Her young son came in with his trademark gun but this time there was no bang! bang! When he saw me, he immediately went and sought for refuge next to his mother, leaning against her and holding the end of her dress.

"Sherry, I have not gone nuts," I started. "Believe it or not but I had to dress like this to get here. Right now there are a couple of bad boys baying for my blood and that is why I need your husband."

Raw fear gripped her but the expression of alarm had vanished. Without waiting, she ran to her bedroom and fetched her husband. When Shylock saw me, he got stunned for a minute and I had to give him a broad smile of reassurance. I had now removed the sweater hence the bruises on my hands were now visible.

"Sherriff, what is going on? What has happened?" he asked.

Unlike his wife, he did not take me for potential material for a home of lunatics.

I did not answer him. I just lifted up the handbag and said, "Let's leave the explanations for another moment. As for now, can I have a shirt and a pair of trousers so that I can get rid of the attire now that the play is over." He looked at me and laughed lightly. "Apart from the clothes, you also need to wash your face to clean the make-up," he said, this time laughing loudly. I joined him in the laughter but he still had more. He first looked at his wife mischievously then added, "And don't forget to get rid of the tampon too." This time even his wife could not resist laughing.

* * *

We sat in his study room next to one another. After I had changed, I found him eagerly waiting for me. I had dragged him aside and told him that I had something private to discuss and we needed to go to his study room since we would need his computer. I decided to give it to him without beating about the bush.

"This will shock you as it shocked me. You will not believe it but Bob Smart's murder is the beginning of this puzzle. It is his death that has triggered this string of assassinations."

"What!" he growled, his eyes almost bulging out of their sockets.

"We will start from the beginning," I went on ignoring his surprise.

"Let's go to the beginning. After the genocide, the government was under pressure to bring those responsible to book and that is when the general called Bob Smart to head a special mission of investigating the genesis of the violence. Smart dug up a heap of filthy things, made a report and handed it over to the general. That is the last that was seen of him. While going home after handing over his report, he was carjacked and his bullet-riddled body was found some hours later. The explosive report accidentally fell in the hands of the general's wife who then went ahead and used it as a weapon of coercion to arm-twist the general into giving in to her demands for a legal divorce." I heard some noise behind us and I paused. His wife came from behind us and placed two glasses of lemonade on the table then walked out. I went ahead to recount to him all what I had gathered until I reached the conclusion.

"All these deaths have been triggered by the general's desire to recover the lost flash disk."

"What is in the flash disk, Sherriff?" His face was now tight and apprehensive.

"This takes us back to the beginning. After the heat of the genocide had died down, the general had called Bob Smart and had given him a job to find out who might have triggered the violence. Smart dug deep into the militia groups, extortion rings, organised thugs and all the criminal cartels which were used by the politicians and the prophets of doom so as to trigger the chaos that almost brought the country on her knees. Smart did a nice job and he was able to penetrate these groups to their core. From Bagdad boys to the Vampires down to Kabul warriors up to the Gestapo; Smart un-earthed everything. He travelled extensively around the country and came up with a comprehensive dossier. His dossier contains all the leaders of these groups, a cluster of politicians including senior cabinet ministers and Members of Parliament who benefitted from the dastard activities of these groups. He came up with a list of prominent businessmen who funded these militias, thus keeping them in business. He also came up with a list of senior police officers who shield these groups in return for hefty monies. To crown it all, Smart managed to discover how some of these groups were used in the electoral campaigns and the bloodbath that rocked the country after the election debacle. That's the picture."

"Then why did they have to kill him after doing such a superb job?"

I could not help sneering at him. I had thought he would be able to tie that on his own.

"I was a bit foxed until I put Smart's murder in the picture. I looked at the set-up and I realised there must be a *mister X* who is missing in this dossier. This mister X is the general himself. Why should he give Smart a job then fight to have a cover-up? This told me that the general is hell-bent on hushing up things for only one reason: he has vested interests. To me, he is the base on which this iceberg rests; the overall godfather and that is why he is ready to make a journey to the bottom of hell if only to make sure that this report does not see the light of day." He drew a sharp breath but I ignored him.

"Come to think of it, his wife would not have blackmailed him unless she was sure that what she held in her hand was a lethal weapon. This is my conclusion Shylock. The general is the hidden shadow who runs the show and I bet Bob Smart didn't discover this otherwise he would not have handed over the report to him. The general is afraid of exposing these crime groups and their godfathers because he either risks exposing some of his friends or risks remaining out of the breadline and I guess that is why he was ready to chance his life if only to short-circuit my efforts. That is the way I figure it out."

Shylock blew out his cheeks then buried his face in his hands like one in mourning. I did not need to look beyond his face to know that what I had told him had hit him like a torpedo.

"Let's see the contents of this flash-disk," he finally said. I was just waiting for that. I produced the flash-disk and he inserted it in the computer and we waited.

His heavy breathing told me that he was finding it hard to believe what he was reading. We watched the photos of the kingpins, the interviews of the witnesses, the confessions of converts and the horrifying rites of the oath ceremonies. Then we came to the photos of the political bigwigs and the fund-raisings and I heard Shylock catch his breath but I understood his reaction. Looking at the list was like reading the list of who is who in the political establishment. When we came to the group of senior police officers involved, Shylock almost bolted. When the report came to an end, we both dropped into a long pregnant silence. The silence would have persisted had he not broken it with a question.

"There is one thing that doesn't fall into place," he said. "You told me that you met the dead DJ. Then, that body that is lying below the grave in the cemetery, to whom does it belong?"

I looked at him, my eyes full of pride and gave him a broad reassuring smile.

"I have tied that up too and its one of my jollies," I said with a beaming face. "In the beginning it had puzzled me but after linking the pieces together, I managed to crack it. That body can only belong to the only actor who can't be accounted for in this play: the chauffeur who is still at large and this you can bet your pension on it."

He now looked convinced though the flecks in his eyes gave a voice to his fear and indecision.

"Sherriff, how are you planning to wrap it up?" I was waiting for just that. Without wasting time, I rolled out my battle plan and explained to him the role I wanted him to play and the logistics we needed.

"It looks a Herculean task but with guts it can be done. We have all the witnesses that we need and once we produce the DJ and pull out that body from the grave, we will be left basking in glory. That man we are still holding at the Passion Box could turn out to be a formidable ally if we manage to squeeze a confession from him."

He nodded silently then said, "I hate to tell you this mate but I guess this potato is too hot to handle. This information can topple the government and I don't want to imagine what would happen if those shoeshine boys walked in just now. We could easily earn ourselves a treason charge!"

"What are you saying, Shylock!" I shouted without wanting to.

"I have always been sincere with you but now I would be lying if I told you that I like this set-up," he said, much to my dismay.

"Shylock, you are not telling me to stop, are you?" I asked in a voice packed with anger. "I am not telling you to stop," he said in a pleading voice. "I am just telling you to be rational and weigh the risks. You are up against a system that is cast in rock and meddling with it is suicidal. If I were you I would shelf my ego and call off this battle."

I pierced him with my fiery eyes and leaned close to him. This was the second time he was letting me down and I wanted him to know that this did not go down well with me.

"Shylock, I can't believe I am hearing this from you. I came here because I believed you are a strong believer in justice, a paragon of virtue, a man who can't be bought and who like Caesar's wife is beyond reproach. Now I know otherwise."

He dropped his head to hide his shame and in spite of my anger, I found myself pitying him. After a while, he looked up and asked, "I am not underrating your plan. On paper it sounds convincing. What worries me is if the general pulls a card we are not expecting and the whole plan goes awry. Do not look at a rained on lion and mistake it for a cat. I warn you not to make the mistake of biting more than you can chew."

"He won't! Trust me," I said, taking my seat again. "Right now he is full of jitters for he is yet to recover this flashdisk. Chances are that he doesn't know I have escaped but if he has, then that increases his worries. If there has ever been a good chance to send him against the wall, then it's now."

He remained silent, scratched the top part of his head and shook his head, saying, "I am sorry to let you down but I don't feel like dipping my snout into this one. It's too dangerous."

I decided I had had enough of him. I threw a quick glance at my wristwatch and realised that time was running out. I stood up and offered him my hand.

"I accept your choice but all the same I am going it alone,"

I said. "Be the friend you have always been and do a last favour for me. Give me the equipment and the gear I need then lend me your car."

"I will give you the equipment but my car keys no," he said flatly. "I will not place my foot where even the devils and angels fear to tread. If something goes awry, everything can come tumbling like a pack of dominos and the consequences can be fatal so I hope you will understand me."

This I was not expecting but I was happy that at least he had ceded on one.

"Thank you, although I was expecting more but as they say, a half is better than nothing." I said calmly. Time had come for me to move but I still had one barb to throw to him.

"I know why you have shied away, Shylock," I began. "For you there is too much at stake; a family, a career and a future. Unlike you, I have lost everything so I have nothing to lose."

"Don't worry, Sherriff," an unexpected voice said from behind us. "If he doesn't give you his car, I will give you mine. Unlike him, I have nothing to fear."

We simultaneously turned our heads. Only then did we realise that Sherry had been standing next to the half-open door following our conversation.

"You should not be here, Sherry!" Shylock hissed. She ignored his outburst, gave me an encouraging smile saying, "I admire your courage, Sherriff, and I pray that you succeed."

"Wives!" Shylock shouted, banging the table with his fist. I almost laughed for I knew he was only trying to divert his embarrassment. Without warning, he stood up and stormed out of the room. His wife gave space to him, then looked at me and made a face with her lips. She then closed the door and followed her husband to their bedroom.

He came back to the room and brought me everything that I needed save for his support. Everything was packed in a rucksack and while giving it to me, he apologised again. "I am sorry Sherriff but this is the far I can go." I did not pursue the matter for I had other things worrying my mind. He walked out of the room and left me to prepare myself. I spent a good deal of time knowing that if I made a slight fault, I would end throwing a spanner in the works. When I was sure all was set, I picked up the gun, checked it then dipped it into my shoulder holster. Satisfied that I was now ready, I murmured a prayer and walked out of the room.

Husband and wife were standing next to one another, their faces rigid with fear and their eyes tense. I had to reassure them that I was in control so I pulled out my phone and dialed the general's number.

"Hallo?" a growling voice said from the other end, a voice that told me that my quarry was at home. I drew in a deep breath, wiped the beads of sweat hanging on my brow with the back of my hand then my voice went into play.

"You have something that belongs to me and I have something that belongs to you," I said unceremoniously. He remained silent for a while then came in again.

"Whom am I speaking to?"

"You are speaking to Sherriff."

I heard him draw in a sharp breath, the way only a scared person would do and I knew I had won the first round.

"What do you want!" he shouted menacingly. I knew he was faking tough but I was ready for him. I ignored him and sent the second part of the plan in motion.

"You heard me well, General," I said sternly. "I have something you are dying to recover and you have something I am dying to save so I propose we meet and make a peaceful swap then everyone can go his way."

"What if I say no?"
Time had come for me to break him down. If I had to level the ground, I thought, I had to make sure that he understood he was dealing with a person of another calibre, not his wife.

"You can't say no, this we both know but in case you do, then what I am holding will fall in the hands of someone who will be more than eager to draw some profit out of it."

A deep silence fell on the line broken only by his heavy breathing, which I could hear very clearly.
"I am here in my house," he finally said. "I will send someone to…"

"No, you won't!" I half shouted. "I prefer to find my way alone. It would be better if I found you alone too. Remember, no blows below the belt and in case you try to pull a fast one, I will blow everything in the air." I hung up on him before he could say anything.

I gave the bewildered couple another reassuring smile then I headed towards the door. Before I walked out, Shylock's raspy voice stopped me in my tracks.

"Are you sure of what you are doing, Sherriff?" he asked, looking at me in the eye.
"No, I am not but I am going ahead all the same," I said after staring at him briefly. "Remember that the tree of impunity is watered by those who see evil but decide to do nothing. Well, I have decided to do something but in case I don't succeed, so long for friendship." With that, I walked out of the door and disappeared in the night.

* * *

The uniformed guard who manned the gate walked towards me and before I rolled down my window, my hand went to my ribs and I felt for my gun.

"I want to see the general. He is expecting me," I said roughly.

He eyed me the way one eyes an unwanted guest who has gate-crashed into your feast, nodded coldly then went ahead and opened the gate. I drove my car on the well-tarmacked drive and stopped it at the parking space. There was no car around neither was there a single soul in sight though I could see some light inside the house. I locked my car, passed my hand over my chest and touched my gun again. *To you Larry,* I murmured while I walked towards the front door.

He was standing behind the table, his callous face as dull as a wall painted in indigo, a half-filled bottle of whisky and an empty glass in front of him. I did not need to look beyond the dead expression on his face and his searching eyes to know that he was a very troubled man, something he was fighting hard not to show. He was dressed in his official uniform, with glittering medals sticking all over, perhaps to bare his fangs and send the message home that this was an encounter between the highest authority in the police force and a junior or even to warn me that what was in the offing was nothing less than a David-versus-Goliath duel. Well, I mused, if he thought that his striking demeanor would scare me, then he was in for a rude shock.

We faced one another and I gave him a meaningless smile just to show him that his little show did not impress me. "If you don't mind you can join me for a drink," he said in a husky voice. In normal circumstances I would have accepted but aware that this was a meeting between a lion and a lamb, I declined. I thought it wise to keep standing; a few metres from him partly to show him that this was not a meeting between friends and partly to keep him under a close watch. He lifted up the bottle in slow reflexes, filled the glass then looked at me suspiciously.

"I knew I would receive a call from you, though I wasn't expecting it this soon," he said. "I had heard about your supernatural acumen but I never expected you to be this good."

I kept my silence. The idea was to let him talk first before I guided him to the guillotine. "When I called you that night, I knew you would dig up a couple of filthy things but I was sure I could handle that. However, I confess that had I known that you would become the thorn in the flesh that you have been, I would have thought otherwise."

He had not yet said something of value so I still remained silent.

"Of course I knew that you would soon discover that my wife's kidnap was stage-managed and that is what made you walk straight into my trap."

"Why did you kill Larry?" I asked point blank, my smoldering eyes watching him keenly.

He took another pull from his glass sending down a dose of whisky then smacked his lips twice and fixed his chilling stare on my face.

"I didn't kill your friend, my whoring wife did it," he said without any feelings. "If my wife hadn't attempted to use him to ensnare me, I would not have gone for him."

I had scored the first goal. Now I needed to know where I stood.

"You said you knew that I would have caused trouble. Then why did you pick on me?"

In such a tense environment, I didn't expect him to laugh but he did laugh; a scoffing laughter that left me utterly irritated.

"Keep your friends close but your enemies even closer,

so they say. When I was going for the whistleblower, I was sure that I would get all the answers but when I remained empty handed, things went haywire. Then they told me that you had gate-crushed into the scene. I knew that the situation had now become as hot as a live wire. I was sure that you would soon pick up some leads then you would begin to cause trouble hence it was tactical to have you at a close range just to monitor you. Then I realised that I could also use you and the opera was complete."

He paused, caressed his clean-shaven chin then went on.

"Sherriff, what you don't know is that besides being a sly schemer I am also an opportunist with a nearly divine luck. I was not handed this glorious perch on a silver plate, I earned it so don't underrate me. When my wife refused to bulge and I realised that your friend did not have the flash-disk, I found myself stuck.

The information in the flash-disk was too valuable and damning to be left to circulate in the free market hence I had to fight to death to retrieve it lest it fell into the wrong hands. I had to get a professional to trace it and bring it back to me and you Sherriff were tailor-cut for the job . As things look now, I guess my bet was right."

Again he sipped some whisky and went on.

Although killing the Whistleblower was a gross mistake that landed me in tricy waters, it turned out to be providential; a kind of a blessing in disguise for it brought me the man I needed, you. When word reached me that you had started making enquiries about your friend's killing, I decided to kill two birds with one stone. I knew everything about you and I knew that you and him were soulmates. Your records also told me that you were exceptionally good and that meant I had found the right man.

I knew that if there was a man who could help trace the lost flash-disk and give it back to me, then that man was you. I also knew that un-tethered, you were a dangerous man hence it was vital for me to have you under close watch. All I had

to do was to plant one of my closest confidants on your way just to trigger you into action."

"And who was this person," I asked for the sake of curiosity.

He smiled sheepishly then said, "Jackline." I could hardly believe what I was hearing.

"She! Jackline!"

"Yes. Jackline. Sherriff, you may think you are a professional but against me you are just an amateur," he said, a brutal expression on his face. I said nothing. The bombshell he had dropped was too hard to take and I started realising that I was up against a sly adversary. He stared at the ceiling, pulled a face then went on. "Tracy thought she was good at cheating but she didn't know that she had to reckon with my omnipresent eyes and ears. She didn't even know that Jackline was my mistress. When her love for me started fading out, Jackline is the one who grabbed the oars and steered me to happiness. To buy her loyalty, I transferred all the pampering to her and promised her that I would kick out Tracy, then she would move in as my wife. That made her my secret informer. She kept me informed about my wife's illicit love escapades and in return, I coated her with gold and false promises."

"Then why did you kill her?"

He spat on the carpet in a gesture of disgust. "She had served her worth," he said heartlessly. He reached for the cigar box and selected a cigar, regarded it for a moment then went on.

"At a certain point, I started getting doubtful. You were proving to be more slippery than a fish in water and I realised that you needed extra watching. When I called you that evening, the idea was to buy you then have you work under my instructions. You rebutted my plan confirming that you were a person of principle and that made me shift gear and activate my plan B button."

"Let's get down to business, General. I am tired of this idle talk," I said, feigning annoyance. He lit his cigar then looked up at me, saying, "Why hurry things Sherriff, when we have the whole night all for us? After all, don't they say that there is no hurry in Africa?"

I said nothing for I had decided to wait until he exhausted his chest thumping before I closed in on him.

"When you took a break from your investigations, I started getting nervous since I still had the flash-disk to recover. I had placed my men to tail you just only to provoke you but when you started to give up hope, I knew I had to change tact.

When they told me that they had traced down the prostitute who had robbed your friend, I decided to use her as the bait.

We forced her to call you giving me a chance to scare you with a murder charge while all along the idea was to connect you with the DJ who had refused to bulge in spite of our tireless efforts to break him down." More light was falling on the mystery. That explained to me why that bully I had encountered in the scene of crime had not shot me but I decided not to follow this up.

"The idea of throwing you in the cell together with the DJ was a brilliant move. Though you managed to fool my juniors you did not fool me. When they told me that the trick of the tape recorder had failed to yield dividends, I knew you had pulled a fast one. I told them to check on your finger prints and when they confirmed that your finger prints were on the recorder, I knew I was back in track."

He blew thick curls of smoke and placed the burning cigar on the ashtray.

"When they told that your finger prints were on the recorder, I knew that the DJ must have told you something of worth meaning that I was now at the tail-end of my mission.

All I needed was to cut you loose and give you free space and this I did with the class of a shrewd strategist. I made them dump you in the forest then planted a good Samaritan to free you. You have a colourful record Sherriff: a selfless, dedicated and a self-sacrificing officer - someone who can easily give his life for a friend. I knew that once you laid your hand on the flash disk, you would use it to bargain for the DJ's life. When I got your call this evening, I knew Ihad backed the right horse."

He finished what was in the glass and made a refill. His eyes were now bloodshot although I could see that he was still in total control of his self.

"Time has now come for us to talk business. You will now give me back my flash-disk," he said with a note of finality that sounded more of an order than a request.

"You know the rule of the game General. You free DJ Cool and you get your flash-disk back. It is that simple," I said firmly.

His blood-shot eyes dug into me like two sparks, then a weird smile crossed his rubbery lips.

"And what will happen if I say no?"

"Then the contents withheld in the flashdisk will go public." I answered, this time adding a flavour of threat to my voice. He gave me one of the most callous sneers I have ever seen, then placed his hand on the table saying, "Strange how history repeats itself! A few weeks ago, my wife was standing right in front of me making demands and showering me with threats but unlike you, she had an upper hand on the bargaining table and she seemed like she would have her way. Of course I would have called her bluff but on the other hand, I knew it could turn sour. *Hell hath no fury like a woman scorned,* so they say. The wife of the general, standing in the dock as a witness against him would not only be sauce to the press but it would also have stirred public emotions."

He paused, crushed his cigar end then looked at me and sneered.

"This is not the same with you. You are Mr No-one and you have no power on the bargain table, so I can afford to call your bluff. Right now you have no credible witness and what you think you can use against me are mere paper tigers."

He was now boxing me to a corner for I knew what he was saying was true. However, I am not the type to go down on my knees begging for mercy thus I wanted him to know that I was still ready to gird my loins and fight back. I was down but not out. I decided to throw what I thought would be the killer jab.

"That is what you think, General," I said standing my ground. "You forget that there is still that body lying in the cemetery. It belongs to your missing chauffeur, doesn't it?

To my surprise, he nodded emphatically.

"Yes, it belongs to him but I have that tied up too. Come day-break and someone will lose that body where not even the gods can find it while the charred remains of your friend the DJ will be resting in peace in its place." I knew the crunch had come. I decided to play his way for I deemed it the only way to go if I hoped to lead him to the slaughterhouse. I dipped my hand inside my jacket, felt for my gun but before

I could whip it out, a stern voice brought me to a halt.

"Sherriff, don't you dare to pull any monkey tricks!" I did not need to be told who had echoed these words. I slowly turned my head and my eyes picked out the commandant standing on the door, the nozzle of his gun pointing straight to my head.

I looked at him and I realised that the chessboard had changed. I was expecting the general to play a dirty card but I was not expecting it this early.

"Ah! Here comes the boy with the heavenly luck!" I exclaimed sarcastically but the commandant said nothing. He was now advancing towards me in small-calculated paces, his gun still held at the ready while his eyes were fixed on the hand in my pocket. When he was close to me, he ordered,

"Let's have the flash-disk and make it snappy!"

I gave him a forced sarcastic smile and turned my eyes to the general.

He too was having a gun in his hand although he was not pointing it at me.

The gloves were now off and the moment for the final showdown had come.

"You are now held between two fires Sherriff so give me back my flash-disk!" the general growled. I had no choice but to play their game. I put my hand in the pocket but before I could pull out anything, the commandant dug his gun in my spine. He then felt for my holster and fished out my gun then made a step behind me. He did not search me further and that made me thank the heavens. I pulled out my hand and showed them the flash disk. The commandant came from behind me, snatched the gadget and tossed it towards the general. Amidst the deathly silence that gripped the room, broken only by the ticking sound of the wall clock, the general picked up the flash disk, eyed it intently and drew in a long sigh of relief. I held my breath and prayed. This was the first trick from my bag and I knew that if it failed to work I was sunk. When he placed the flash-disk on the table, I drew in a long sigh of relief.

"I guess you have already made a copy, haven't you?" he asked.

"Yes, I have and you can bet that by tomorrow the media will flash it in banner headlines." He stared at me fixedly then gave me a wide glee.

"That is what I call a hollow threat Sherriff," he said.

"I am sure that once you are out of the way none of your paper tigers will attempt to provoke a storm for that could be akin to digging their own graves. With all the first hand witnesses gone and without any credible witness to create any ripples, the defence lawyers will have a field day. Hearsay, trash, a cock and bull story: this is how the jury will rule."

He came back to the table, picked up his glass and sipped his whisky. He looked at me triumphantly saying, "This is the course the things will take. After you are dead and the DJ's body is lying in that grave, no one will risk creating ripples. You are the remaining witness who may have first-hand information and this drives all the tides blowing in my favour."
I was no foreigner on how the corridors of justice operated hence I knew what he was saying was true. Once I was out of the way and with the prosecution and the judges on his side, he would enjoy himself while skewing justice.
I threw a quick glance at the wall clock and my heart skipped a beat. I noticed that time was running out yet I still had the most crucial part of my plan to put into action.

"Please, don't act foolish General," I said in a stammer. "The law will finally catch up with you." He moved his head sideways.

"If I were you I would not worry about the law, I would worry about myself," he said. "The law is a cobweb as one sage once affirmed. The small flies get caught while the big flies break through." I would have jumped on him and broken his neck but he still had his gun pointed at me. I knew that keeping my eyes on the hand that held the gun was crucial and I didn't want to move even a muscle.

"You are a patriot Sherriff, I will give you credit for that." He went on. "Patriots use their hearts and that is why they are even willing to die for their countries while leaders like me use their heads to make hard choices. That explains why many patriots never make it to leadership; hard decisions are made with the head and not with the heart."

I was not listening to his chest thumping for I was keenly watching his finger while he pushed back the safety catch. He levelled his gun and his lips parted in a vicious grin.

"You are a patriot Sherriff hence you deserve the death of a patriot; a bullet through the heart," he said in a wicked voice.

I knew that this was the moment to draw him to the trap. I had gathered all what I wanted and now the crunch moment had come.

"Before you kill me, how sure are you that you have what you were looking for?" I asked with a half smile.

He narrowed his eyes and his face hardened. His confused eyes went to the flash disk that was lying on the table then back to me. Without saying a word, he placed his gun on the table, picked up the gadget then walked to a computer that was sitting at the far end of the office and switched it on. When it was ready, he eyed the flash disk then slid it into the computer.

The crunch moment had come. My adrenaline shot to the

zenith and I said a million prayers hoping that Shylock had done a good job.

The deafening explosion that came after the flash disk had touched the computer confirmed that indeed the trick had worked.

The computer exploded and the general threw himself to the ground. I turned quickly to face the commandant knowing well that if I made a wrong step my plan would go up in smoke. He still had his gun held at the ready hence I knew I had to watch him keenly. I made as if to attack him all the time watching his finger which was curled around the trigger.

I felt a heavy blow around my chest which was followed by a deafening noise of a gunshot that shook the palace to its foundations.

I had never been shot before and I had never known that a bullet could be this strong. I had banged my head on the floor and this had made my brain go for a while. Then slowly I started to come round and I could hear the faint voices of two men talking. I became aware that my senses were back and this made me enter into panic mode. I held my breath and my muscles hoping and praying that they did not come to check on me.

"All set?" I heard the general say.

"All set, Sir," replied the commandant.

"We are running short of time," the general went on.

"Leave me to handle this body. In the meantime, go and get rid of that DJ then make sure his body is in that grave by tomorrow. Take the remains of the chauffeur and leave them where not even the gods can find them."

Then I heard the howling noise of a siren and I almost lept with joy.

"The law is already here but I don't know who called them. Get yourself into one of the rooms and lock yourself in while I handle them. Once I get rid of them you can carry on with the rest of the plan," the general said in a scared voice. I heard the noise of the general's quick footsteps and the creaking of the door while he opened the front door and walked out into the night.

When I was sure I was alone, I rose up from my 'death' and tiptoed towards the window and peeped through. What I saw made me almost jump through
the window with joy.

The guardian angels squad was sealing the entire parking space. They were around twelve of them, all dressed in full combat gear as if they had come for the world's most wanted terrorist. Although the howling of the sirens had ceased, they were still flashing. All the men had their guns lowered but they all gazed meanly at the general. I saw the general look around then address the man who was in the lead. It was Shylock.

I drew in a deep sigh of relief.
Even as I walked out of his house there was persistent red light that kept telling me that Shylock would change his mind. In spite of everything I knew that our friendship was not build on quick-sand and that told me that he could not just abandon me to my fate. As I watched him walk towards the general, I remembered what he had told me.

"I know he will shift the goal posts thus you must have a trick ready. There is some explosive in the disk. Once it comes into contact with any electric current it will just explode. This will be enough to distract him. The rest depends on you," he had said while giving me the flash disk. This was when I knew he would change his mind.

"Good night officer," the general said in a groaning voice. "You have just arrived on time. He is in there lying on the floor. Thank heavens I was faster than him otherwise I would be dead." No one moved except Shylock. He lifted up his gun and pointed it to the general who immediately stood back, a horrified look in his eyes. The fear on his face increased even more when the other men, following their leader lifted up their guns and pointed them at him.

"What do you think you are doing Shylock," he growled, his face tightening and his eyes widening with alarm. "Are you going crazy?"

"No, I am arresting you," said Shylock in a polite but hard voice. "You have the right to have a lawyer and the right to remain silent. Anything you say may be used against you in the court of law."

The editor of *Mambo-Leo* and some reporters stepped from behind the men and started filming the unfolding events. The general's knees wobbled and he found himself losing control over his bowels.

"Shylock, I hope you know what you are doing," he said in a husky voice that betrayed all the fear and alarm that was boiling inside his belly.

"Yes, I do," Shylock replied, then turned to one of his men. "Jeff, clip the handcuffs on him." While the man moved forward with a pair of gleaming handcuffs, the light of flashing cameras filled the air while the policemen struggled to push back the battery of reporters who were surging forward to film all the details of this historic arrest.

* * *

They led the general into a waiting car as I walked into the scene. I knew that this was the most crucial part of the plan and I had to act fast if I hoped to unmask him in full public glare so I elbowed myself through the surging reporters and journalists. When Shylock saw me, he firmly ordered the reporters to give way and they obeyed hence I found myself standing next to the car door facing the general.

When he saw me, his mouth opened agape and his eyes grew round. He wanted to say something but words choked him. There was real horror printed all over his face and he looked like he needed air. I gave him a triumphant smile and unzipped my jacket exposing my bulletproof jacket. "You called me a patriot and you couldn't have been more right than this," I said, digging out the bullet and showing it to him. "Leaders die and people forget them but patriots never die for they live forever in the hearts of the nation."

It was exciting to watch the scared look in his eyes for it was a look of a vanquished man – beaten fair and square. His handcuffed hands were shivering like a leaf on a windy day. What scared him most were the threatening noses of the cameras as the pressmen filmed the unfolding events. What he didn't know was that I had more rabbits to pull from the hat.

I unzipped my jacket fully and removed the bulletproof gear. I then unbuttoned my shirt and pulled out a tape recorder that was fastened around my waist with an adhesive tape.

"I don't know what kind of president you would have made but I want to play some sweet music for you before you leave the flock of the lawful," I said while playing back the tape. I then pressed the play button on and turned up the volume.

I didn't kill your friend, my prostitute wife did. If she hadn't gone to him, I wouldn't have gone after him.

The night became dead silent, a silence broken only by the unmistakable voice of the general, which came from the tape. The journalist fixed their cameras on the general's face, which now looked like a statue while all the other men looked like erect rocks.

Yes, it does belong to him but I have that tied up too. Come tomorrow, that body will have disappeared and the charred remains of your friend the DJ will be sleeping peacefully in that grave."

He gasped then buried his face in his handcuffed hands in a gesture of resignation. I knew I was now holding his jugular. All that I needed was to tighten the noose and deny him air.

This is the course things will take. After you are dead and the DJ's body is lying in that grave, no one will risk creating ripples. You are the remaining witness who may have first-hand information and this drives all the tides blowing in my favor.

Sure that I had driven the last nail in his coffin, I stopped the tape and handed it over to Shylock. I then turned to my fallen foe and gave him my parting shot.

"The wheels of justice turn slowly, General, but they turn," I said with a smile. "Let's see how you sneak out of this one."

When I lifted up my hand and gave him a mock salute, he made as if to get out of the car and grab me but a powerful hand pushed him back. He lifted up his handcuffed hand and thrust his thick pointing finger into my direction.

"You are a dead man!" he snarled threateningly. "I may not get you but someone else will!"

I did not say anything for I knew the journalists and the

cameramen were taking down everything. I just smiled at him saying, "You won the battles, General, but I have won the war. See you in court for the awarding of the medals."

I watched with a beaming face as Shylock gave his orders to his most trusted men and minutes later, the convoy carrying the general left for the headquarters. The chase cars of the press closely followed the police cars with the reporters and cameramen hanging from the rooftops.

What I didn't know is that all what had transpired had been aired live in all the media houses thanks to my comrade-in-arms the editor. Only a few men and some pressmen remained behind. I walked to where Shylock was and took his hand in mine.

"I knew you would come," I said in gratitude, shaking his hand firmly.

"Don't thank me, thank Sherry. She is the one who worked it out for you."

We embraced each other like in the good old times until he pushed me away.

"I guess you will need some rest," he quipped. "I will give this palace a thorough check-up just to see whether there are more skunks then I will join you."

"What is the idea, Shylock? Do you want to steal my show?" I asked sarcastically.

He patted my shoulder playfully saying, "Remember the paradox of the horse and the horse rider. The horse does the racing and gets only hay but the rider scoops the prize and all the honours that come along with it. You are the horse, I am the horse rider."

We both laughed until a stern voice brought us to a stand.

"Sherriff!"

I quickly turned around but a sharp pain tore through

my shoulder. This was followed by a loud bang and I knew someone had shot at me. While I fell to the ground clutching my bleeding shoulder, Shylock's gun cracked. I lifted my face from the ground and caught sight of the commandant as he lifted up his gun aiming at me.

Shylock's gun cracked again and this time he caught him in the head, sending his brains splashing against the wall. "I had forgotten about that bastard!" I said when Shylock bent down to check my state. My left shoulder was damp with sweat and I was still writhing in pain. Shylock looked me over then caressed my head with his hand. "It's nothing big but I guess the scar will be a precious souvenir to carry for the rest of your life." I would have wanted to join him in the laughter but my tearing pain could not allow me.

"I will send you to the hospital while I iron out the rest," he said while helping me to my feet. "There is a dead man to trace out and another living one to dig out from the grave."

This reminded me that our mission was not yet done for until we traced out DJ Cool, we could not let go the cry of victory. I gave Shylock the clues of the possible places to check on. "It's my bet he is still in the intelligence headquarters. Check that one first but just in case you don't succeed, send some men to the Passion Box and you will meet a certain Kimbo who will help you squeeze the truth from that bastard." Still clutching my paining shoulder, which was now damp with blood, I boarded the police car and headed to the hospital.

***

The sunrays pierced through dawn and helped suck away the dew of the memories of the night before. Their soothing effect helped calm the pain of my heavily bandaged arm and the new light of the day helped to bring back to life my once dead hope.

Time was now ripe for me to turn a new leaf and make a new beginning.

While they were digging out the bullet from my left shoulder, Shylock was running berserk, ripping open all the police stations until he managed to trace out DJ Cool. Although I had told him to zero his searchlight on the intelligence headquarters, he was not taking chances. With the commandant gone and the general's mouths tightly stitched, it was not an easy task. Finally, he took the commandant's cell phone and looked at the pattern of the calls. One call kept recurring and finally he traced the call to a private residence and that is how he managed to burst it.

They had moved DJ Cool to a private house where they had tortured him almost to death. When they rescued him, Shylock gave an order that he was to be taken to hospital then appointed one of his most trusted men to guard the ward round the clock. No one was supposed to talk to him until there was an order from Shylock. Although he was in pain, Cool managed to talk to me through the phone. He thanked me tearfully and promised to come and see me after he had traced his girlfriend.

While Shylock was searching for Cool, another bunch of the GUARDIAN ANGELS squad with the press at their side, was guarding a grave at the cemetery waiting for the warrant of exhumation. Shylock had made it clear to them that not even a fly should go near the grave until he himself came with the warrant, a warrant he managed to get in the wee hours from a city judge.

Finally, under the full glare of the press, the chauffeur's

body was exhumed and taken straight to the mortuary where an independent pathologist was waiting to make the tests. The news that a dead DJ had come back to life sounded like a fairy story in the ears of the populace. Journalists flocked to the hospital in droves. These were joined by the ardent fans of Cool who like the doubting Thomas vowed not to believe until they saw him with their own naked eyes. However, his resurrection was overshadowed by the capture of the general. This one stole the thunder for it was the first high-level arrest the people had ever witnessed. When early morning came, Shylock had managed to get warrants for other exhumations. Larry, Tracy, Jackline and Milly's bodies were all exhumed for further forensic tests. When the pathologist finally confirmed that the body that had been lying in the cemetery indeed belonged to the chauffeur, the press went wild knitting the pieces together and what came out was a mouth-watering story that sounded like a dramatic Hollywood movie.

This is when hell broke loose.

By the time mid-day came, hurried press conferences were called and resignations tendered. For the die-hards, those who vow never to resign until they are forced to, bad news started flowing in in the afternoon. The highest authority cracked the whip and soon big heads came rolling down like huge boulders leaving thunders and dust behind them. Prominent men who were fond of smiling before the cameras suddenly turned camera-shy and some retreated to bunkers.

To the populace, the events were received with a mixture of awe, anger and wonder. The nucleus of organised crime and national plunder had been exposed and most of them could not believe that their country had all along been held hostage by turn-coats who smarted like good citizens during the day but donned the garbs of out-laws when night came.

Slowly, the anger swelled until it burst the banks making everyone turn to the guillotine. The citizens were now hungry for raw flesh. They wanted to see heads rolling and the blood of the culprits spilling to over flowing heights. When handcuffs started shining in the hands of the high and mighty and the cells started receiving aristocratic tenants who were hitherto untouchable, claps and shouts of joy rent the air.

At last, the long awaited journey to halt the train of impunity and lawlessness had begun.

As for me, I lay on my hospital bed watching the events from the screen of the small television that Shylock had placed in my ward before he retreated to his bed after a gruelling day. What I saw and what I heard made me smile with self-pride and I closed my eyes for a prayer of thanks giving.

Finally, the one week odyssey was over.

* * *

The party was well attended. There was a big banner *'Equal service to all'* hung above the front gate. It was not just a party to celebrate the rare but deserved achievement of a comrade; it was a meeting between friends. When an announcement was made in the airwaves that Shylock had been appointed the new Police General, my joy was uncontainable. This was made even juicy by the fact that his deserved appointment was a result of the furore of the populace. It was the first public appointment coming after a heated public demand.

THE END